THE VALANCOURT BOOK OF
HORROR STORIES

VOLUME THREE

THE VALANCOURT BOOK OF

HORROR STORIES

VOLUME THREE

edited by
JAMES D. JENKINS & RYAN CAGLE

VALANCOURT BOOKS
Richmond, Virginia
2018

The Valancourt Book of Horror Stories, Volume Three
First published October 2018

Published by Valancourt Books, Richmond, Virginia
http://www.valancourtbooks.com

ISBN 978-1-948405-13-3 (hardcover)
ISBN 978-1-948405-14-0 (trade paperback)
ISBN 978-1-948405-15-7 (special Tiki edition)

Also available as an electronic book.

All Valancourt Books publications are printed on acid free paper that
meets all ANSI standards for archival quality paper.

Cover by M. S. Corley
Set in Dante MT

CONTENTS

ACKNOWLEDGMENTS

The Editors acknowledge with thanks permission to include the following stories:

'Don't Go Up Them Stairs' © 1971 by R. Chetwynd-Hayes. Originally published in *The Unbidden*. Reprinted by permission of the Estate of R. Chetwynd-Hayes.

'The Parts Man' © 2018 by Steve Rasnic Tem. Published by arrangement with the author.

'The Life of the Party' © 2013 by Christopher Beaumont. Originally published in *Mass for Mixed Voices: The Selected Short Fiction of Charles Beaumont*, edited by Roger Anker. Reprinted by permission of Don Congdon Associates.

'The Poet Gives His Friend Wildflowers' © 2018 by Hugh Fleetwood. Published by arrangement with the author.

'Monkshood Manor' © 1954 by L. P. Hartley. Originally published in *The White Wand and Other Stories*. Reprinted by permission of The Society of Authors.

'Blood of the Kapu Tiki' © 2018 by Eric C. Higgs. Published by arrangement with the author.

'On No Account, My Love' © 1955 by Elizabeth Jenkins. Originally published in *The Third Ghost Book*, edited by Cynthia Asquith. Reprinted by permission of the Estate of Elizabeth Jenkins.

'Underground' © 1974 by J. B. Priestley. Originally published in *The Illustrated London News*. Reprinted by permission of United Agents and the Estate of J. B. Priestley.

'Mr Evening' © 1968 by James Purdy. Originally published in *Mr. Evening and Nine Poems*. Reprinted by permission of W. W. Norton & Company, Inc.

'Mothering Sunday' © 1960 by John Keir Cross. Originally published in *Best Black Magic Stories*, edited by John Keir Cross. Reprinted by permission of the Estate of John Keir Cross.

'The Bottle of 1912' © 1961 by Simon Raven. Originally published in *The Compleat Imbiber*. Reprinted by permission of Curtis Brown, Ltd.

'Beelzebub' © 1992 by Robert Westall. Originally published in *Fearful Lovers and Other Stories*. Reprinted by permission of the Estate of Robert Westall and David Higham Associates.

EDITORS' FOREWORD

IT'S OCTOBER AGAIN, and you know what that means: it's time for another volume of Valancourt horror stories! Reader response to the first two entries in the series has been so positive that we're thrilled to be able to offer this third volume, and we think it may be the best yet.

As in past volumes, we've selected a wide range of stories – all by Valancourt authors – spanning the 19th, 20th, and 21st centuries, which means you will find rare ghost stories from the Victorian era alongside brand-new material that has never appeared in print before. And, as in the first two volumes, we have taken a broad view of what constitutes a 'horror story' and have tried to assemble a good mix of styles and themes. As you might expect from any good collection of spooky tales, ghosts and hauntings are amply represented in this book, but you'll find plenty of other types of horror as well: a monster in the attic with a taste for human flesh, an unpopular man who discovers a macabre new way of making friends, a particularly horrible baby who might be the spawn of Satan himself, vengeful Polynesian spirits, a subway train whose next stop is somewhere much hotter and further underground than one passenger expects, and even – why not? – a sinister snowman brought to life by the black arts.

Some of the authors in this collection will be well known to horror fans, such as the prolific R. Chetwynd-Hayes, the multi-award-winning modern-day master of weird fiction Steve Rasnic Tem, or legendary *Twilight Zone* scriptwriter Charles Beaumont. But even the most avid readers of horror anthologies will likely encounter some names with which they are not familiar, like the almost-forgotten Victorian-era writers Helen Mathers and Ernest G. Henham, biographer Elizabeth Jenkins, or the cult American novelist James Purdy. Many of the tales in this book have been long out of print, some of them never reprinted since their initial appearances many years ago, and three contributions – by Tem, Eric C. Higgs (who sadly passed away shortly after submitting his story), and Hugh Fleetwood – are appearing for the first time ever.

In compiling our first three Valancourt Books of Horror Stories, we've been astonished at the substantial number of high-quality, seldom-seen horror tales we have been able to compile from the relatively small number of authors we publish, especially given that many Valancourt authors are not known as horror writers. This just goes to show how much excellent, underappreciated fiction is out there, waiting for those willing to take the time and effort to seek it out. We hope that you'll enjoy this collection and also that you will take a moment to visit our website and click your way through the dark corners of the rest of the Valancourt catalogue – you never know what else might be lurking there . . .

JAMES D. JENKINS & RYAN CAGLE
August 2018

R. Chetwynd-Hayes

DON'T GO UP THEM STAIRS

An extremely prolific author and editor of horror fiction, R. CHETWYND-HAYES (1919-2001) published over a dozen novels and more than twenty volumes of short stories; he also edited numerous paperback horror anthologies in the 1970s, including volumes of the Armada Monster Book *and* Fontana Book of Great Ghost Stories *series. Chetwynd-Hayes's stories usually feature a mixture of horror and humour, and he often wrote about monsters, both traditional ones like vampires and werewolves and others of his own creation, such as the Shadmock and the Jumpity-Jim. His brilliant collection of interlinked monster stories,* The Monster Club (1976), *was adapted for a cult classic film version in 1981 starring Vincent Price and John Carradine and has been republished by Valancourt, as has a volume of the author's complete vampire tales,* Looking for Something to Suck (1997). *Like his 'The Elemental', which appeared in* The Valancourt Book of Horror Stories, Volume 2, *'Don't Go Up Them Stairs' showcases the author's trademark blend of the horrific and humorous. It first appeared in 1971 and seems not to have been reprinted in more than forty years.*

G RANDFATHER SAID HE WAS NEVER TO GO UPSTAIRS. By 'upstairs' he meant, of course, the second flight, the uncarpeted treads that led to the gable attic. His mother also stressed this unquestionable order in no uncertain terms: 'Never, never, go up them stairs.'

These were the first words he learnt to utter when still in the pram stage, not all at once of course. First it was: 'Never,' that drooled off his baby tongue, then: 'Go-o-o,' followed by: ''em stai-r-rs,' in a few months. 'Mama' came afterwards, 'Dadda' was never an issue – he was dead.

Lionel was ten before he began to consider the implication of this order. He could go to school, go to the pictures, go to visit Aunt Matilda who lived two miles away, but he could never – not if he lived to be a hundred – go upstairs to the attic. It was like Adam being told he must keep off apples. One day he approached his mother when she was in the midst of jam making.

'Why?' he asked.

'Why not?' she snapped, being in that kind of mood.

'Why can't I go upstairs to the attic?'

Her plump face turned to the color of unbaked pastry, so that the veins in her cheeks looked like streaks of strawberry jam.

'What did you say?'

Lionel's courage evaporated, and he muttered, 'Nothing,' but it was too late, he was seized by his shirt collar and dragged into the presence of his grandfather who was dozing before the living room fire.

'He asked me why,' his mother gasped in a voice that could scarce be heard.

'Why!' Grandfather's faded old man's eyes gleamed with fear, his mouth sagged as though he were about to cry, then he was on Lionel, cuffing him about the ears, but without much force, for he was very frail.

'You-don't-ask-why.' He screamed the words, and Mother admonished tearfully, 'Careful, Dad, you'll do yourself an injury,' whereupon the old man returned to his chair panting like a worn-out steam engine.

'Never ask why again,' he nodded weakly, 'just never go up them stairs.'

This outburst must have hastened the work done by umpteen years (no one knew how old Grandfather was), for one morning, just over a week later, Mother found Grandfather dead in his bed. Two men came and put him in a coffin, which was laid on two trestles in the front, to-be-used-only-on-special-occasions, room. Strange uncles and aunts, the existence of whom Lionel up to that time never suspected, came to pay their last respects. There was much drinking of grocer's sherry and munching of biscuits; Lionel, scrubbed, brushed, and imprisoned in a tight black suit, sipped his lemonade, and wondered why they had all come so early, after all the funeral was not for two days yet. Aunt Matilda was there, a vast bundle of lavender and old lace, for she weighed all of eighteen stone; her false teeth were continually slipping, which gave her a somewhat sardonic, amused expression, not at all in keeping with the occasion.

'How'd you like to stay with yer old auntie?' she enquired, after ruffling his hair, an operation which irritated him exceedingly.

'All right,' he conceded with reluctance.

It so happened he was spared this particular ordeal; news came some two hours later that a branch of the Tabernacle of Divine Wrestlers had burnt Aunt Matilda's cottage down. Mother looked particularly worried and tried to palm him off on the other uncles and aunts, but with no success.

'Give him a black D-R-A-U-G-H-T,' advised Aunt Matilda, who seemed in no way put out by the destruction of her home, ''e'll never hear a thing.'

They both overlooked the fact that Lionel could spell.

Mother was not a good actress. The next day she made continual and loud comments, stating he looked poorly, and how much good a nice basin of broth would do him, if consumed just before bedtime. She also unwisely added how well he'd sleep afterwards. When she was outside hanging up the washing Lionel inspected the kitchen. Apart from minced chicken, onions and chopped vegetables, there was a quantity of black powder in a white envelope. This he washed down the sink, and substituted black pepper in its place, then ran back to the living room just as Mother came back with her empty washing basket.

That evening all the uncles and aunts came back and a red-faced man who had been introduced as Uncle Arthur arrived with a wheelbarrow filled with bricks. Mother in a loud stage whisper told him to put them round the back, adding, quite unnecessarily, that 'little jugs had big eyes.' Then they all sat round and watched Lionel drink his broth.

'Lucky boy,' bellowed Aunt Matilda, 'I only wish somebody would make me some nice broth.'

'Luvly stuff.' Uncle Arthur smacked his lips. 'Makes me mouth water, it does.'

It is extremely doubtful if their appreciation would have lasted beyond the first sip; the pepper had made the broth very hot, and Lionel's mouth felt sore by the time he had emptied the basin.

'Feel sleepy, son?' enquired Mother.

'Yes,' lied Lionel.

Everyone gave a sigh of relief, and there was quite a procession to escort him to bed. He was tucked in, kissed a disgusting number of times, then they all trooped out, but Lionel had a suspicion someone was posted outside his door, if not indeed peering through the keyhole, to report progress. He closed his eyes and even snored in what he hoped was a realistic manner. The door creaked open, footsteps tiptoed across the room, and Lionel was gently shaken.

'You asleep, son?' asked Mother.

Lionel snored even louder, and fought down a traitorous sneeze.

'Is 'e off?' enquired Aunt Matilda's voice from the doorway.

'Like a tombstone,' Mother replied. 'He'll be under for eight hours at least.'

They left him and locked the door, unmindful that a rim lock has screws on the inside which are easily removed by a penknife, a present from Grandfather last Hallowe'en.

There was an awful lot of bumping in the front room, and the door was obligingly ajar. Two uncles were lifting Grandfather out of his coffin, and after they had laid him on the floor, they began to fill the coffin with bricks which Uncle Arthur was passing through the open window. The entire family, if they were related, were attired in strange costumes. Mother and all the aunties wore tall black tapering hats, and long matching dresses, while the uncles were naked, save for a knee-length black apron. Presently the coffin was filled with bricks and Uncle Arthur, after climbing in through the window and closing it after him, started to screw down the lid, while everyone else intoned a dirge that sounded to Lionel something like this.

> 'Grandfather was with us, long, long, long,
> Now he has gone, gone, gone,
> Where did he go, go, go?
> Down where the dark river flow, flow, flow.
>
> Now his body is dead, dead, dead,
> But the Black One must be fed, fed, fed,
> Give him meat to munch, munch, munch,
> And lovely bones to crunch, crunch, crunch.'

Uncle Arthur had finished screwing the lid back, and they lifted Grandfather, who looked very frail and cold in his white flannel nightgown, and laid him on the coffin. They now joined hands and danced round the corpse, this time singing a gay little tune that sounded rather like 'Knees Up Mother Brown.'

> 'Upstairs we all must go,
> He-Hi-He-Hi-Ho,
> All must be done just so-so,
> He-Hi-He-Hi-Ho.
>
> Do we fry his liver, braise his lights?
> He-Hi-He-Hi-Ho.
> Bake his kidneys, stew his tripes,
> He-Hi-He-Hi-Ho.

No, the Black One likes 'em raw,
He-Hi-He-Hi-Ho,
He's waiting for us behind the door,
He-Hi-He-Hi-Ho.

Now together let us sing,
He-Hi-He-Hi-Ho.
Black One's dinner we do bring,
He-Hi-He-Hi-Ho.'

The dancers took a much needed rest; Aunt Matilda was puffing in a most alarming manner; Uncle Arthur was leaning on Grandfather's feet, until Mother gave him an angry push that sent him sprawling. Lionel would have laughed if it had not been for their eyes. Even when they were singing their silly little ditty their eyes were bright – glazed with horror; smiles were grimaces, mouths twitched, hands trembled. Uncle Arthur clambered to his feet, then looked upwards in one revealing glance. Everyone repeated the movement; Aunt Matilda gave utterance.

'We must go up.'

Lionel fled, ran up the stairs silently on bare feet, to take refuge in his bedroom and listen behind his unlocked door. There came the tramp of feet, the thump-thump of the heavily laden, the creak of protesting stairboards, and something moved in the room above. A slithering, followed by a soft bumping, then as the procession on the stairs began to intone yet another dirge, whatever was above started to dance.

'Black One, Black One, here we come,
Bearing something for your old tum,
Grandad's ripe and ready now,
Come out quick, and get your chow.'

The ceiling shook, a picture moved, and the noise above

became a patter of sheer joy. Grandfather and his escort passed Lionel's door and carried on up the second flight. Lionel waited. There was a bump on the top landing, the family came running downstairs so fast someone slipped and tumbled down the last few steps; the dancing ceased and a heavy tread crossed the ceiling. The murmur of subdued voices below indicated the family were waiting also, and Lionel gently pulled his door open and peered out. A black candle was burning on the bottom stair of the second flight. It sputtered, and gave out a thin plume of white smoke, then the door of the attic creaked open and a strong draught blew the candle out. The family chanted again as Lionel closed his door.

> 'Ugly Black One up above,
> Accept this offering with our love,
> But come not down, stay up there,
> And we'll remain just where we were.'

There was a terrible silence, and Lionel knew, even if he did not understand, that some very important decision would be reached during the next minute. Downstairs someone began to cry, then Uncle Arthur swore; both sounds were frozen when a crash made the banisters tremble, followed at once by a swift dragging, a take-away; but Lionel knew it was Grandfather being pulled into the attic, for the sound continued on over his ceiling. A door slammed, and the family sent their sigh of relief shivering up the stairs.

They all dispersed shortly afterwards, save for Aunt Matilda and Mother. Lionel had only just screwed the lock keep back into place when he heard them coming up the stairs; he got into bed and turned over on one side, shutting his eyes tight when the key turned.

'Is he still asleep?' Aunt Matilda's whisper was a muted shout. 'Is he still under?'

'Yes,' Mother was leaning over him, 'the black draught will keep him still as a week old corpse till daybreak.'

'When will you tell him?'

'Not until he's fourteen.' Mother straightened up. 'I think he'll have a real bent for it then.'

'Sure, 'e's a natural,' Aunt Matilda chuckled, 'them green eyes. And the way his ears taper. He'll be lording it over his own B.M. before you know it.'

Mother shut the door when she left but did not lock it, and Lionel lay awake and listened. There was much movement in the attic above; soft thuds with an occasional thump, and once a loud bang as though something heavy had been dropped on the floor. Two hours or more had passed before he decided it was safe to climb out of bed and approach the door. The black candle had been relit and its flickering flame fought the writhing shadows in a losing battle. Aunt Matilda, who must be sharing Mother's bed, sent out reassuring snores, and even Mother confirmed her state of unconsciousness by a spasmodic snort.

Lionel took up the black candle and slowly mounted the stairs. He was not afraid, only tensed by excitement; at last he would know why he must not, or rather, should not, 'go up them stairs'. The top landing was festooned with cobwebs, the floor carpeted by dust in which lay the imprint of Grandfather's form, plus a long path along which the corpse had been dragged to the black-painted door. Lionel put his candle down, and pressed his ear to the keyhole.

Something was munching; there was a sharp crack followed by a sucking sound, then a soft ripping like thick felt being torn. Lionel peered through the keyhole, but it was pitch black inside, and he could not see a thing.

He did not mean to open the door, for commonsense told him such an action would be asking for trouble, but he could not help himself. His hand crept up to the handle of its own accord, the muscles in his wrist hardened, and then, before his brain had time to flash out a panic-inspired order, the handle turned and the door slid open. The candlelight attacked the inner darkness, and was at once repelled. A graveyard smell came to him, and with it memory of things which breed in old and forgotten tombs; life that is born of death corruption and must never see the light of day. He retreated a few steps, and the candlelight, grateful for this small respite, came with him. A soft padding thumping was approaching from the inner darkness, and a deep shadow shape turned to a dirty white. It was lean and tall, clad in a long gown made from unbleached linen shrouds; the face was green-white and shone with a soft luminous light; the eyes were white, pupilless pools, and it had no nose – only two holes. It shuffled out on to the landing, right into the circle of yellow light, and reaching out a skeleton hand, opened its black-toothed mouth:

'Glug – glug.'

Lionel dropped his candle and ran; slipped down a few stairs, fell down the rest, and a bellowed: 'Wassat?' followed by the creaking of bed springs told him Aunt Matilda was awake. He looked upwards. The 'Thing' was holding the still lighted candle and peering down at him over the banisters; the mouth was open, expressing what could well be a grimace of pleasure. Whatever it used for a voice also suggested unholy satisfaction.

'... Glug ... glug ...'

'Satan's knee britches!'

Aunt Matilda gripped his shoulder, then dragged him into Mother's bedroom. The two women stared at him with fear-inspired rage.

'You've been up there?'

Lionel nodded.

'He's seen young flesh,' stated Mother.

'Living flesh,' added Aunt Matilda.

'With warm blood in it,' Mother nodded.

'Tender meat.'

'No gristle.'

'A succulent morsel,' Aunt Matilda licked her lips, 'untouched by undertaker, juicy, such as 'e's been looking for these past three hundred years.'

'Satan preserve us,' Mother made an X sign and the aunt quickly imitated her, 'what shall we do?'

''And 'im over,' replied Aunt Matilda without hesitation. 'Now He's seen, He'll want.'

'But – I can't,' Mother clutched Lionel to her ample bosom. 'I can't give Him my son.'

'Do you want Him down here?' The woman's vast fat face was pitiless. 'Do you want Him loose?'

'No,' Mother's grip slackened. 'No, that don't bear thinking about, but Lionel's me son, Matilda. Remember that, he's me son.'

'It'll be a sacrifice,' agreed Aunt Matilda. 'There's no denying, it'll be a sacrifice.' She froze and raised a hand. 'What's that? Hark, damn ye, hark.'

The three figures became statues; they looked at each other, mutely pleading for confirmation that the silence was absolute. But a stairboard creaked, a banister squeaked, then for a few moments there was nothing, a pause before the rack was turned another notch. Something bumped against the wall, then a short croaking cough, followed by a spluttering sigh; another stair protested – there was no doubt now, whatever lived in the attic was coming down.

'What is it?' Even now Lionel could not resist his craving for knowledge.

'A Ghoul,' snapped Aunt Matilda. 'What did you suppose it was?'

'A King Ghoul,' Mother corrected. 'You remember, Matilda, Grandmother always said it was a King Ghoul.'

'Hark!' Aunt Matilda glared her terror. 'It's trying to get in. Come on, we've got to barricade the door.'

Lionel watched the women manhandle the wardrobe into position, and tried not to see the door handle slowly turn, but he could hardly ignore the spluttering roar that proclaimed the Ghoul's rage when it found the entrance barred. Mother and Aunt could do no more than make the X sign and mutter completely futile incantations, while the wardrobe was trembling in a most alarming fashion. Lionel could see only one other exit from the bedroom, and he decided to use it. Aunt Matilda glanced over one shoulder.

'Here, Maud, the little perisher is getting out of the window.'

The descent for a ten-year-old was simple. The ivy was tough, well rooted into the mortar, and Lionel had used this natural ladder before. Once on the ground he looked up and decided Aunt Matilda was foolhardy to attempt the same feat. She was not built for it, but what with the shifting wardrobe and the appeasement morsel on the road to freedom, she really had not much alternative. The ivy parted company with the wall, and Aunt Matilda came down with a sickening thud. She lay quite still, but possibly she was not dead, only Mother settled the matter beyond doubt by climbing out on to the window sill and jumping down on to Aunt Matilda's back. Lionel distinctly heard the spine snap, and wondered idly if Aunt's head would wobble should it be possible for her to stand up.

'See what you've done now,' Mother complained, clambering to her feet. 'Look at poor Matilda.' She bent down and shook an unresponsive shoulder. 'You all right, Matilda?'

Aunt Matilda did not, indeed could not, answer, but a voice from the bedroom window did its best.

'Glug . . . glug . . .'

The Ghoul was leaning out of the window; its green luminous face gleamed like an over-ripe melon. Mother grabbed Lionel by the scruff of the neck and pushed him forward, while at the same time doing her best to lift him upwards, but the Ghoul was looking down at Aunt Matilda's immense sprawling figure. He pointed with one chalk-white finger.

'. . . Glug . . . glug . . .'

'Oh!' Mother relaxed her grip and Lionel twisted like an eel to break free. 'Yes, of course. Never thought of that.' She looked up at the Ghoul who was drooling with anticipation. 'You get up them stairs and stay there, and we'll let you have her when it's right and respectable.'

'Glug,' the Ghoul pointed again.

'Don't be so greedy,' Mother admonished. 'It isn't as though you haven't anything to go on with. I mean to say, normally you would have had to wait a very long time for Matilda.'

The marble eyes moved slowly, then stopped when Lionel came within their vision, but Mother was fearless now she had, so to speak, a generous amount of ammunition to hand.

'No you don't. You've had me father, and you'll have me sister, but you'll have to wait for me son. So get back up them stairs or I'll throw a crooked cross at yer.'

This threat seemed to disturb the Ghoul for it jerked back from the window sill, and roared like a wolf.

'A crooked cross,' Mother repeated. 'Now up with yer.'

The Ghoul withdrew, but with reluctance, for the luminous face peeped round the window frame twice, and the white eyes glared down at Lionel, while a black tongue licked grey lips.

'Crooked crosses.' Some of Mother's new-found confidence was seeping away, and her voice squeaked.

The Ghoul went; they could hear his feet slouching up the stairs, then the attic door slammed, and Mother gave a vast sigh of relief.

'That was a near thing, and it was all your fault. Look what's happened to poor Matilda, and she not ready to take the steep path. Thank your dark stars she fell out of that window all the same. There's enough to keep the Old One busy for a long time, to say nothing of what remains of poor Grandfather.'

'What's a crooked cross?' asked Lionel.

'A cross that's crooked,' Mother explained. ''E don't like 'em,' she shuddered, 'neither do I. But they's poison to a Ghoul.'

'Now,' she squared her shoulders, 'you must go and fetch Uncle Arthur.'

'Where does he live?'

'I'm going to tell you, ain't I? Go down through the village and you reach the cross roads where yer Great-Aunt Bridget is buried, you'll see a sign post which says, TO DEVIL'S WOOD. Follow the footpath till you come to DEAD MAN'S BRIDGE; cross, and two hundred yards further on you'll find HANG-MAN'S CORNER. Turn left, and yer Uncle's cottage is on the right. Got that?'

Lionel nodded.

'Right. Tell Arthur what's happened, and say he's to get here pronto. Off you go, and look out for 'is cat. Don't get familiar with it.'

Lionel ran through the village, and the full moon watched him run. He walked through Devil's Wood and felt strangely at home in the eerie gloom; Dead Man's Bridge was a narrow wooden structure that creaked when he crossed it, and Hangman's Corner was marked by the ruins of an old gibbet Uncle Arthur's cottage was almost hidden under a dark canopy of large trees, and as Lionel pushed open the wicket gate an immense black cat emerged from the shadows, and after arching its back, spat at him.

'Crooked crosses,' Lionel experimented.

The cat spat again, then turned and was off; a black streak that was soon lost in the deep darkness. Lionel went up the garden path and tapped on the weatherbeaten door. The door flew open and Uncle Arthur faced him, a bulky figure outlined against the dim candlelight that illuminated the room beyond. Lionel tried to see what was in the room, but Uncle Arthur kept bobbing about, so he was left with the impression of toads in bottles and a heap of old bones.

'Must be trouble,' Uncle Arthur commented, 'otherwise Maud would never have sent you.'

'The Ghoul came downstairs.' Lionel thought it wise to be brief. 'Aunt Matilda fell out of the window, she's dead, Mother said get there pronto.'

'Satan!' Uncle Arthur took a deep breath. 'Let's get going.' He peered into the darkness. 'Lucifer!'

The black cat appeared and glared at Lionel. Uncle Arthur slammed his front door.

'Curse loud, curse deep,
All those who try to peep.'

The cat swore and took up a position on the doorstep. Uncle Arthur swept Lionel up into his arms, and after muttering some words that the boy was unable to hear, jumped forward. The return journey was accomplished in no time at all. Uncle Arthur may have run, but more likely he flew. Hangman's Corner was gone in a flash; Dead Man's Bridge did not creak when they passed over; Devil's Wood was a blur of startled trees, the village was barely reached before it was left behind, and there was Mother standing by Aunt Matilda's recumbent form.

'What kept yer?' she snapped.

'Out of practice.' Uncle Arthur was indeed a little breathless. 'Let's get her inside. Can't afford to waste time now the Old One has remembered the way downstairs.'

Mother nodded again, then together they carried Aunt Matilda indoors, and laid her out on the front room table.

'She's going to take a bit of getting upstairs,' Uncle Arthur observed.

'But it'll be worth the effort.' Mother wiped her forehead

on Aunt Matilda's skirt. 'The Old One will sleep for years after her.'

'I dunno,' Uncle Arthur shook his head doubtfully, 'he's seen young meat.'

'Serve him right,' she glared at Lionel, 'if he hadn't gone up them stairs, Matilda would still be brewing her black stew with the worst.'

Next day Grandfather's brick-filled coffin was interred in the village churchyard, although popular opinion maintained the cross roads was the right and proper place, and that evening the undertaker put Matilda in her narrow box. Uncle Arthur went round to the builder's yard for another barrow-load of bricks, while Lionel pondered on the problem of crooked crosses. He decided to question Uncle Arthur.

'It's like this, young 'un,' he sat down on the wheelbarrow handle, 'when you've been initiated a cross of any kind is bad medicine, but a crooked cross is fatal. If I just sees one, I goes all squeezy in me stomach.'

'What's init . . . ?'

'Initiated? That's when you takes an oath of allegiance to Old Nick. A Ghoul of course is worse off than us warlocks. I mean to say, he's from down under, and a crooked cross would liquefy him. That's why the Old One is in your Mother's attic. Years and years ago he used to haunt the churchyard, but people got wise and began putting crooked crosses on their tombstones. But in an initiated house, he's as safe as if he was in the dark place itself. Get me?'

That night Lionel sat on the side of his bed and thought the matter out.

'I'm not initiated,' he said aloud.

He finally made a crooked cross out of a bent bed spring.

The Ghoul upstairs had been quiet for the past two days; having an after-dinner nap, Lionel supposed. Mother, worn out by the need to keep an eye on Lionel, and still blissfully unaware of the uses a penknife can be put to, was snoring. He crept downstairs clutching his crooked cross in one hand.

A black candle, large enough to last the entire night, burnt by Aunt Matilda's coffin. She looked far from peaceful, for her teeth were bared, and this grimace gave Lionel the idea he needed. But the teeth were tightly clenched, and his penknife had to be inserted to force them apart so that the little crooked cross could be pushed in over the stiffened tongue. Once open the mouth was reluctant to close again, and Lionel had to upper-cut Aunt Matilda with his small fist before he could safely retire to bed.

It was offering night again. Uncle Arthur brought along his barrow-load of bricks; Aunt Matilda was lifted out of her coffin (no mean task), and the family danced and sang.

> 'Old One, Old One, here we come,
> Bringing goodies for your tum,
> Fat Matilda, plump and white,
> Succulent flesh, the kind you like.
>
> Sup well, eat your fill,
> There's plenty here, and no bill,
> Rump, sirloin, liver, lights,
> Kidneys, breasts, and unstewed tripes.
>
> Suck the marrow from the bones,
> Chew the gristle, spit out the stones,
> Have the brains on breadless toast,
> Prepare the topside as a non-heat roast.
>
> Five-toed trotters on a stick
> Her wishbone will make a fine toothpick,
> Haunch of Matty, what a treat,
> Munch, munch, munch, such lovely meat.'

All this advertising had brought the Ghoul into active,

feet-stomping life. The ceiling shook, the lamp trembled, and Lionel could scarce control his glee when he joyfully anticipated what was to come.

It took a lot of effort to bring Aunt Matilda up the stairs, and there was certainly no breath left for further singing. They had a brief rest on the landing outside Lionel's door, and Uncle Arthur could be heard swearing.

'He's very active up there,' he said after a while.

'He's always a bit frisky before meat,' another uncle suggested.

'You don't suppose,' Mother hesitated, 'he'll come out before we come down?'

' 'Course 'e won't,' Uncle Arthur replied, without, however, much conviction, 'I mean, he never has.'

The journey upwards continued. Lionel heard the shuffling footsteps move over the ceiling to the attic door. Aunt Matilda was dumped on to the upper landing, then there was a mad scramble as the family poured down the stairs; once safely in the hall, they huddled together and chanted the final dirge.

> 'Old One, Black One, listen please,
> From our fears, you must give us ease,
> Come not down, stay up there,
> And we'll all give a hearty cheer.'

The attic door opened, and Aunt Matilda was dragged across the floor. When the door slammed the cheer was not very hearty, little more than an overgrown sigh, then the family retired to the front room for some well-deserved celebrating, while Lionel sat on his bed to listen.

There was much rattling and bumping, as though a vast collection of bones were being cleared to one side. Then came some soft bumps, a few flops, a moist flap, and one mighty crash, then a series of cracking sounds: Lionel giggled, and said aloud, 'You wait – you just wait.'

He waited for a long time. Downstairs Uncle Arthur was singing an obscene song and the rest of the family seemed to be dancing. Then the Ghoul grunted; an enquiring, almost disbelieving growl, that must have been heard in the front room, for Uncle Arthur was stopped on a high note, and the dancing ceased.

The scream began as a whistle. Like an overheated whistling kettle it grew in volume, became an ear-splitting shriek, rose up to a bellowing roar, then reached full maturity as a roof-raising, rasping scream. The ceiling shook, there was a mighty crashing, thrashing; a terrifying bouncing, as though countless very large lead balls were being tossed about. Then a shuddering crack streaked across the ceiling, a lump of plaster fell down on to the dressing table, another crack appeared, then another. Lionel crouched down by his bed, and as an afterthought, crawled under it. The room rained plaster, something crashed down on to the bedside rug, and Lionel stared into the empty eye sockets of a bleached skull; a couple of thigh bones followed, then a gleaming shoulder blade; something soft and floppy flapped on to the bed, and Lionel decided not to think about it.

The scream sank, became a gurgle, then a hiss – then ceased. A few more bones fell, another hunk of plaster, but at last there was peace – an absence of sound before the murmur of frightened voices came up from the room below. Lionel looked upwards and crooned with joy. The Ghoul's head was hanging down through the jagged hole in the ceiling. The green face was no longer luminous; just nasty, crawling slightly, and seemed in imminent danger of parting company from whatever was left of its main body.

'Got yer,' said Lionel.

The family crowded into the room; they looked upwards, they looked down, then they looked at Lionel. Mother put the communal thought into words.

'How did you do it, Son?'

Lionel was brief; action, after all, spoke louder than words.

'Crooked cross,' he said.

'Little monster,' said one aunt.

'A horned toad,' agreed Uncle Arthur.

'What,' enquired Mother, 'will he be when he grows up?'

Silently Lionel pointed to the head dangling from the ceiling.

Forrest Reid

COURAGE

FORREST REID (1875-1947) *is still regarded by most critics as the finest writer ever to emerge from the North of Ireland. Though popular success eluded him during his lifetime (and after), his novels were almost universally praised by contemporary critics, and* Young Tom (1944), *perhaps his greatest achievement, was awarded the James Tait Black Memorial Prize for best novel of the year, the equivalent of today's Booker Prize. Though Reid is widely recognized as a great writer, he is not often discussed as a practitioner of supernatural fiction, an odd omission, given that the supernatural runs through almost all his work, from* The Spring Song (1916), *in which a ghostly tune seems to be luring a boy to the world of the dead, to* Uncle Stephen (1931), *in which a young lad has a spectral playmate, to* Denis Bracknel (1947), *the story of an unworldly boy who practices strange occult rituals by moonlight. Late in his life, Reid set out to rewrite much of his early fiction, including 'Courage', a story that originally appeared in 1918; the version reprinted in this collection is the seldom-seen revised text of 1941. Many of Reid's novels are available from Valancourt, and a previously unpublished horror story, 'Furnished Apartments', appeared in* The Valancourt Book of Horror Stories, Volume One.

WHEN THE CHILDREN CAME TO STAY with their grand-father, Michael, walking with the others from the station to the rectory, noticed the high stone wall that lined one side of the long country lane, and wondered what lay beyond it. Over the top of the wall trees stretched green arms that beckoned to him, and threw black shadows on the white dusty road. His brothers and sisters, stepping demurely beside a tall aunt, left him, as usual, lagging

behind, and when a white bird fluttered out for a moment
into the sunlight they did not even see it. Michael called to
them, and four pairs of eyes turned straightway to the trees
but were too late. 'A pigeon,' Michael said to nobody, and
trotted on to take his place among the rest.

'Does anybody live there?' he asked, but the aunt shook
her head: the house, of whose chimneys he presently caught
a glimpse between the trees, had been empty for years; there
was not even a caretaker in the lodge.

Michael, a rather persistent little boy, learned more than
this, however, from Rebecca, the rectory cook, who told him
that the house was empty because it was haunted. Big boys
at the right time of the year would climb the wall and strip
the apple-trees, but they took care to do so in broad daylight.
The ghost had been seen of course – that was a silly question – how else could people have known about it? It was
the ghost of a lady who had lived there once and been very
wicked; and probably unhappy too, since she couldn't rest
in her grave. Then Rebecca added, more prophetically than
explicitly (though Michael understood her perfectly), that
there were boards up, with 'Trespassers will be Prosecuted'
on them, and that his grandfather would be very angry. . . .

It was on an afternoon, when a game of croquet was becom-
ing increasingly acrimonious, that Michael slipped away
unnoticed, and set out to explore the stream running past the
foot of the rectory garden. He would follow it, he planned,
wherever it led him; follow it just as his father, far away in
wild places, had followed mighty rivers into the heart of
unexplored forests. His father was a traveller, and had written a book, with lots of photographs in it. Michael had never
been able to finish the book, or for that matter even the first
chapter of it, but he had looked at the pictures, and now, by
an easy process of imagination, he was a traveller too.

The long, sweet grass brushed against his legs, and a white

cow, with a rejected buttercup hanging from the corner of her mouth, gazed at him in mild curiosity as he passed. He kept to the meadow side, and on the opposite bank the leaning trees formed little magic caves tapestried with green. Black flies darted restlessly about, and every now and again he heard splashes – the splash of a water-hen, of a rat, of what might have been a fish, though this was unlikely – and then, behind him, the heavy, floundering splash of the cow herself, plunging into the stream up to her knees. He watched her plough laboriously through the sword-shaped leaves of a bed of irises on the farther side, while the rich black mud oozed up between patches of bright green weed. A score of birds made a quaint chorus of trills and peeps, chuckles and whistlings; a wren, like a small winged mouse, flitted about the ivy-covered bole of a hollow tree. But a few yards further on he came disappointingly to the end of his journey, for a rusty iron gate was swung here right across the stream, and on either side of it, as far as he could see, stretched a high grey stone wall.

He paused. The gate was padlocked, and its spiked bars were set so closely together that it would not be easy to climb. While he gazed, a white bird rose out of the burning green and gold of the trees, and for a moment in the sunlight was the whitest thing in the world. Then the bird flew back again into the mysterious shadow, and Michael stood breathless.

He had realized where he was, and that this wall must be a continuation of the wall in the lane. The stooping trees leaned down as if to catch him in their arms. He looked more closely at the padlock, and saw that the spring was half eaten away by rust. He took off his shoes and stockings. Stringing them round his neck, he waded through the water, and with a stone struck the padlock once, twice – twice only – for at the second blow the lock dropped into the stream. Michael tugged at the rusty bolt and in a minute or two the gate was open. Passing through, he clambered up the bank on the other side, and it was while he was pulling on his stockings and his shoes that he saw the gate swing slowly back into its old position.

That was all, yet it slightly startled him, gave him an uneasy feeling that his movements had been watched and that he had been shut in deliberately. Of course the gate must have moved of its own weight, he told himself; nevertheless he had abruptly ceased to be an explorer in remote, untrodden forests, and Rebecca's quite different kind of story had taken the uppermost place in his mind.

Before him was a dark moss-grown path, roofed by trees, whose overarching branches shut out any gleam of sunlight. The path seemed to lead on and on through a listening, watching stillness, and Michael hovered at the entrance to it, doubtful, gazing into its equivocal shadow, not very eager to proceed further.

A nice explorer he would make! His lips pouted and he frowned. Then he made up his mind, and though still frowning, walked on determinedly, while the noise of the stream died away behind him, like a last warning murmur from the friendly world outside.

Quite unexpectedly, for the path turned at an abrupt angle, he came upon the house. It lay beyond what must once have been a lawn, but now the unmown grass, coarse and matted, grew right up to the doorsteps. And to Michael the house itself had a daunting, forbidding look. Lines of dark moss and lichen had crept over the red bricks: the shutters looked as if they had been closed never to be opened again; yet next moment his heart gave a violent jump, for one of them, with a loud and most dismal rattle, flapped back from a window on the ground floor.

He stood motionless while he might have counted fifty. He was on the verge of flight, but fought down the impulse, and there was no further alarm. Moreover, even from his present distance he could see that the window was broken and most of the glass missing – the work, no doubt, of the apple-raiders. A puff of wind had blown back the shutter, that was all. In the reassuring sunlight the spirit of adventure revived and he advanced to make a closer inspection. With his hands on the low window-sill, he peered into a large room. Next, kneeling on the sill, he unlatched the window and pushed it up. The other boys had not dared to enter, he thought, for if they had he was sure they would not have troubled to re-latch the window. Then he clambered across the sill.

Instantly, and most cheeringly, all sense of fear vanished. He could *feel* that the house was empty, that not even the ghost of a ghost lingered here. And with this certainty everything dropped comfortably, if half disappointingly, back into the commonplace. He opened the shutters, letting the rich afternoon light pour in. Though the house had been empty for so long, it still smelt sweet and fresh, and not a speck of dust was visible anywhere. This was surprising, but though Michael drew an experimental finger over the top of one of the little tables, his finger remained clean; the table might have been polished that morning. He also touched the faded upholsteries and curtains, and sniffed at the dried rose-leaves in a china jar. Above the wide chimney-piece hung a picture – the portrait of a lady, still quite young. She was seated in a chair, and beside her, with one hand resting on the back of the chair, stood a boy of about Michael's own age. It was easy to see that they were mother and son, and Michael's thoughts immediately turned to *his* mother, and they were rather strange thoughts, and rather sad, so that presently he wished he had not looked at the picture at all. He drew from his pocket a letter he had received that morning. She was better, she said, and would soon be quite well again. Yesterday she had gone out for a drive, but today she felt a little tired, which was why her letter must be so short.

But he was to enjoy himself, and be a good boy, and give her love to the others . . .

He went out into the hall and unbarred and flung wide the front door before ascending to the upper storeys. There he found a lot of interesting things, and in one room discovered a whole store of toys – soldiers, picture-books, a bow and arrows, a model yacht, and a musical box with a small silver key lying beside it. He wound up the box, and a simple melody tinkled out, faint and fragile, losing itself in the empty silence of the house, like the light of a taper in a cave.

He opened the door of another room, a bedroom, and sitting down near the window, began to turn the pages of an old illuminated volume he found there, full of pictures of saints and martyrs, all glowing in gold and bright colours, yet somehow vaguely disquieting. It was with a start that, on glancing up from his book, he noticed how dark it had grown. The pattern had faded out of the chintz bed-curtains and he could no longer see clearly into the further corners of the room. It was from these corners that the darkness seemed to be stealing out, like a thin smoke, spreading slowly over everything. Surely he had not fallen asleep! yet he did not see how else the time could have passed so quickly without his noticing it. It was so dark now that the bed-curtains were like pale drooping wings, and outside, over the trees, the moon was growing brighter. He must go home at once . . .

He sat motionless, trying to realize what had happened – and listening, listening – for it was as if the secret hidden heart of the house had begun very faintly to beat. Faintly at first, a mere stirring of the vacant atmosphere, but as the minutes passed it gathered strength, and with this consciousness of awakening life a fear came also. He listened in the darkness, and though he could hear nothing, he had a vivid sense that he was no longer alone. Whatever had dwelt here before had come back, as a beast returns to his lair, and was even now, perhaps, creeping up the stairs. A paralysing dread held him weak and inert – though only for a few seconds. It had not – whatever it was – come for him, he told himself. It could not know about him, and perhaps he could get downstairs without meeting it. He glided swiftly across the room and opened the door.

Out on the landing, he had before him the great yawning well of the staircase, that was like a pit of blackness. His heart thumped as he stood against the wall. With shut eyes, lest he should see what he had no desire to see, he took two steps forward and gripped the banister. Then, with eyes still tightly shut, he ran quickly down, unconscious instinct guiding his feet in safety.

At the turn of the stairs the open hall-door showed as a dim silver-grey square, and once he had reached this his panic left him. Fear remained, but it was no longer blind and senseless. He even halted on the threshold, and while he stood there a voice from far away seemed to reach him – yet not a voice, really, so much as a soundless message. He waited, and the message became clear. The way of escape lay there in front of him, but there was something he must do before he took it, and if he left this undone, then he would have failed.

He looked up at the dark, dreadful staircase. Nothing had pursued him, and he knew now that nothing would. Whatever was there was not there with that purpose, and if he were to see it, to face it, he must go in search of it. And if he left it? Nothing would happen; he would be quite safe. Only he knew this, that he would be leaving something else as well, for the message most surely, though he did not know how nor why, had come from his mother. It was her spirit that was close to him at this moment, as if holding his hand, holding him there upon the step. But why? – why? She wanted him to stay, but she did not or could not tell him why. He was free; the choice was his. Yes; but if he were a coward she would know, he would have to tell her, he could not hide it from her. She would accept it, she would forgive him, but that would be wretched, he did not want her to have to forgive him. He steadied himself against the side of the porch. The cold moonlight washed through the hall, and died out in a faint greyness half-way up the first flight of stairs. With sobbing breath and wide eyes he retraced his steps, but at the foot of the stairs he stopped once more, dreading the impenetrable blackness of those awful upper storeys. He put his foot on the lowest stair, and slowly, step by step, he mounted, clutching the banisters. He did not pause on the first landing, but continued straight on into the darkness, which seemed to close about his slender figure like the gates of a monstrous tomb.

Groping his way, he opened the door of the room with the toys. It was bathed in moonlight, and he prayed, 'Let it come now,' for he felt he could not bear the strain of waiting. But nothing came; the room was empty. And he knew, perhaps had known all along, that this was not the right room. Yes, he had known, and with the blood drumming in his ears he now made his final effort. He opened the other door, and was at first conscious only of a sudden, an immense relief, for this room, too, seemed blessedly empty. Then, close by the window, in the pallid twilight, he saw something. At first hardly more than a shadow, a thickening of the darkness, and then, drawing inward and gradually defining itself, a human form. It made no movement towards him, and so long as it remained thus, with head mercifully lowered, he felt that he could bear it. Yet the suspense tortured him, and a faint moan of anguish rose in his throat. With that, the grey marred face he dreaded to see was lifted. He tried to close his eyes, but could not. He felt an increasing weakness and clutched at the doorpost for support. But in the stillness, as he waited, the strange realization slowly came to him that it, too – this shadow – was afraid, and that what it feared was his fear. He saw in the dim, sad eyes the doubt and despair that could find no utterance, and as he did so another and more generous emotion began to stir within him. Why was she like this? – so different from the picture downstairs – and where was the boy who had stood so close to her, who had seemed so close to her? Michael made no effort to retreat though now she was approaching him – timidly, uncertainly. He looked at her steadily; he wasn't going to run away. He was quite sure now, and was no longer afraid. She wanted him, so he came to meet her, and when she held out her arms he came nearer still and held up his face to hers. But as her arms went round him it was as if he were wrapped in an icy mist, through which he had a last brief vision of a radiant happiness shining down on him – and then he was alone....

Alone in a moonlit house that no longer held any terror for him. Alone, but with a strange glow of happiness that seemed not only within, but all around him. He must certainly go home, and yet now he felt loath to do so. Only, they would wonder what had happened to him, must have begun to wonder long ago; and he was very hungry. He pulled back the curtains as far as possible to let more moonlight in, and on the window-ledge a box of matches was revealed. This was lucky, for now he could light the two tall candles on the chimney-piece. And it was while he was doing so that he became more vividly aware of what he had felt subconsciously during the past few minutes. A subtle change had come about in the surrounding atmosphere, though in what it consisted he could not tell. It was as if the earlier stillness were no longer empty, had become, rather, a hush in the air, like that which accompanies the falling of snow. But how could there be snow in midsummer? – and, moreover, this was within the house, not outside. He lifted one of the candlesticks and saw that a delicate powder of dust had gathered upon it. He looked down at his own clothes – they, too, were covered with that same thin powder. Then he knew what was happening. The dust of years had begun to fall – silently, slowly, like a soft and continuous caress, laying everything in the house to sleep.

Dawn was breaking when, with a candle in either hand, he descended the broad whitening staircase. As he passed out into the garden he saw lanterns approaching. It was a search party, he guessed; and guessed that, after many hours, Rebecca must have remembered an early conversation. Yet, to his surprise, nobody scolded him, nobody asked questions. Nor was it till the next day that he learned of the telegram which had come in his absence.

Ernest G. Henham

PETE BARKER'S SHANTY

The career of ERNEST G. HENHAM (1870-1948), *whom a critic for the* Times Literary Supplement *in 2013 called 'one of England's lost novelists, a writer of startling ability', was a strange one. From 1897 to 1907 he built a minor reputation for himself under his birth name of Henham, publishing a number of moderately successful novels, including the weird decadent tale* Tenebrae (1898) *and the haunted house novel* The Feast of Bacchus (1907), *both republished by Valancourt. But for reasons of health, Henham was obliged to move to Dartmoor, where he apparently disowned his earlier works, adopting the pseudonym John Trevena and publishing a series of highly accomplished mystical novels which were ranked by a contemporary* Los Angeles Times *critic as being on par with the classics of Turgenev and Dostoevsky. Given the enthusiastic response Henham/Trevena's tale 'The Frozen Man' received from readers of our first* Valancourt Book of Horror Stories, *we are pleased to be able to offer another very rare story by this elusive author. First published in 1898, 'Pete Barker's Shanty' features an unusual setting for a horror story – a desolate stretch of prairie in late 19th-century Canada – that no doubt draws on the author's early life experiences in Canada working for the Hudson Bay Company (the 'H.B.' referred to in the story).*

K LINE REINED IN HIS HORSE, and pointed to a patch of prairie, thickly covered with small rose bushes and other vegetation, springing from a brown, furrowed soil. 'It's just as I told you half-an-hour ago, Talbot. We're a way off.'

'How do you know we're wrong?' I asked.

'That field yonder. There's no broken prairie alongside of the trail we should have travelled. We're some points too far north.'

'There may be a shanty near.'

Kline frowned, then wheeled his horse off to the patch of land, and trampled down the dwarf briars for some paces. 'It might be any time from five to ten years since a plough went over this,' he announced, as he rode back. 'If we do strike a shanty a piece on, it'll be empty.'

'Case of camping out here, then?'

'I guess,' he assented, casting another glance around.

There wasn't much to see. Behind, the waving prairie rolled away, broken by poplar bluffs, and spotted by little mounds of black soil that marked badger or gopher holes. On each side, and in front, the bush spread thickly.

I was bound for a station of the H.B. on the Sand River, and we had reckoned on reaching our destination about midnight. This was now impossible, owing to my guide's mistake in the route. Already the shadows were lengthening and the sun dipping down to the line of the glowing horizon.

Kline nodded towards a tall bluff of white poplar. 'There'll be a good place.'

'But this is a trail,' I said. 'It must bring out somewhere.'

'Only wants half a look to tell it's an old one – hasn't been used for years. Likely it's an old H.B. route. Look at the way those bushes crawl over the ridges, and see how smooth the soil is – just as the spring thaw left it. There hasn't been a wheel over here this summer.'

'Well, we'd better fix up our camp,' I said, gathering up the reins. 'We'll want a couple of smudges, for the mosquitoes are going to be a terror.'

Again we set off, my companion as usual taking the lead. The barely defined trail ran straight into the heart of the bush, then disappeared in the rapidly falling darkness. But we had not covered more than thirty paces, when Kline pulled up, so suddenly, that my Kitty started back. He sprang to the ground, fell on his knees, and closely examined the centre of the trail.

'What have you got there?' I called.

After a few moments he raised his head. 'It's been a clear day, eh, Talbot?'

'Yes,' I said, wondering.

'Hasn't been anything more than a breath all day, but last night was a bit windy?'

When I again replied in the affirmative, he sprang to his feet. 'There's been a man along here since morning.'

'How shod?'

'Barefoot.'

'Must have been a *nitchi*.'

'Might. But they don't often tramp singly. We'll shove along before it gets darker.'

He sprang again to the saddle, and we plunged into the bush. After about five minutes' travelling, the leader pulled up again. He turned his head with the announcement, 'The trail splits. It's too dark in the bush now to make out a foot-print.' Then his voice changed. 'Ah! Do you see that?'

'What?'

'Look at your Kitty.'

My old mare was sniffing up the air that came down the trail to the right.

'That's a better sign than footmarks. If old Kitty was the fellow's donkey in the Bible that talked, she couldn't put it plainer.'

'Can't make much out of it,' I said, patting her neck.

'She says that, if we push along this side bit of trail, we shall come out on a clearing where there's a shanty. How do I make that out? Why, easy enough. Kitty's thirsty, and she can smell water in the air. When there's water to be found in a place like this, there's a well. Where there's a well, there must be a man who's dug it. A man lives in a shanty, and a shanty stands on a clearing. See?'

'You can't tell that the shanty will be occupied now.'

'What's the good of that footprint, then?' returned Kline, riding off.

We crashed steadily through thick bush for some time, then came upon a thicket which barred further progress.

'Where's your opening now?' I asked, secretly a trifle disgusted with my guide.

'Somewhere round,' replied Kline. 'Here, Billy, take us out of this.'

He flung the reins on his horse's neck, and touched up his flank with the saddle thong. The animal stood pawing the ground uneasily, and sniffing from left to right. Then, with a suddenness which might have unseated a less skilful rider, he turned into the bush on the left side of the trail. It was very dark as the foliage was thick, so the next moment I found myself alone on the path, with Kitty snorting and pulling impatiently.

'Come on,' a voice below me was calling. 'Mind out for your face, and sit close – it's down hill.'

I faced the thicket, with hands held before me. I felt innumerable twigs and bunches of cold leaves sweeping around. Kitty was half-stepping, half-sliding, down a steep and crumbling incline.

'What's the matter with this?' was Kline's question as I reached him.

A path lay before, running in a straight line through bush, and ending in open prairie. In another minute the legs of our horses brushed through the waving grass of a flower-decked circular patch, not more than a hundred yards in width, and bound in every direction by the dark tree line. We glanced around this open space. Then I looked at Kline, and he at me.

'I guess we're over sixty miles from Sand River. Far as I know, there isn't any shanty between here and there. It's thick bush, like that we've just come through. Who in thunder can live over there?'

He nodded towards the opposite side, where, in the dim light, we could easily make out a grass-thatched log shanty, surrounded by a neglected fire-break. We rode across, dismounted, and knocked upon the closed door. But nobody stirred within.

'See if it's fastened,' said Kline.

I raised the catch, and pushed. The door gave at once, and we entered.

'Owner's out. Let's water the horses, Talbot. Then we'll sit inside for a smoke.'

The well was close to the house, with a bucket handy. We turned into the shack as soon as we could, for the insects were ravenous. Discovering a lamp, we lighted up, and made ourselves fairly comfortable.

The shanty was old and crazy, with floor composed of bare soil, and grass thatch protruding through the sloping roof. A folding-bed stood in one corner, a table in the centre, and a cupboard near the single window, by the side of a box, upon which lay a few books and an axe. Perceiving a worn Bible, I picked it up, and found a name inscribed upon the flyleaf. The markings were faint, written evidently years before, but on bringing the book to the light, I made out the words, 'Pete Barker, from the old father, likewise named Pete Barker.' I laughed at the curious wording, and Kline, who was chopping tobacco at the table, asked what I had discovered.

'Name of the owner. Ever heard of Pete Barker?'

'Never,' he replied. 'But I'd like to know what he's doing out here.'

We began to fill the dreary place with comfortable clouds of smoke, Kline seated upon the bed, and I upon the box under the window. Outside it grew darker, for the moon had not yet come up; inside, the melancholy lamp cast sickly rays around the bare room. Had there been no mosquitoes, I would as soon have camped in the bush.

Kline had bent to pick up a dry grass to clear his pipe stem, when I suddenly asked him a question. He looked up to reply, but, as I met his glance, I saw a strange pallor creeping up beneath his dark skin. His lips were moving as though in speech, but no sounds came to my ears, and I noticed that the hand which held his pipe tapped foolishly upon his knee. He was staring at some object near my right shoulder.

I started round hastily, but immediately the hair began to bristle beneath my hat. For there was an awful picture behind my shoulder. Presently I knew that I was staring at the square window pane, and that pressed close to the glass was the upper portion of a human face – white, ghastly, wild-looking. As suddenly it vanished, while the pane became again blank and dark.

'It must be the owner of the shanty,' I said unsteadily.

'It's owned by the devil, then,' Kline muttered.

The door opened gradually. The next moment a remark-able figure entered – an old man, clothed in a mouldy suit, patched all over with scraps of skin and sacking. His feet were bare; scanty hair trailed in greasy ringlets down his dirty neck; his nails were long and crooked, while the fingers were curved like eagle's talons; his teeth were few and yellow. The steely-blue eyes rolled unceasingly, as though striving to light upon a certain object which always remained invisible.

Kline recovered wonderfully when he beheld the kind of individual he had to deal with. 'Crazy,' he said, in a low tone.

After a pause I spoke. 'Talk to him, Louis.'

Kline pulled the pipe from his mouth, cleared his throat vigorously, then remarked in a conversational voice, 'Say, Pete.'

But he might as well have addressed the table.

'How are you making out, Pete Barker? Are you going to put us up for the night, and set us on the Sand River trail in the morning?'

The result was the same, and Kline turned to me with a puzzled expression.

'Darn it, Talbot! don't believe old moonhead knows we're here at all.'

The situation was so peculiar that I laughed. Kline joined in with a deep cachinnation, and, strangely enough, the sounds aroused the old man into action. He held his head to one side, like a man trying to catch a sound from afar, then suddenly came to my side, grabbed at the axe, and left the shanty.

'Too bad to have hurt his feelings,' said my companion, who was dropping into a lively vein. 'He's after practising surgery on someone.'

Presently old Barker returned, and set down the weapon. His eyes kept on rolling, while low mumblings proceeded from his thick lips.

I have never passed a more extraordinary evening. The madman ate his strange meal, then took up the shabby Bible, and sat down on the bed, which Kline promptly vacated. There he remained for over two hours, holding the open book in his claw-like hand, his eyes roving around the room, the mumbling growing sometimes louder and deeper.

We had our own store of provisions, and there was plenty of water at hand, so we might have fared worse. Presently I pulled out a pack of cards, and we started a game of euchre, while the proprietor sat opposite, sometimes groaning loudly as though in pain. It was rather horrible to be cooped up with such a creature in that lonely spot. I know Kline didn't like it, for he kept screwing round his head, and snatching sidelong glances at the figure behind.

Suddenly the old man, without any sort of preparation, threw himself down along the bed, and turned his face towards the log wall.

'He's the craziest old fool upon this earth,' said Kline, uneasily.

'All the same, we might follow his example,' I suggested.

'I suppose,' he said, fingering the cards nervously, 'he won't try any monkey tricks upon us while we're asleep, you reckon?'

We arranged ourselves as circumstances would allow, then I blew out the lamp. There was a bright moon shining – the pale rays poured through the window, and flooded the shanty with weird light, while a night breeze had arisen, and was moaning softly round the shanty. Presently I heard heavy footsteps; immediately after, black shadows fell across the illuminated window, and I started up – to fall back laughing, when I remembered the horses. Later, I was annoyed to hear Kline's deep breathing; I felt he had played a mean trick in dropping off to sleep, and leaving me to keep an involuntary watch. Then I opened my eyes.

The madman had turned, and the moonlight shone full upon his ghastly countenance. It was ridiculous to feel alarm, still I could not restrain a strong shudder. Insanity is always terrifying to the sane.

Then I managed to direct my thoughts towards that day's journey, and in wondering at what particular point we went astray, I dozed off. . . .

I woke cold and nervous, and, as I turned heavily, conscious of stiffness in each limb, my eyes opened, and lighted at once upon old Barker, sitting on the bed, his claw-like hands resting upon his knees, his body bent forward.

'Curse the old fool!' I muttered. 'Why can't he hide that hideous face?' But, as I grew more awake, it struck me that there was something in his expression I had not observed before. I half rose on my elbow, and looked round – the next moment I felt cold water trickling along my spine.

Upon the box by the window, full in cold moonrays, sat a young girl, clad in a black dress, which was fastened at the throat by a red, heart-shaped brooch, her hands clasped together, her eyes fixed upon the old maniac opposite. She was frightened, for her face was very pale, and her dark eyes large and fixed. She appeared to quiver from head to foot, but this effect might have been produced by the surrounding waves of light. Suddenly her head came for a moment in front of the window pane. Then I shuddered, for I could still see the dim unbroken outline of the lath through her head.

Bathed in perspiration, I watched the unnatural figures gazing one at the other. At length I summoned courage to free myself. I dragged my stiffened limbs from the ground to the door, opened it and stepped into the white night, passing the girl so closely that I might have touched her shadowy shoulder. Then I wrapped my head in a coat, and slept on the grass, until strange sounds aroused me soon after sunrise.

I rubbed my eyes blankly, while Kitty came up and whinnied a good morning. A cry certainly hung in my ears, but I thought I had been dreaming. Suddenly a voice rang out loudly, 'Here, Talbot – if you're alive!'

I was upon my feet in a flash and at the door. Dashing inside, I found Kline upon the ground, with old Barker kneeling upon his chest, the axe raised in his right hand, the left clutching his captive's throat. Seizing the madman – it was an easy matter, for he completely ignored me – I threw him aside, while Kline hastily dragged himself up.

'You came in time,' he panted. 'Old moonhead was just going to strike me down with that axe.'

'I was sleeping outside,' I explained. 'Your shout woke me.'

'If it hadn't, he'd have made cold meat of me. He took me foul, when I was asleep; but he's terrible strong, I tell you.'

The strange creature was now trembling like a beaten dog. Kline followed him to the corner, and struck him upon the shoulder. 'You old moonhead! You'd fix a man when he's asleep in your shanty, eh? You old rathead!'

'Leave him alone, Louis,' I cried. 'Remember he's mad, poor old chap!'

An hour later we rode away from Pete Barker's shanty, by the way we had come. Kline went ahead, silent and moody, but as we came towards the cultivated patch, he started and said, 'Say! did you see that wolf?'

'No,' I replied. 'Where did it go?'

'Right into the bush. Wait a few minutes, while I see if I can get in a shot.'

I was impatient to finish my journey, but, as I didn't want to put him in a worse humour, I consented. Presently I heard a shot in the distance, and soon he returned, pale and excited, but empty-handed. 'I had one shot, but he was too far,' he explained.

Early on the following day we came safely to Sand River.

That winter I spent at my usual headquarters – Winnipeg. One afternoon, shortly after Christmas, I was returning to my lodgings, by means of the short cut afforded by some side streets, when I caught sight of the slim form of a young girl, in Persian lamb jacket and cap, walking a little way in front. There was nobody else to be seen along the silent, snow-covered street. I gained upon her rapidly, but, when she was about to round the corner of a block, I noticed her catch quickly at her throat, while the next moment she began to search for something on the beaten snow of the sidewalk.

Just then I came up, and at once perceived a small object gleaming redly from a side drift. I stepped across, picked it up, and at the same time the girl turned towards me with a slight exclamation.

It was a small, heart-shaped brooch. The whole strange scene of the previous summer flashed back into my mind, so I looked up quickly, expectantly, to see – standing before me in the dull winter light, the same girl I had looked upon sitting in the shanty beneath the moonlight, with fearful eyes fixed upon the old madman opposite.

'If you please – it is mine,' she said timidly. The wonder crept into her eyes when she beheld the expression in mine.

For I was almost stupefied. Here was the girl in the substance, whom I had seen in the shadow. On this occasion I could not pick out portions of the wall through her head.

She was quite a little girl, plainly dressed in black, and

pretty in a quiet way, though very pale. I kept staring at her, until she began to grow afraid. She shrank back, and said in the same low voice, 'I can't prove that it is mine. Still, I am telling you the truth.'

'I know you are,' I burst forth. 'I saw you drop it.'

Her mouth took a curious shape; she was divided between fear of me and anxiety to regain her brooch.

'Tell me your name,' I said, almost sharply, for my nerves were overstrung.

She hesitated a moment, and then replied simply, 'Jessie Barker.'

I spoke almost without knowing it. 'Does your father live here?'

That stirred her. Her cheeks grew still whiter. 'Why do you ask?' she whispered, bending forward. 'What do you know about him?'

'Listen,' I said, taking her by the arm. 'Away north there's a shanty standing on a patch of prairie in the heart of the bush. An old man lives there, an old madman. His eyes—'

She screamed, and covered her face with her hands. 'Don't – it's too horrible.' Presently the strange confession came forth slowly. 'I have seen him – often – but I not know who he is; I do not know where that shanty is, though I have been in it every night—'

'I have seen you there.'

'No – no,' she sobbed, for she was crying now. 'That is impossible.'

'But you must know his name – it is Pete Barker.'

She screamed again, and tottered as though she would fall. I came forward to support her, but she pushed me away with her weak little hands. 'Please let me go. I do not want my brooch now – I want to go home.'

At length she recovered a little, and stood wiping her eyes with a tiny handkerchief, her shoulders heaving with suppressed sobs. 'It was my father's name,' she faltered.

'Then *he* is your father. But how did you recognize the description?'

She gave a shudder. 'By my dreams.'

'Dreams!' I repeated, though I began to understand.

'I always dreaded sleep. I was sure to find myself in that horrible place, staring at that – that madman. Night was a time of horror for me. I got weak and ill – I think I should have died, but the dreams suddenly ceased.'

'You never go there now?' It was a strange way of putting the question, but my brain was whirling.

'No. The dreams stopped one night last summer. They have never come back.'

'What night was that?'

'The seventeenth of July.'

I remembered the date well. Her dreams had ceased the night after we had left the shanty. Mysteries were falling like snowflakes in October.

The girl was too ill to talk any more, so I saw her home, and returned her the brooch. Soon afterwards I saw her again, and then she told me the little she knew of her family history.

'My father married at an advanced age. He was very fond of his wife, who was an English girl, but I have heard that the affection was not altogether mutual. I was their first child, and a few months after I was born my mother disappeared. People thought she must have made away with herself; anyhow, she was never heard of again. Everybody noticed that my father was very strange after his wife's disappearance, so they weren't much surprised when he suddenly left the place. Since then, nobody has seen him, except you – and I.'

The following summer, the Indian Department again ordered me to the Sand River Station. I had no idea who was to accompany me as guide and interpreter, until I reached the starting-point. There I found Kline awaiting me.

'They've bothered you with me again, Talbot,' he said, by way of greeting. 'Well, I guess I know the trail this journey. We won't go fooling off down side tracks and paying visits to private lunatic asylums, eh?'

For the first days of our outward journey everything went smoothly. Certainly the trail was very difficult. I noted it more especially on this occasion, and wondered how Kline managed to keep right, for side trails bristled from the main like a herring bone. But the prairie was his home, and he understood it well.

It was late in the afternoon. We were trotting along easily, with a cool wind fanning our faces. Gaudy tiger lilies and marigolds brushed our horses' legs. Suddenly we passed a tall poplar that stood quite by itself, near the trail, the lower part of its trunk black as ink, the upper white as flour. It seemed to be familiar.

A curious sensation that! Often have I travelled across the prairie, and been attracted, almost hailed, by some slight object, which has fixed itself into the memory, yet been forgotten, until the sight of it has again restored remembrance. You recollect, perhaps, the actual phrase you used when passing on the previous occasion.

But Kline had also noticed this tree, and continually cast mysterious glances towards it, standing gaunt and motionless in the lessening sunlight. He was leading, but I soon perceived that he was uneasy, for he was gazing from right to left, sometimes half checking Billy, at others turning and looking at me out of the corner of his eye.

Still we pushed on, without speaking, but I kept my eyes upon the guide. Moisture glistened beneath the wide rim of his hat, and I felt that this was not caused by heat. He held his gaze fixed ahead, riding like a man who has lost control over his actions.

The sun was dissolving into the colours of evening, and the shadows were growing blacker, when the explanation came. Kline reined up with a frightened oath; he turned his face to me and pointed beyond. Following the direction of his hand, I saw, quivering in the rising breeze, a thick mass of stunted vegetation springing from a patch of once cultivated land!

'How the h—l have I gone to work and made the mistake again?' he almost shouted, and I was surprised to find him so thoroughly alarmed. 'I knew I was wrong for the last hour.'

'Well,' I said, 'let's go on. We'll spend the night with old Barker again.'

He shrank back in horror. 'Not me! I'd sooner camp right here, without supper or drink.'

I only replied shortly, 'I'm going, anyhow. I want to see him again.'

Kline saw the imputation upon his courage. Presently he said sulkily, 'You're boss, Talbot. If you say, "come" I've got to.'

On this occasion I was leader. Down the slope we struggled, along the narrow path, and out once more into the open. There stood the shanty ahead, but as we rode across the open space, I noticed that the weeds had grown up thickly all round, even in front of the door, which stood slightly open.

Though I was quick in dismounting, Kline was ahead of me. He had entered before I touched ground. We met at the door, and he exclaimed, 'The old chap's hopped the twig.'

'Dead?' I cried, though I was scarcely astonished.

'As this log post. I'll fetch him out, though he's not much in the beauty line.'

He disappeared again, and I heard him muttering and groaning. Presently a harsh sound of bones creaking and dry skin stretching and cracking reached my ears and made me shudder. Then he reappeared, dragging a dreadful skeleton, over which the brown skin, partially covered with wretched shreds of clothing, still hung tightly. The twisted beard and greasy locks were still there, the dry, sunken eye-balls; yellow teeth protruded from the grinning jaws. Finger bones and misshapen feet scraped gruesome furrows in the dusty soil, as Kline, whose sudden nerve I wondered at, dragged the heap of bones from the shanty and rested them on the grass.

'Why! there's blood on his beard!' I exclaimed, as I bent over the remains.

'Pshaw!' muttered Kline, 'that's no blood.'

'It is,' I said testily. 'He must have fallen and struck his head against the wall.'

'That's it, Talbot,' agreed my companion, hastily. 'He went off in a fit. All these crazy chaps do that.'

We interred Barker's bones with scant ceremony, simply removing the turf, scooping out a couple of feet of loam, then laying in the body, and finally replacing the earth. This done, we fumigated the hut by means of a smudge, and made it as habitable as before.

As we sat smoking after supper, I reflected upon the curious repetition of events. Before turning in, I ransacked the box, but found nothing of significance, though later I observed something which sent a thrill through my body.

After I had deprived old Barker of the axe with which he was about to cut short Kline's career, I had driven it into one of the logs near the window, and had left it so fixed. Now I noticed that the weapon was still in the very position in which I had placed it a twelvemonth back. So the old man must have died almost immediately after our departure, for he would have found some use for the axe every day of his life. This convinced me that Jessie Barker's release was owing to her father's death, which, according to her state-ment, must have taken place on the very day of our depar-ture. The excitement had probably brought on a fit, which had finished him off.

Before we settled down for the night, Kline insisted on

hanging his coat before the window. 'It's going to be a bright night,' he explained. 'I don't want to wake up and see his bony face sticking against the panes outside.'

I think I went off to sleep almost directly. The room being partially darkened was scarcely an improvement, for shimmering rays crept in on all sides, lighting up parts of the room, and leaving the remainder in a deep darkness. However, I was tired, and not in a mood to be easily disturbed.

It is not pleasant to be suddenly aroused, even in your own unromantic bedroom. But to be awakened at dead of night in a lonely hut, miles from civilisation – to be called into action, moreover, by a voice that is hoarse with horror, and stirred by a hand that is well-nigh powerless with fright – is an experience that few would wish to undergo.

I started up, and, by the wan light of a wandering moon-ray, saw Kline hanging over me. His face was distorted, and his eyes half shut; the lower jaw fell, while he panted like a dog; shining drops coursed down his nose.

I tried to speak, but my tongue was bound; I tried to rise, but my limbs were frozen. I tried to make signs, but my muscles refused to act. Still he hung over me, quivering and sweating.

At length I managed to ejaculate, in a voice which was not mine, 'Speak, Louis!'

The answer came, but not from him. There was a gentle knocking at the door. Gentle, but soon it grew louder, until hollow echoes ran around the hut. The silence returned, a silence more awful than the disturbance. Kline had fallen forward, right over my body.

'It's him,' he moaned, twisting his foolish fingers round my arm.

The shanty stood out in the open. No tree grew by; no branch could fitfully tap against the door.

I would have torn the coat from the window, but Kline held my arm. 'Don't, for the Lord's sake! Do you want to see him grinning at us? He's outside there – tearing round the shanty – crazy as ever.'

I trembled horribly; then the knocking came again. Kline clutched me frantically, burying his head close to my side, moaning and sobbing like a child.

'They say dead men don't talk. I tell you, they howl, and they yell. A living man can't get in a word with them!'

'What are you driving at?' I muttered, but he only groaned and slobbered, so I made as though I would get up.

'Don't do it,' he panted. 'If you open the door, he'll murder me. That's what he's waiting outside for. I killed him, Talbot – fixed him last year.'

I sank back in horror, while he rambled on. 'I was terrible mad with him for trying to fix me, so I slipped back and shot him. There it is! Oh, Lord!'

I could feel his convulsive tremblings as the knocking arose again. But when it died away, I pulled together my few shreds of courage and rose, shaking off Kline, who clung to me pitifully.

'Don't leave me, Talbot. We're done for, if you open the door.'

I tore down the coat, and the moonlight poured into the room, lighting up every corner. Kline covered up his face with the fallen garment, while I staggered to the door, and took a deep breath, like a man about to plunge into cold water. I put my hand towards the catch – then the bony fingers rattled upon the partition, and I fell back into the room.

It ceased. Five times I caught hold of the catch, but my arm dropped powerless. At last I flung open the door, though I weakly closed my eyes at the last moment. Then I laughed at my folly, for there was nothing – nothing, except the long, waving grasses, the dark line of bush, with the moonlight playing over all. So I stepped outside, keeping, I must confess, a watchful eye upon a certain black mound that rose hard by.

I leaned against the log wall, and gazed at the motionless line of trees. Suddenly I fancied a breath of cold air passed across my cheek. The night was exceedingly warm – there was scarcely a ripple of wind. The next instant there were two small blue lights, close together, moving over the grass. They looked to be about five and a half feet above the ground. I could think of nothing but Pete Barker's eyes.

As I stood there, frozen outwardly, on fire inwardly, my left hand was seized. Invisible fingers closed around mine; rough bone pressed against my hand; long talons pricked my flesh. It pulled, and though my knees tottered, I had to obey, to follow the dreadful thing, with a moaning in my ears, and the blue lights hovering at my side, through the trembling grass that swept against my legs, across the open space, into the bush. Through thick brake and over great stones, crashing through tangled bushes that cut and lashed my face, on and on, dragged by that horrible, irresistible hand. . . .

I sank upon a rock, and struggled to regain breath and senses. I could see that a hand had formerly been at work in that spot, clearing away the undergrowth, which was now commencing to spring up again. At length I rose, and stepped from the circle of pines. In an instant the dreadful grasp fell upon me, and I was forced back, this time to the centre of the clearing. The moonlight poured down through the mournful trees, so I bent to examine the ground at my feet. Probably the soil had been disturbed in the past, though there were no signs to assure me. So I drew out a knife and bent to my task, loosening the earth, and chopping through roots. I had scarcely dug to the depth of a foot, when my nails – I was shoveling aside the loam with my hands – scraped against a smooth surface. After a little more burrowing I unearthed a small box, the lid of which was fastened by nails. With this I passed from the group of pines without hindrance, and returned to the shanty, where I found Kline lying in a dead faint.

Later, in the grey dawn, I told my story. Then we opened the box, and discovered three things, each telling a separate tale of that dreadful life. A photograph – at first glance I thought it was intended for Jessie, subsequently I guessed that it was her mother's likeness. Then a baby's coral, with two little silver bells attached. Lastly, a roll of dirty paper, covered with almost illegible writing. This was a confession, written and signed some years before by old Barker, setting forth the fact that he had murdered his wife in a mad fit of jealousy.

Kline quickly recovered from his conscience-stricken fear, and to this day I do not know whether to blame him for his act. Certainly the madman's death preserved the daughter's reason, and her life was of more value than his, I take it. He must have possessed some hypnotic influence over her, though I don't know whether he was aware that he exerted this power nightly. I have never again been near the shanty, though I daresay it still stands upon the bush-encircled patch of prairie, sixty-five miles north-west of the Sand River.

I never saw Jessie again, as she had left Winnipeg when I returned, so I had no opportunity of letting her know the truth regarding her mother's end. I confess I was disappointed, for she was a pretty girl, and once or twice I had thought – but that has nothing whatever to do with this story.

Steve Rasnic Tem

THE PARTS MAN

One of the finest and most original speculative fiction writers of our time, STEVE RASNIC TEM *has published over 430 stories, seven novels, and ten collections in a career spanning four decades and has won nearly every major award in the field, including the World Fantasy Award, British Fantasy Award, and Bram Stoker Award. His work blends elements of horror, dark fantasy, science fiction and surreal nightmare into a genre uniquely his own. 'The Parts Man' was written especially for this volume and ranks alongside the author's best work. A retrospective collection of thirty-five of Tem's finest tales,* Figures Unseen: Selected Stories, *appeared from Valancourt in 2018.*

THE CAR WAS RIGHT OUT OF THE MID-THIRTIES: jet black with a chrome grill, skirted fenders, multibar bumpers, and the dashboard rich in shiny silver knobs and trim. Cranks on either side of the dash allowed him to tilt the two halves of the split windshield. Christian loved that classic look, but this vehicle, with its endless lines and confusing interior shadows, not so much.

The car stretched as it roared through intersections and bent around corners. The side windows were so short it appeared to be squinting. The inside, so full of dark, had enough room to fit pretty much every person Christian had ever wronged.

'Drive faster. You have limited time, and so many passengers to pick up,' said the parts man from one of the back seats. The parts man moved around in the car by means of unfathomable physics. He seemed everywhere at once. Sometimes he appeared large enough to fill the interior, other times so thin and two-dimensional he disappeared when turning his head.

Christian kept a nervous eye on the rear view mirror. 'I'm still getting used to the shifter.'

'Push the gas pedal down, Christian.' The voice was close behind him, breath stinking of spoiled meat and cigar. Christian gazed into the rear-view and the parts man stared back, only his sleepy brown eyes and a twisted stretch of pale nose showing. Thankfully not the mouth of no lips, the saw-like teeth, the long white tongue. 'Or are you having second thoughts?'

Christian glanced into the mirror again, this time seeing his own face, sixty-eight years of deep lines and broken blood vessels. Or was it sixty-nine? When he first slipped into the driver's seat his arthritis made his joints scream as he bent his legs. 'No. A deal's a deal.'

He counted off the intersections, scanning the sides of the street for landmarks, looking for that certain spot he remembered from decades ago. He couldn't remember precisely where, until the parts man said, 'Stop!'

Christian hit the brakes and saw the church through the split windshield, and that tan apartment building still standing on the corner. He remembered. This was more or less where it occurred.

'First, the payment,' the parts man said, and reached around the back seat and between the buttons of Christian's shirt.

Christian gasped as he saw the fingers go in – so terribly long and pointed, spiderleg narrow, slim enough to go through a key hole. They entered somewhere below his heart, pinched, and withdrew. The sensation of a cold wind leaking into his insides consumed him. 'What was it?'

'I took nothing you cannot live without. A surgeon's exam would find nothing missing. Still, you have paid a dear price.'

Christian reached under his shirt but felt neither blood

nor wound. But that notion of a cold leakage continued. He stared out the driver's side window. A glossy spot shimmered in the pavement a few feet away, an oil stain perhaps. But as he watched it spread into a pool, shimmered, and then long tendrils of smoke and liquid rose into the air, entwined, filling in with patches of pale mesh, dripping, bleeding into veins and arteries and the brilliant white of bone, red of muscle, wrapped rapidly by umber flesh, flowering into a brain, eyes, tongue and head, the coiled corkscrews of her Afro, and then that face that still haunted his dreams: it was Cheryl, still wearing the yellow sundress she'd died in.

The rear driver side door opened and Cheryl staggered toward the car with a dazed expression. The door closed around her as if she'd been swallowed. Christian watched her in the mirror. When he caught her eye she leaned forward and grabbed his arm. 'Christian? What happened?'

The parts man was now seated in the front passenger seat. His head was long and triangular-shaped, snailskin pale, topping a long too-pliable neck whose many creases suggested segments. He was enveloped in a soft gray coat which flapped and shuddered with a life of its own. The parts man murmured with his lipless mouth, 'Tell her she had a bad moment, but that she's fine now. She will be, until tonight's ride is over.'

Christian shook his head, more at the parts man's proximity than the lie he had to tell his long dead girlfriend. 'It's okay, honey,' Christian said. 'You're okay. You just had a bad moment. Everything's fine – just enjoy the ride.'

She laughed hazily. 'I'm just so tired. Don't take it personally if I can't hold up my end of the conversation, 'kay?'

Christian watched her reflection as her eyes closed, then caught a glimpse of himself: the smooth brow and the clear eyes, maybe eighteen years old. He'd been driving a '71 Mercury Comet back then, blue as the sky. He and Cheryl had been arguing all afternoon about something – he couldn't even remember what – something unimportant, with him not understanding what she was even talking about, and her furious with him for not caring enough to understand. She'd shouted at him to stop the car – she was getting out. He'd been so mad he'd foolishly slammed on the brakes, right there in traffic. He knew he'd made a terrible mistake when she grabbed the door handle. Before he could object she'd opened the door and was standing out there on the pavement, not even a second before something large and silver slapped her away.

So forty-five plus years later when the parts man dragged Christian out of bed and made his offer, how could he refuse? A few hours more life for Cheryl, and for all the others he'd let down over the years, the ones he'd left behind dead or dying while he survived. And at such a reasonable cost for an old man, although the pricing details had not yet been specified when he'd accepted the deal.

He heard the sounds behind him, and twisted around as the parts man touched her with his spider leg fingers, pulling her close for an intimate whisper. Christian wanted to object, but had no idea what he was objecting to.

A half-hour later they were parked in front of a block-long brick box of a building. It looked grayish, wrapped in dirty fog. The upper story was ragged and transparent. It was the old YMCA building, torn down ten years ago.

'We're here for Tommy, aren't we?'

'Thomas O'Toole. Less accomplished than your other friends. "Slow," you thought.'

Actually they'd called Tommy much worse. It wasn't that they disliked him. Tommy had been quiet, didn't defend himself, and they had no one else to pick on.

'I don't think he was even slow. He was probably as smart as the rest of us. Maybe if we'd left him alone he would have been okay.'

They walked up the steps and a slight tug opened the

double doors. The parts man apparently knew the way, guiding them through a series of halls until they entered the dusty gym. Christian avoided looking at the far end of the court. The bleachers on both sides were partially collapsed, the wall banners in tatters. Moonlight made a series of narrow vertical shadows on the far wall. One of the vertical shadows suddenly began to swing.

He followed the parts man until they were almost under the hoop. A small boy hung from a clothesline tied to the rim. Christian hadn't looked at the body when it happened; he felt he had to now. The noose made such a deep crease in the neck the folds of skin obscured it. 'There's a ladder leading up to the beams,' Christian said. 'He must have climbed up with the clothesline, walked the beam to where the backboard supports are attached, and then shimmied down those supports to the hoop. That took a lot of guts.

'We didn't know why, if it was something we did. There was no obvious . . . *precipitating* incident.'

The parts man ignored him. He was staring at the little boy. 'Thomas? Are you ready to come down and join us?'

Tommy's head rose from its hinged position. Small hands dug into the groove in dull pewter flesh and pulled the noose out. He dropped gently to his feet and looked around. He stared at Christian but said nothing.

The parts man came up to Christian and one hand went deep into his upper belly, fumbling around. Christian heard a loud snap and felt intense pain. He doubled over as the parts man brought out a bloody piece of rib.

'Not *so* bad,' the parts man said. 'I understand that some starlets *choose* to have the lower ones removed. It makes them look thinner.'

Tommy and the parts man strode for the doors. Christian, still in pain, struggled to keep up. When they got to the car Cheryl looked curious as Tommy climbed in. Later, when Christian checked his rear-view, the parts man was whispering to Tommy, who appeared to be laughing hysterically, but no sound came out.

Several more stops followed, picking up people Christian hardly knew. The choices surprised him: former neighbors and distant relatives, casual college friends, a remote co-worker. The locations weren't always familiar; some he didn't remember at all, but they stirred feelings strong enough to make him weep.

The fares for these passengers were modest. Whatever the parts man took from Christian caused barely a twitch or strain. Yet damage adds up, as someone of Christian's age knew all too well. Soon enough he suffered from a constant barrage of aches.

The bald man with the sad eyes waited at the curb in front of his decaying cottage as if this was a ride he'd expected. He stepped gingerly onto the running board and then appeared confused as to what to do next. After a rush of offered hands and a tangle of advice he stumbled in and navigated to the back, so far into the rear of the vehicle the car appeared to stretch to accommodate his desire for isolation.

Christian said to the parts man, 'I think this is a mistake. I don't recognize him.'

'You were a child. Perhaps you recognize his home.'

The cottage had a partially collapsed roof and sagging windows, large water spots patterning the warped lap siding. 'I've dreamed about this house.'

The parts man was now in his ear, whispering. 'When you first read that John Donne poem in college, you thought of him. "Any man's death . . ."'

'. . . Diminishes me,' Christian finished. The man's name had been Wilson, and he'd lived at the end of their street. The neighborhood kids teased the poor man, ringing the doorbell and running away, throwing trash in his yard, calling him names as they hid in the bushes. Christian didn't know why they'd singled the guy out. Maybe because he was one of the few adults they knew who seemed totally power-less, and who was so frustrated by their actions.

Then one day the man was gone, and Christian's parents said he died. It was the first time he could attach a face to death. Some of the other kids laughed about it – a forced, embarrassed laughter – and he remembered trying to join in, but couldn't.

'What's the fare for . . . for Mister Wilson?'

'Hmmm, first tell me, when you first heard about his *demise*, did you cry?'

'I didn't really *know* him. I didn't know *how* to feel. I was just a child.'

'Very well then.' The parts man reached for Christian's face, fingers hovering over Christian's right eye. Thinking the parts man aimed to take it he closed his eyes tightly. Then he felt a tug on a single eyelash, and the swift pluck that forced a single tear. 'That will do,' the parts man cooed, and Christian felt ashamed.

As he drove the car full of passengers through the long dark night and into the day and again into dusk he tried fruit-lessly to keep track of where they were, in what part of his current city or in what part of his past, down narrow lantern-lit lanes where lovers strolled, past saloon-lined blocks play-ing the best jazz he'd heard in decades, out into the dusty roadways between fields where the headlights were the only illumination.

Behind him in the seats the revived chattered on as if speech were a gift soon to be taken away (which, of course, it was). He wondered how their mouths felt to be active again. He didn't listen, too busy wondering about the next stop, the next passenger. Once you've lived more than six decades you become accustomed to friends disappearing from the world a few every year, and then a few every month, and then every week seems to be this march of everyone familiar into everything unknown.

Was he expected to mourn them all? Was he supposed to think he was the one deserving to go and not them? Christian could barely remember their names. There were moments when he would wonder what so and so was up to these days before remembering that so and so had died ages ago.

They picked up his grandfather coming out of a dilapidated church. Christian thought it might have been the church where they'd held the old man's funeral, but he couldn't be sure; he hadn't attended. He'd been so busy with his own life he hardly remembered getting the news. This man had been the only grandparent Christian ever knew, the others dead before he was born.

His grandfather was dressed in a snug-fitting sand-colored suit, blue shirt, and bright red tie. The outfit made his tawny complexion resemble gold. He sat down next to Cheryl and immediately struck up a conversation. She looked enthralled. Christian was so glad to see him he almost didn't mind losing a kidney for it, although the taking of it proved to be a long and lingering extraction.

Soon thereafter, the car found the factory where Christian's father died. The angry-looking man in the blood-stained coveralls at first refused to get in when he saw that Christian was driving. Christian saw the side of his father's face and his left hand, both chewed to pieces when he'd fallen into the machinery, and looked away. The casket at the funeral had been closed. He wondered what age he was in his father's eyes. In his mid-twenties was when their relationship fell apart.

He watched as the parts man tried to talk his father into getting into the car. He looked at his grandfather, who appeared to have lost his good humor. His grandfather had never approved of his son-in-law.

Eventually the parts man re-entered the vehicle, holding onto his father's good hand, leading him like a child. His

THE PARTS MAN 65

father settled somewhere near the back, pressing himself so tightly against the window Christian could only see parts of his bloody coveralls.

Christian clutched the wheel and jerked recklessly into traffic. It appeared as if the hood passed through a Ford station wagon without a ripple. He heard random complaints from the back but paid no attention as he hit the gas and floated into the passing lane. He was furious, but not sure why, except that his father was present. He'd been the same way at the funeral, staring at the back of the pew in front and clenching his teeth as a succession of speakers attempted to find something nice to say.

'For this passenger you have a choice of payments,' the parts man abruptly said from nearby.

'For *him*? I'm not paying. I didn't request his resurrection, and I'm aware of no guilt over his death. *His* was the funeral I should have skipped.'

The parts man said nothing more, but Christian felt the long fingers inside his back, and the twist and jerk as additional bone was taken away. He bit into his tongue, choked on the thick metallic liquid that filled his mouth, but uttered not a sound. After a few more miles the fire of the pain had dampened, but he felt as if the parts man's fingers were still in his back, prodding.

The car had become so hot and humid Christian was having trouble thinking. Assuming a little air on his face would clear his head he looked for the AC controls before realizing a car of this age had none. He began to turn the crank to tilt the split windshield on the driver's side. But after only half a turn the handle broke off. Frustrated, he tossed it to the floor.

'No worries,' the parts man said, reaching past him with one hand and playing with the dashboard. When he took his hand away Christian could see that the broken handle had been replaced by the bloody rib the parts man had taken earlier. He couldn't bring himself to touch it and cranked up the other half of the windshield instead.

It dawned on him where they were. Large, aging maples obscured most of the houses from the street, but regularly-spaced narrow driveways cutting between dark lawns led up to each one. 'You must turn soon,' the parts man said, so close behind him he might have been inside Christian's head. 'Remember? The alley behind the back yard.'

The parts man didn't have to guide him. This was where his mother moved after Christian married and moved out west, about twenty years after his father died. He turned into the alley and drove until he was behind the fourth house on the right. He could see the brilliant orange glow coming over the top of her fence.

His mother had started to fail the next to last year of her life. It wasn't anything obvious at first: the occasional lost name, a little more observable awkwardness, the random fall. She claimed to be okay, just a bit 'distracted'.

Christian had noticed these things, but they hadn't worried him. She wasn't that old, and she'd been living by herself for over fifteen years and doing fine. She had her friends and her volunteer work. She didn't need him looking after her. She'd told him so herself, 'I have lots to do, too much. You have your own life now, a family to start.'

But something *had* changed. He'd noticed the accumulating differences. But he *did* have his own life to worry about, and a marriage to nurture, a new wife who demanded most of his attention. When he came back to visit at Christmas they would have more time together; he would be able to observe his mother and evaluate whether there was any real cause for alarm.

There were no witnesses, but the fire department was able to piece together an approximation of what must have happened. She'd been cleaning house, getting rid of out-dated files, tax returns and bank statements. She'd talked about doing that for years. The problem was how to dispose of so much paper. 'I don't want some criminal stealing my information.' That had become a constant worry. Apparently she decided to carry it all into the back yard and burn it. It must have exhausted her. The fire was going strong when she decided to add one more box to the flames. She either became unsteady and fell, or tripped.

The parts man joined Christian at the gate. The glow was so bright it showed through the narrow spaces between the boards, casting tiger-stripe shadows over both them and the car.

'What are you charging me for her?' Christian asked.

The parts man didn't answer right away. Then, so softly Christian could barely hear him, 'The price will need to be a grave one.'

'Then take it now. The pain will help me focus.'

The parts man circled in front of him. The invasion of Christian's chest was immediate and devastating. Afterwards, the parts man held up a shapeless bag of pinkish gray organ meat. 'You can live with only one lung. You don't need this one.' He stuffed it into his coat pocket.

A corrosive ache filled the cavity where his lung had been. Christian dwelled on that as he pushed open the gate.

What he witnessed was not fire, although it did project a kind of heat. A large volume of what was not fire but perhaps the idea of fire occupied the middle of the yard. It had much of the brilliance and the color, but was a little too transparent. It warped and mutated like some kind of amorphous organism made of light, filling the air with the smell of frying beef. Down at the bottom of it a darkened figure lay writhing, featureless head drawn back and white teeth gleaming across the gaping mouth. One cindered arm stretched in his direction.

'We have to drag her out of there!' His father was standing beside him, fresh blood like a shimmering veil obscuring

the ruined part of his head. His one remaining eye locked
onto Christian's gaze. 'Help me, boy!' His father entered the
flaming apparition and grabbed his mother's arm, suffering
no apparent harm. Christian's remaining lung raged with
pain as he involuntarily sucked in air. He stepped into the
center of the flames and grabbed her around the shoulders
and the two of them carried her out of the flaming illusion.
It withered into nothing with a whistling sound.

They helped her into the front passenger seat and his
father retreated wordlessly into the back of the vehicle. Ridic-
ulously, Christian buckled his mother's seatbelt with care.

She attempted to speak. 'You've ... gotten ... old.' Her
voice was like crackling leaves at the height of autumn.

He glanced at her head. Two narrow slits had opened in
the scales of black crust to expose the whites of her eyes, but
her iris and pupils had partially adhered to the underside of
her lids so she couldn't look directly at him. He focused on
the road ahead. 'I thought you would see me as younger, the
way I was when you were alive.'

'I'm your mother. I see you as you are.'

'M – mama. Was it bad, my bringing you b-back?'

He heard her teeth clack together and didn't know if it
was involuntary or some version of mirth. 'I'm glad I . . . can
see you again.'

As they drove on the sky was no longer completely dark
and the last faint stars disappeared. Christian felt fatigue
unlike anything he'd ever experienced, and wondered if he
might be dying. His passengers had little to say, although
his mother and Cheryl did exchange pleasantries about the
brief time they'd once known each other.

Christian had given everything possible to give, and if the
guilt had not been thoroughly exorcised it never would be.
Like so many days in his life which he had anticipated with
either excitement or trepidation, this one had devolved into
yet another day he just had to get through.

Someone stepped in front of the car. She was tall and gangly, with little flesh on her frame. Her nursing uniform swallowed her. She carried a small bundle. He stopped. Beside him his mother clacked her teeth.

The skeletal nurse stood wobbly, one hand reached for the hood for stability as she fixed him with an angry glare.

'Ba-by,' his mother croaked. 'She has a ba-by.'

Then Christian recognized who she used to be. 'No, this is *not* something I need to do. He wasn't a child yet, more like our *hopes* for a child.'

The parts man was then so close Christian could feel the tongue's moist touch on his earlobe, and the soft scrape of those well-sharpened teeth. 'Can you say you felt *no* guilt when they took him away? Which did you regret more, looking at him, or not looking at him *long* enough?'

He and Grace had been trying to have a child for a long time, had almost given up when Grace became pregnant. She was wearing one of those oversized T-shirts that said 'Baby On Board' – she joked about how odd it looked on someone her age – when her water broke months too early. Her voice was broken when she called for him from the bathroom. He remembered looking at her as she stood awkwardly with her feet apart on the wet floor, her eyes tightly closed. He didn't know what to say, and that became his mode for the rest of the evening.

In the car on the way to the hospital she kept saying it was far too early and they were going to lose the baby. He kept repeating that she wasn't a doctor and she didn't *know* that. But at the hospital the doctor said the baby was dead or dying and for her sake recommended that they remove it rather than wait. *Dead or dying?* He would always wonder if he'd heard that correctly, and if there was significance in the difference they should have paid more attention to. Grace would later say she could remember nothing about that conversation.

From that point on – even as they took her into the delivery room and allowed him to sit beside her – he held her hand and kept whispering 'we'll get through this day.' He could hear the sounds of babies being born in nearby rooms, the mothers' cries of both joy and pain.

The tall nurse with the piercing eyes stood at the end of the bed and stared at him with what he thought was disapproval, but it was a very bad time – probably her stares meant nothing. She narrated the procedure in an oddly matter-of-fact way. As they removed the small body there was a moment of silence, then she said 'a boy, perfectly formed, approximately . . .' and Grace cried out 'please, I don't want to hear this,' and the nurse replied 'it's just for the record' and Christian wanted to call her a liar, and realized they were in a Catholic hospital and wondered if that made any difference.

Before they took him away, Christian stood up clumsily and stretched so that he could see his son. It was only a momentary glimpse, but he thought the skin was a dark red, almost purple, and the closed eyes looked molded on, doll-like and unreal. He sat down feeling like an awkward teenager. He thought he'd done something wrong – either he shouldn't have gotten up, or he should have taken a longer look.

As they wheeled Grace into another room he'd kissed her, and the lethargic way she looked at him, the stillness of her body, convinced him he would one day lose her, but at least not that night.

Now the skeletal nurse was handing him the bundle through the window, and unwilling to hold him Christian passed the child into his mother's charbroiled arms, who carried him into the back to share with the others, and although they all exclaimed at the delicacy of his fingers as he held on to theirs, at the beauty of his eyes and of his smile, the baby made not a sound. Christian got out and walked around struggling for breath. The nurse had disappeared.

'It is time for my payment, Christian.'

Christian stared at the parts man, who huddled in his great coat as if cold, only his sad eyes and part of his twisted nose showing above the tall collar. 'I didn't *need* to see him again! Haven't I paid you *enough?*'

'I do not make the rules.'

Christian sat down in the road, his arms hugging his knees. 'Then *who* does?' Getting no answer, he stretched out on the pavement and looked up. Color had flowed back into the sky. He was seeing the dim edges of different clouds, and he struggled to find resemblances.

'This will be the last time I charge you.' The parts man loomed over him. 'After this we will return you to your home.' Then the parts man hunkered down, and serious exchanges were made, essential and irretrievable items were taken, and secret locations within Christian's body made empty. He knew he would never be the same. The pain was . . . *clarifying*, and although Christian cried he did not scream. The worst of it was glancing over and seeing that all his passengers were watching from the car.

They pulled up to his house in the drowsy light of morning. It was difficult climbing out of the car. Whatever adrenalin had driven him through this journey had dissipated, and all he had left was this constant mental haze of deterioration enlivened occasionally by an ambush of pain. He wondered how much of his future had been amputated, but of course there was no sensible math for such things.

He didn't say goodbye to any of them. He wondered if they recognized the kind of bargain he had made.

They'd bought this small house almost ten years ago. They'd gotten rid of much of their belongings, keeping only a few pieces in remembrance of their best of times. This place required little maintenance. Grace had fallen in love with the tree-shaded porch, and they'd spent many evenings there during her final few years. He'd liked the well-lit corner where he could read his much reduced collection of books.

He'd left the house tidy when he went away with the parts man; he always liked to leave rooms picked up and put away. Now the surfaces were cluttered with tissues and pill bottles and a variety of medical debris. The air smelled of strong disinfectant, but not so strong as to hide the basic sourness underneath. A wheelchair sat in one corner of the living room, a walker and a potty chair in another – everything he'd thrown away the week after Grace died.

The woman sitting in the green wing-backed chair was not the Grace of her last few days – thin and suddenly older and breathing explosively – but the Grace from a few weeks before, smiling and teary-eyed and still able to speak her mind.

With some effort he got down on his knees in front of her and cupped her trembling hands inside his own. They stilled immediately and she smiled at him. 'Christian, where were you? I've been waiting.'

'I had ... errands.' He struggled not to cry and it made him almost laugh. 'But I'm here now. We never said ... our proper goodbyes. I wanted to tell you how grateful I was, for all those years. And how, now I ache for you every day.' And then he rose awkwardly and embraced her, kissed her desperately on her eyelids, her lips, and when she failed to respond he sagged onto the floor.

'I'm sorry,' she whispered.

'You didn't speak your last few days,' he said, 'and you could hardly tolerate my voice. I assumed it was because, in a way, you had gone on to another ... life, and were done with this one. Is that the case? This ... place, it means nothing to you now?'

She was silent for a very long time. Then the words came slowly, but at least they came. 'I remember, going away, to college. I saw no one from home for three years. Not my parents, not the boyfriend I left behind. Then I came back for a week. I still, loved my parents. They were the same. But I was different. I cared not a bit for my hometown, my old friends, even my old boyfriend. They meant nothing because I was now in another place. It wasn't as if I'd fallen out of love, out of anything. They'd just become . . . irrelevant.'

She'd angered him. 'You're saying I'm like some high school flame? Our marriage was, what? Trivial?'

'You're upset. No, it is *not* the same. But I'm just trying, to find some words you might understand. Take my memory of going away to college. Multiply it by a thousand. Times ten thousand. Imagine that. It's not that I don't want to care. It's that I cannot. Want, or care. Now.'

He took this in, and found he wasn't surprised. He didn't know what else to say to her. But then he thought about what he really wanted to know. 'So tell me this. You're the only one I can ask. We weren't believers, either of us. So is it like heaven? Is it like hell? Something else? What is it? What is it like?'

She stared at him blankly, and then there was a slight tremor in her mouth. She looked as if she were in pain. 'Don't ask me that. That is something you cannot ask. What good . . .' She stopped, glancing around as if she'd forgotten where she was. 'What good would it do you? There's nothing I can do to save you from it. Just, live your life, Christian. Live your life as long as you can.'

He sat there without speaking. Occasionally he would glance at her, expecting her to be gone, but she still sat there with no expression, occupying the chair. He struggled to his feet and went to the front window. To his surprise the car was still out there, the parts man standing beside it, watching the house. Christian opened the door and limped down to the street. 'You're still here,' he said.

'I wanted to see how your visit went,' the parts man said.

'Is that humor? Is that the way you see us?'

The parts man grinned a toothy grin. 'That is life – make of it what you will. Enjoy the rest of your journey. Now that our arrangement has completed it is time that I ended *theirs*.'

The parts man spread his great coat making it appear as if he'd increased his size. He re-entered the car, but instead of getting into the driver's seat he climbed in through one of the back doors and joined the full complement of passengers. Christian couldn't tell what was happening inside the car – the interior was too dark and the windows were too small – but there was a great deal of movement and a great number of teeth and when the car glided away it appeared to be empty.

Helen Mathers

THE FACE IN THE MIRROR

HELEN MATHERS *was the pen name of* ELLEN BUCKINGHAM MATHEWS *(1853-1920), an extremely popular and prolific author of the late Victorian period. Her first novel, a romance entitled* Comin' Thro' the Rye *(1875), was extraordinarily successful, remaining in print for decades and going through at least 160 editions as well as being adapted for a 1923 film. But Mathers also had an interest in the weird and supernatural, as evidenced by 'The Face in the Mirror', the title story of a 1903 collection, and two novels published in 1896:* The Sin of Hagar *and* The Juggler and the Soul, *both stories of mad scientists and occult experiments; the latter involving transference of living souls into dead bodies. She was also one of the authors of* The Fate of Fenella *(1892), an experimental 'round robin' novel republished by Valancourt, each of its twenty-four chapters penned by a different popular novelist of the day, a lineup that also included Sir Arthur Conan Doyle and Bram Stoker. The present story, which as far as we can tell has not previously been reprinted, features the classic trappings of the Victorian ghost story, including a spectre, a haunted chamber, ghostly images in a mirror and messages from beyond the grave.*

THE LETTER WAS GONE. In vain I shook out my satin gown, and blamed the folly that had made me take this, the only love letter that had ever been dear to me, downstairs to dinner in that vast house, where even human beings were liable to get lost, how much more so, then, a scrap of paper!

My thoughts threw back – it was safe at dinner, for occasionally I touched it in my pocket, and thus bore with a dull neighbour gladly; and afterwards I had not moved from a deep ottoman where different persons had come and talked to me till bedtime. If I drew my treasure out with my handkerchief, it might still be there perhaps, crushed out of sight – or if visible, the men probably found it when turning out the lights, and it was furnishing rich food for merriment in the servants' quarters at that very moment!

But there was a bare chance that I had left it in the drawing-room – that they had overlooked it – and I was resolved that as soon as the house was perfectly quiet, I would steal down, and make a search.

It was not yet twelve – but the women kept early hours, and the men would be in Lord William's smoking-room, an immense distance away, and the servants' wing was yet farther – so I thought I was pretty safe, and at five minutes to twelve I took my candle, and stole softly down the corridors and staircase, crossed the wide hall, and, turning the handle of the drawing-room door, went in.

How ghostly it looked – how strange! At night, familiar things wear unfamiliar faces – the very colours of the flowers are different, and one has a feeling of intrusion, as if inanimate things had also their hours of rest, and resented disturbance from outside humans. At a distance, the deep orange-pink brocade of the ottoman I sought looked almost black, but what was my joy, on reaching it, to behold, sticking up between the cushion and the padded side, a tiny gleam of white, that proved to be the corner of my letter!

I pounced upon, and pressed it to my lips. All thought of fear, of isolation in the vast sleeping place forgotten, I almost danced to the door, the pictured faces on the wall seeming to advance upon me, as in passing, the light in my hand struck them, though they looked, I thought, as if they, too, were angry at my unseasonable visit. As I closed the door behind me, something stole on my ear, and ravished it; so enthrallingly sweet was it, so enticing, that with eager ear bent towards it, and neck outstretched, I instantly followed that exquisite music – not knowing whence it came, not knowing whither it would lead me – just because it drew my feet, my spirit, and would have drawn me over a precipice, I truly believe, had it passed beyond it, so little control had I over my own body at that moment.

Swiftly I went, scarce heeding through what doors I passed, which way I turned – only presently I became aware that I was in the deserted corridors of a disused portion of the house, and still, now far, now near, that haunting melody drew me on, such melody as surely human hands never drew out of earthly instrument, yet, such melody as while thrilling me with the most exquisite pleasure, also brought tears to my eyes, for anguish there was in it, and love, and deep despair!

On every side were closed doors that looked as if they had never been opened; on the ground was dust – dust that might have lain there a century – damp and chill was the air, but I felt neither cold nor fear, as, dying away in a lingering cadence of mournful beauty, the music crossed the threshold of an open door beyond me, and I stood alone with thumping heart in the midst of an apartment hung with mouldering velvet draperies that in colour, methought, had once been green.

The candle light in my hand but made the gloom, the desuetude of the room, deeper; the charm, the power that had irresistibly brought my feet hither, had ceased with the music; I was no longer a creature subjugated through my ears, entranced into ecstacy by sweet sounds that realised my dreams of heaven – I was just a lonely, shivering girl, lost in a remote part of a castle the size of a village, and almost certainly unable to find the way back by which I came.

Have you ever known what it is to feel murder in the air – to feel it all about you – to know that by stretching out your hand you can actually touch the murderer; has no telepathic message ever passed to you from some mere stranger, warning you that he has committed, or will commit, an awful crime? Such a feeling came overpoweringly upon me when, looking down, I saw on the dusty boards at my feet a great discoloured splash, as if a ewer of blood had been spilt violently, and no one had washed the pool away . . . Suddenly an unreasoning terror laid hold of me, ungovernable, as when in panic men strike women down – and I turned to escape headlong. But even in turning, my body froze – my eyes were drawn to a mirror (the only one the room contained) on my right, and across which there passed slowly the face of a girl no older than I . . . lovely indeed was it, with a loveliness haunting and penetrating as the melody that had drawn me hither, but what horror, what agony were there – and on it the look that few have seen, and none in all its intensity save the murderer . . . for this girl was in the act of being murdered, and was looking at me as if I – I were actually committing the crime! This was her spirit – so she may have looked in the flesh when her blood gushed out, and left that stain showing dim at my feet . . . all the hatred of death, the passion for life, summed up in the flashing moment that seemed an eternity to murdered and murderer alike, aye, and to me as the mirror showed clear – and the only thing that moved in that accursed room was I!

I know not to this day how I got myself away from the stain, the mirror – or how I found my way through those passages and corridors back to the inhabited part of the castle . . . perhaps the letter, which I had never once let go, gave me courage, perhaps I knew that I must not, dared not stumble or fall, with that behind me . . . but when at last I reached my room, and sank down before an almost burnt out fire, I cried like a child, cried for that murdered girl who had once been young, and perhaps loved even as I – and I wondered if that enchanting melody had been used to draw her to her death, even as it had drawn me to behold her spirit, revisiting the scene of the crime.

At breakfast next morning a servant entered, carrying a salver, upon which was a shoe buckle of brilliants that I knew, and he asked to which lady present it belonged, as it had been found that morning in a passage of the disused portion of the castle.

I claimed it for mine, and as I took it, met Lady William's eyes full – then she looked at her husband, who was looking at her, then both went on talking as if the incident were quite natural, though some of the women smiled, others regarded me curiously, then turned inquiring glances on the men, as if asking with which of them I had held a tryst. But the men's faces expressed nothing save surprise, and though afterwards I got chaffed about my nocturnal wanderings, no one present seemed to know what Lord and Lady William and I knew – if the look I had seen them exchange meant anything at all.

Only when I told my hostess later, she laughed my story away – 'You had been dreaming,' she said; 'was not the fire out when you woke up?'

I asked her, then, 'What of the buckle?'

'You lost it in some other part of the house – and a servant picked it up, and meaning either to restore it, or not, dropped or deliberately placed it in the disused wing, which, nevertheless, is often used by the servants when up to nefarious practices,' she said.

'And my dress?' I answered. 'Come and see it' – and she came.

The ivory satin train was half a yard deep in dust and dirt – the front was disfigured by the candle grease that had fallen on it as my hand trembled. I could never wear the gown again.

'Clearly you walk in your sleep,' Lady William said with perfect *sang-froid*; 'Kenneth must cure you of such tricks – if what I hear is true?'

I said that it might be true – and my hand stole to my bosom, where, for greater safety, the letter whose loss had brought about such a striking experience lay, and to which I had not yet written an answer – though long ago, had not my heart and eyes given it?

'I have asked him for Christmas,' she said, 'and he comes on Saturday.' She smiled, and came and kissed me, but was resolute not to discuss what had happened to me overnight.

'And you must let me give you a new frock,' she said, 'as a punishment for living in an old castle with miles of dirty passages!'

And she sent for her maid, and would not go away until the woman had got my measurements, and she promised me that my frock should arrive before Kenneth, and so it did.

But before that, and this is a true and strange thing, each night, close on twelve, I would be seized with an intense longing to hear that melody again, and my feet would begin to move of their own accord towards the door, and there would be so fierce a struggle between my will and their intention, that I would have to sit down, and hold fast to the arms of the chair, and wish that Kenneth were here to hold me in his, and keep my feet from itching to follow the music, that I knew was ravishing the silence, and which I was at too great a distance to hear. And I longed to see once more that face in the mirror – to question it – to ask if the murderer had escaped, or if he had walked free among his fellow-men with the blood stain on his hand hidden – and for that awful injustice done to her, she must come back for ever and ever to her death chamber, luring with the spell of ensnaring music, strangers to the spot where, helpless, she met her death, unavenged to this day!

Night by night, the longing grew – taking such fierce hold upon me, that the sweat would pour off my brow, and by main force I would hold myself still till half-past twelve, when the fierce struggle relaxed, and, exhausted, I would fall into deep slumber.

And even in the day time the ebullient gaiety that used to distinguish me was gone, and I could not lose myself in thoughts of Kenneth and his coming; I could not even feel that I loved him very much; I was as one in a thrall, and even when I read his love-letters, I wondered if that murdered girl had been loved as Kenneth loved me – if it were because love had made her life so sweet, and she so loath to leave it, that the horror of her fate had made such imprint on her face as life departed . . . and the desire burned and burned in me to find out the real truth of the apparition and the ghostly melody, and which my hostess knew, but would not tell me.

I found the gown that she had ordered for me laid out on my bed when I came home from driving, on the day before I expected Kenneth, and I gazed upon it with no pleasure – I would so much rather have had the secret of the melody, and the face in the mirror, that she would not give me.

I had brought no maid, and as the woman lent to me by Lady William laced my frock for dinner, I looked idly at her face – reflected behind mine in the glass, and then I looked again, struck by something faintly familiar in it – not the features, which were very pretty, but the expression – where had I seen one like it, and when?

Her trained fingers did their work deftly, but there was no spring in them, and no life in her aspect; looking closely at her, I could see that she was completely absorbed in one idea – and that one of *fear* – and the fear in her face was the faint shadow of the vivid, overmastering one that I had seen in the face of the murdered girl in the mirror.

I know little of magnetism, of the power of the physical touch, or I might argue that her fingers carried a nerve message to my brain, but somehow I realised that the girl was in trouble, that a man was at the bottom of it, that if ever one woman stood in need of another woman's help, this one did now.

She arranged the flowers on the bodice of my dress, gave me my gloves, fan, and handkerchief, all without the least relaxing of that strained, waiting look on her face, and it was on my lips to ask what her trouble was, though I knew how frankly the lower orders resent such sympathy from their betters, and seldom forgive those who offer it.

But the dinner bell was ringing, and I went downstairs, and at dinner I contrived to study each one of the men-servants present, and before dessert had arrived at a conclu-sion – the man who had brought me my buckle was at the bottom of the trouble. Also, by the perfectly infallible rule that makes the prettiest and brightest women choose the very worst possible men, this one was as sorry a knave, for all his powder and smart livery, as ever I saw.

He, too, seemed in a dream, and made several small mistakes in waiting at table – and it was an ugly dream too, judging by his expression, an expression that became a direct menace to some person unknown, when, watching him closely, I saw him, alone for a moment at the sideboard, slip into his coat-tail pocket a sharp knife, that the butler had used for carving game. I could see the dent it made in his coat as he moved to and fro, and I knew that he had hidden it there for no good purpose, yet how was I to hinder him from carrying that purpose out?

A deaf old man, greedily intent on his plate, had taken me in, and a man desperately enamoured of the girl next to him, was on my left, so I had plenty of time in which to think the matter out, and in which to put two and two together, the maid's looks upstairs, the man's below, and yet I was too dense to do so – then.

At dessert a telegram was handed to Lady William, and she left the table at once, after sending round the message to her husband, and within an hour had left the castle to go to her mother who was dangerously ill.

I could not worry her with the matter of a footman's vagaries at such a time, and having begged us all to stay on, and insisted that I should not put off Kenneth, she departed, and after a dull evening in the drawing-room among women, half of whom meditated flight on the morrow, I went upstairs to bed.

The maid, Esther, was usually in waiting to unlace me, but tonight she was not there, and, expecting her every minute, and unable to unfasten my frock for myself, I took up a book, and read on for quite half an hour. I can never quite account to myself for not ringing, but I did not; and only when I looked at the clock, and saw that it wanted five minutes to twelve, did I realise that I had felt no overpowering desire to explore the haunted room, as at this hour I usually did.

But I could not sleep in an evening gown, and I was about to ring the bell, possibly to get no response, when suddenly there came over me an entirely different sensation to any I had felt before; *this* was one of overwhelming horror, something that froze my marrow, palsied the tongue with which I tried to cry out, engulfed me as in a billow of icy water that knocked breath and sight out of me as it passed . . . through that sense of disaster, of peril, flashed the thought, 'Why is not Esther here – and why did that man hide the knife? He knows of the haunted chamber, or he could not have found my buckle there . . .'

I snatched one of the lighted candles from the toilette table, and the matches that lay beside it, and sped down the staircase, across the hall, along those corridors and passages through which a haunting melody had beckoned me; but there was no strain of music now – not even the far-off cry of a woman lured to her fate by the lover who had betrayed her; but was not that a light athwart the dark passage, and did it not come from the haunted room? I was yet some fifty yards from it, when a stifled moan, stifled in the uttering, spurred me on, and I dashed in at the door to find Esther gagged and on her knees, while the man, who had secreted the knife at dinner, stood over her, about to strike.

He breathed hard, and glared at me as I struck the weapon out of his hand, then set my foot upon it, and I have since thought it strange that he did not regain possession of it, for we were but two weak women against six feet of ruffian manhood, and he could easily have killed the pair of us if he had had the pluck, and the presence of mind.

But my unforeseen entry, the hour, the situation, unmanned him; and also he had been drinking, and looked a mere loutish brute as he backed away from me, and so through the door, and out of sight.

Then I kneeled down, and took the gag out of the poor girl's mouth, and the look of the murdered that had been on her face when I burst in (involuntarily my eyes sought the mirror, but it was vacant) gradually faded. She kissed my hand, and burst into tears over it, and, as we kneeled together on the dusty floor, she told me her story. How this man had courted only to deceive her, and now was paying his addresses to one of the ladies' maids staying in the house, to whom she had threatened to tell the truth, if he persisted in his attentions to her.

They had been wont to meet here, in the haunted chamber, and Esther had kept the tryst William had made with her, when he had suddenly set upon, and gagged her, and but for my appearance would have killed and hidden her away in one of the old cellars, where her bones might have remained undiscovered to all time.

'He found your buckle, miss,' said Esther, 'and only brought it back for fear you should come by daylight to look for it – and bring others with you who might find their way here again. But 'twas God Himself sent you here tonight' – then suddenly she screamed out '*Look!*' and pointed to the mirror, across which a face flitted that seemed to be looking directly at us, a face that smiled at me, and looked a blessing at me, if ever a spirit face did.

And I knew then, that she had called me, first by that haunting melody, to show me the way, then by spiritual means to save another loving woman from the tragedy that had been her own, and now having prevented it, she would 'walk' no more, since she had accomplished what was better than revenge.

Esther has been in our service many years; her child is at school, and she is fairly happy. The man Rufus was never heard of again, and it is thought that he lost his life in the floods that were out that night. And sometimes I sit down to the piano and try to put into notes the melody that still sounds so plain in my ears, and the children laugh, and say, 'mother is picking out a tune,' but Kenneth knows better.

Charles Beaumont

THE LIFE OF THE PARTY

One of the premier American speculative fiction writers of the mid-20th century, CHARLES BEAUMONT (1929-1967) *was until recently remembered chiefly for his film and TV work, including scripts for several of the most memorable episodes of* The Twilight Zone *and a number of Roger Corman films. When Beaumont died at age 38 of a still-unexplained illness, he left behind three published collections of short fiction; a novel,* The Intruder (1959), *basis for a film starring William Shatner; and a wealth of unpublished material, all of which in recent years has enjoyed a remarkable revival. Starting with Valancourt's reissue of* The Hunger and Other Stories (1957) *in 2012, Beaumont's work has received substantial new attention, including collector's editions from Centipede Press and a best-of collection from Penguin Classics. 'The Life of the Party' is a rare Beaumont tale that had gone unpublished until its inclusion in a now out-of-print limited edition volume in 2013. In addition to its inherent interest as a macabre tale with a trademark Beaumont twist ending, the story is also significant for its autobiographical elements: according to Roger Anker, the events at the high school dance 'happened to Beaumont in 1944 ... exactly as he depicted them in the story'. Beaumont's* The Hunger and Other Stories, A Touch of the Creature, *and* The Intruder *are all available from Valancourt.*

'I CAN'T TELL YOU HOW PLEASED I AM,' said Mr Hulbush, smiling shyly at his companion. 'Of course, I'd always meant to invite you, but somehow I could never find the courage. I suppose I was afraid of being turned down.' He laughed. 'I agree! It *is* silly. But that's what comes of being an only child. You'll meet my mother and then you'll understand completely. Not that I blame her. She behaved like any normal mother, I suppose. Under the circumstances. I mean, with the first three dying and all, and my father running away. It was natural that she should want to protect me, coddle me, keep me out of harm's way. Don't you agree?'

The white-haired man beside him said nothing.

'Still, it wasn't the best start in the world. And my appearance didn't help much, either. From the age of twelve I was plagued with acne, you see. What with that, my crooked ears, and my bulbous nose, I did not present a very attractive appearance. But of course mother always told me I was a lovely child, and I believed her. Until I started school. And you can imagine what happened then. The children mocked me. They told me my face looked like a relief map of the Adirondacks. I remember that one. I didn't know exactly what Aiderondacks were, but I got the point, nonetheless. And it crushed me. Mother said the children were simply jealous of me because I lived in a big house and got high marks, but I wasn't sure. I thought perhaps it was simply that I was ugly. So I went to the doctor for shots and sent away for ointments and salves and gave up sweets altogether, but nothing did any good. Every night I would stand before the mirror, touching the great tender sores and weeping. Do I bore you?'

The white-haired man did not reply.

'Well,' continued Mr Hulbush, 'I heard of a dance coming up about that time. I had seen a girl in class and, though she and I had never exchanged a word, I found that I was dreaming about her. I would go to sleep and dream about her smooth tan skin, the little tiny hairs on her legs shining gold in the sunlight, the heavy ring dangling from a chain between her breasts. And I determined that I would go to the dance and see her. For hours I worked at preparing myself. First I squeezed all the pimples and boils. Then I applied a special salve. Then I covered it all up with a white powder, which I patted just so. Then came the combing of the hair, again just so, and the donning of my best, and only, suit.

Mother warned me that I was making a terrible mistake, but I wouldn't listen to her. I was *determined*.' Mr Hulbush laughed sadly. 'Did I go through with it? Yes. I went alone, long after the festivities had begun. It was at Barker Hall, which at that time stood in the midst of a dark field. I walked across the field and presently I could hear the sounds of music and laughter. Barker Hall was blazing in the night like a beacon, I thought, or a lighthouse. With every step my fear grew. My palms were hot and wet. My heart was hammering.

But the fear forced me on. Much as I wanted to turn and run, I could not. So I stood for a moment at the door, wiping my hands on my trousers, and then I went in. It was bedlam. Thousands of young people – or anyway it seemed like thousands – were dancing and laughing and drinking. The air was full of smoke and the smell of alcohol. There were all the children I saw at school, only now, in their dark suits and tight gowns, they didn't look like children, but young Apollos and Dianas. No one noticed me, of course. I continued to stand by the door, trying to swallow. Then I saw her. If she was lovely seated at her desk with the sun on her legs, she was incredible now. The gown she wore was black velvet. It hugged her. God! She was so beautiful, and I wanted her so much, then, so very much ...'

Mr Hulbush turned off the main highway onto a rutted, unpaved road walled on either side by thick dark trees. Then he glanced at his passenger, Professor Brady. 'Remember, though we were classmates, we'd never spoken to one another. Less than a foot away from her every day for two years, I'd worshipped her from afar. Now she was pressing her body close to a young man and laughing. I admit that I thought terrible, unwholesome things then. I will tell you because we are friends now. I thought of her flesh beneath the dress, and of the young man's flesh, and of how close each was to the other now. Their naked flesh separated by less than a fraction of an inch! And what I would have given then to exchange places with that fellow, I cannot tell you. Consummation enough, only that, and far more than I ever dreamed possible for me. The music stopped after a moment. The young people uncoupled, and the boy walked away from the girl with the golden legs, leaving her standing there, alone. I rushed forward, pushed from behind by the desperate fear of fifteen agonized years. She turned her head. She saw me. Recognition flickered. I said, 'Hello.' And she answered me. Do you know what she said, that Diana with the golden legs, that object of my dreams and hopes? She said: "Who let *you* in?" '

Mr Hulbush drove in silence for several minutes. Then he smiled at Professor Brady. 'That was a long time ago. And there's a happy ending. When she left her husband last year, we became friends, you see – as you and I have – and one thing led to another and now she's Mrs Hulbush! In fact, you'll meet her tonight!' He chuckled and reached into his breast pocket. 'Cigarette?'

The white-haired man did not reply.

'Admirable,' said Mr Hulbush, drawing fire into his cigarette and hacking out a gray cloud. 'However, "Better one major vice than a host of minor ones." D'you know who said that? You, Professor Brady. *The Quintessence of Morality.* Chapter Seven. And besides, "It ain't the cough that carries you off, it's the coffin they carries you off in!" ' He laughed heartily, then lapsed once again into silence. 'I suppose you find that a crude joke, considering my occupation. Well, let me tell you, if I didn't make a joke once in a while, I'd go mad. Being what I am isn't easy.' He dragged on the cigarette, then turned his head quickly toward his companion. 'No, of *course* I didn't choose it. One's life is determined from the moment one is born. That's what I've been trying to say. It was my father's occupation and so – naturally – it had to be mine. We can thank my mother for it, too, and the Adirondacks. But what's wrong with it, anyway? Somebody has to do the job, isn't that so?' He stuffed the cigarette into an ashtray and tapped on the car's high beams. The road ahead snaked through a veritable forest. 'People couldn't understand, for a long time. Even after my pimples disappeared, they shunned me. Mother and I lived alone. Sometimes I would go to a film, but always it was by myself. I would sit in the darkness, alone, looking at the bright pictures, and wonder if I would ever have a friend.' He shook his head. 'Though it seems so far away now, I remember that people wouldn't even shake my hand in those days. When I would enter a restaurant, they would shrink away from me, as though I were diseased, as though I were some sort of strange beast that didn't belong in society. Never once was I invited to anyone's house. Never once would anyone accept an invitation of mine. And my mother kept saying, "They're jealous of you" but I knew that it went much deeper. They hated me because I reminded them of something they didn't choose to think about, and because every town needs at least one person to shrink away from, to despise, to hate.'

The beams of the car suddenly illuminated a large two-story house. The limbs of dead trees scraped against its unpainted boards. No light shone from its shuttered windows. Mr Hulbush turned off the car.

'I'm trying to explain,' he said, 'why I never asked you over before. If I sound self-pitying, it's because I haven't told you the conclusion. I gave up hope, of course, when I realized that a man in my position – or, at any rate, myself in my position – could never enjoy what is called a normal life. But at that moment, at the moment I decided to adjust to a lifetime of loneliness, everything changed.' Mr Hulbush grinned at his companion. 'Suddenly I began to make friends. People began accepting my invitations. The very best people in town, too! The ones who wouldn't have spit on me before, who turned their backs, who laughed at me, who called me "that strange little man". Now, suddenly, they were my friends. Not all, of course. You couldn't expect that. But little by little they've been coming around. In fact, my at-homes are threatening to become the social event of Hilldale!'

Mr Hulbush got out of the car, extracted a wooden device from the back seat and folded it into a chair.

'I *can't* account for it,' Mr Hulbush said, easing the chair up the steps of the house to the front door. 'Perhaps it was the change in my attitude. Or perhaps they realized that my line of work is no less respectable than any other. Who can say?'

He inserted a key in the lock and turned it. They entered a dark hall, hung with paintings of Indian maidens in canoes and mountains. 'My mother's,' Mr Hulbush said, 'but don't be embarrassed. I don't like them, either.'

He rolled the chair down the hall, past many doors.

'It's wonderful, having you,' he said to the white-haired man. 'Somehow I knew we'd hit it off, but – well, I've told you all about that. I suppose it's just that I can't accept the fact that I'm popular, after all these years. I can't *accept* it. Isn't that silly?'

Mr Hulbush removed another key from his pocket and inserted it into another lock. He pulled open a heavy door.

'I see they've started without us,' he whispered, smiling.

A number of persons stood and sat about a large living room. Some were old, some young. All were dressed formally. Mr Hulbush entered the room with his companion. After closing the door securely, he turned and waved his hand.

'Excuse me. Folks, excuse me! I'd like to introduce Professor Edward Brady. Some of you know him already, but to those who don't, I'd like to say that Professor Brady is one of the outstanding citizens of Hilldale. In addition to coming from one of our oldest families, he is an educator of the first rank. His books on psychology are considered indispensable in universities throughout the world. He is listed in Who's Who, the Social Register, and Celebrity Index. In high school, they voted him the most popular boy on campus. Throughout his life he has won the respect and admiration of all who have known him. He is one of my best friends.'

So saying, Mr Hulbush guided his companion slowly through the room to a couch whereupon sat an old woman in a violet dress. 'Professor Brady, my mother, Edna Hulbush.' In a low voice, he said to the white-haired man, 'She has been dying to meet you for years.'

They moved on toward a woman in a black velvet gown. She appeared to be in her late forties. 'Isn't she lovely?' Mr Hulbush said, softly. 'But of course you've guessed who she is. Marianne, the girl with the golden legs. How long I waited for her! But somehow I think I knew, even as I stood burning with shame and praying that the ground would swallow me up, even then I think I knew that we would be together some day.' He placed the chair next to the woman, who stood looking off in the direction of a window. 'You two get acquainted, while I find us a drink,' he said.

Mr Hulbush greeted his guests as he walked to a bar in the corner. He mixed two martinis and returned to the white-haired man, who had not moved. He placed a glass in the man's hand and then, holding his own drink at arm's length, said: 'To good companions, to acts of kindness, to pleasant conversations, and to hell with everything else!' He drank the martini in one long swallow and hurled the empty glass at a fireplace.

'Careful,' he said to the white-haired man, 'or she'll ask who let *you* in!' He laughed and wheeled the chair around. His progress through the room was slow as he halted by each guest.

'Miss Tatum, chairman of the ladies' league, she owns the oldest house in Hilldale. Built in 1787. The house I mean!' 'Mr Pedderson, of O'Brian, Ingley and Pedderson, our leading law firm. He was the boy who held my Marianne in his arms that night, though I doubt he remembers it.' 'Peter Grant, student body president. You remember that witty description of my face? It came from Pete. Now we're inseparable.' 'Mrs Crandall, here, once lost her appetite because of me. They'd served her a fine meal and she was about to eat it when she looked over and saw that I was in the restaurant. She left the table. And look at her now, enjoying my hospitality!'

After each person in the room had been approached, Mr Hulbush turned on a radio, selected a program of music, and went to the woman in the black velvet gown.

He lifted her slightly off the floor and, holding her closely, danced until dawn.

Then he went out looking for new friends.

Hugh Fleetwood

THE POET GIVES HIS FRIEND WILDFLOWERS

Born in England in 1944, HUGH FLEETWOOD *is a writer and artist whom a critic for the London* Sunday Times *has dubbed 'the master of modern horror'. His second novel,* The Girl Who Passed for Normal, *won the John Llewellyn Rhys Prize, and his fifth,* The Order of Death, *was adapted for a film starring Harvey Keitel and John Lydon (Johnny Rotten of the Sex Pistols). Fleetwood's* Foreign Affairs *(1974), a thriller about a famous concert pianist tormented by a deranged stalker, is available from Valancourt, and his weird and haunting short story 'Something Happened' was included in* The Valancourt Book of Horror Stories, Volume One. *This macabre little treat is original to this collection.*

P ALE BLUE AND DELICATE, they smelled both sweet and faintly of death.
'Thank you,' she said, 'they're *beautiful.*'
Yet, perhaps just because they were –
or because of that unsettling scent –
although she smiled as she took them,
her eyes expressed a certain
fear.
As if she'd been reminded
she had always found him chilly,
and he liked to say that beauty, and art,
required sacrifice.
Still, monster or no,
she had loved him for many years,
and she was grateful and touched
by the gift.

So she tried to mask her disquiet,
and didn't insist
when she asked where he had found them –
and he replied, 'Oh, you know,'
and gave a vague, uncomfortable wave . . .

Shortly after, he left,
looking sad, but relieved she hadn't pressed him;
that he hadn't had to tell her
he had picked those flowers from her grave.

L. P. Hartley

MONKSHOOD MANOR

Like many of the authors in our Valancourt Book of Horror
Stories *series, L. P.* HARTLEY *(1895-1972) is well known and
justly acclaimed for his mainstream literary fiction but underappreciated for his fine contributions to the genre of horror and
supernatural literature. Hartley is most famous for* The Go-
Between *(1953), a novel of childhood in Edwardian England that
opens with the oft-quoted line 'The past is a foreign country: they
do things differently there'; it was adapted for a classic 1971 film
directed by Joseph Losey. His other work includes the* Eustace and
Hilda *trilogy, the final volume of which won the James Tait Black
prize for best novel of the year, as well as* The Harness Room
*(1971), the only explicitly gay-themed novel written by Hartley,
who was otherwise discreet about his sexuality. He published several volumes of fine macabre and supernatural stories, the best of
which were collected in* The Travelling Grave and Other Stories
*(1948), republished by Valancourt in 2017. 'Monkshood Manor',
an atmospheric tale set, as with many of the best traditional ghost
stories, at a large, old English country house, first appeared in* The
White Wand and Other Stories *in 1954.*

'HE'S A STRANGE MAN,' said Nesta.
        'Strange in what way?' I asked.
    'Oh, just neurotic. He has a fire-complex or something of
the kind. He lies awake at night thinking that a spark may
have jumped through the fireguard and set the carpet alight.
Then he has to get up and go down to look. Sometimes he
does this several times a night, even after the fire has gone out.'
    'Does he keep an open fire in his own house?' I asked.
    'Yes, he does, because it's healthier, and other people like
it, and he doesn't want to give way to himself about it.'

'He sounds a man of principle,' I observed.

'He is,' my hostess said. 'I think that's half the trouble with Victor. If he would let himself go more he wouldn't have these fancies. They are his sub-conscious mind punishing him, he says, by making him do what he doesn't want to. But somebody has told him that if he could embrace his neurosis and really enjoy it—'

I laughed.

'I don't mean in that way,' said Nesta severely. 'What a mind you have, Hugo! And he conscientiously tries to. As if anyone could enjoy leaving a nice warm bed and creeping down cold passages to look after a fire that you pretty well know is out!'

'Are you sure that it *is* a fire he looks at?' I asked. 'I can think of another reason for creeping down a cold passage and embracing what lies at the end of it.'

Nesta ignored this.

'It's not only fires,' she said, 'it's gas taps, electric light switches, anything that he thinks might start a blaze.'

'But seriously, Nesta,' I said, 'there might be some method in his madness. It gives him an alibi for all sorts of things besides love-making: theft, for instance, or murder.'

'You say that because you don't know Victor,' Nesta said. 'He's almost a Buddhist – he wouldn't hurt a fly.'

'Does he want people to know about his peculiarity?' I asked. 'I know he's told you—'

'He does and he doesn't,' Nesta answered.

'It's obvious why he doesn't. It isn't so obvious why he does,' I observed.

'It's rather complicated,' Nesta said. 'I doubt if your terre-à-terre mind would understand it. The whole thing is mixed up in his mind with guilt—'

'There you are!' I exclaimed.

'Yes, but not real guilt. And he thinks that if someone caught him prowling about at night they might—'

'I should jolly well think they would!'

'And besides, he doesn't want to keep it a secret, festering. He would rather people laughed at him.'

'Laugh!' I repeated. 'I can't see that it's a laughing matter.'

'No, it isn't really. It all goes back to old Œdipus, I expect. Most men suffer from that, more or less. I expect you do, Hugo.'

'Me?' I protested. 'My father died before I was born. How could I have killed him?'

'You don't understand,' said Nesta, pityingly. 'But what I wanted to say was, if you should hear an unusual noise at night—'

'Yes?'

'Or happen to see somebody walking about—'

'Yes?'

'You'll know it's nothing to be alarmed at. It's just Victor, taking what he calls his safety precautions.'

'I'll count three before I fire,' I said.

Nesta and I had been taking a walk before the other week-end guests arrived.

The house came into sight, long and low with mullioned windows, crouching beyond the lawn. This was my first visit to Nesta's comparatively new home. She was always changing houses. Leaving the subject of Victor we talked of the other guests, of their matrimonial intentions, prospects or entanglements. Our conversation had the pre-war air which Nesta could always command.

'Is Walter here?' I asked. Walter was her husband.

'No, he's away shooting. He doesn't come here very much, as you know. He never cared for Monkshood, I don't know why. Oh, by the way, Hugo,' she went on, 'I've an apology to make to you. I never put any books in your room. I know you're a great reader, but—'

'I'm not,' I said. 'I go to bed to sleep.'

She smiled. 'Then that's all right. Would you like to see the room?' I said I would.

'It's called the Blue Bachelor's room, and it's on the ground floor.'

We joked a bit about the name.

'Bachelors are always in a slight funk,' I said, 'because of the designing females stalking them. But why didn't you give the room to Victor? It might have saved him several journeys up and down stairs.'

'It's rather isolated,' she said. 'I know you don't mind that, but he does.'

'Was that the real reason?' I asked, but she refused to answer.

I didn't meet Victor Chisholm until we assembled for drinks before dinner. He was a nondescript looking man, neither dark nor fair, tall nor short, fat nor thin, young nor old. I didn't have much conversation with him, but he seemed to slide off any subject one brought up – he didn't drop it like a hot coal, but after a little blowing on it, for politeness' sake, he quietly extinguished it. At least that was the impression I got. He smiled quite a lot, as though to prove he was not unsociable, and then retired into himself. He seemed to be saving himself up for something – a struggle with his neurosis, perhaps. After dinner we played bridge, and Victor followed us into the library, half meaning to play, I think; but when he found there was a four without him he went back into the drawing-room to join the three non-bridge playing members of the party. We sat up late trying to finish the last rubber, and I didn't see him again before we went to bed. The library had a large open fireplace in which a few logs were smouldering over a heap of wood-ash. The room had a shut-in feeling, largely because the door was lined with book-bindings to make it look like shelves, so that when it was closed you couldn't tell where it was. Towards midnight I asked Nesta if I should put another log on and she said carelessly, 'No. I shouldn't bother – we're bound to get finished sometime, if you'll promise not to overbid, Hugo,' which reminded me of Victor and his complex. So when at last we did retire I said meaningly, 'Would you like me to take a look at the drawing-room fire, Nesta?'

'Well, you might, but it'll be out by this time,' she said.

'And the dining-room?' I pursued, glancing at the others, to see if there was any reaction, which there was not. She frowned slightly and said, 'The dining-room's electric. We only run to two real fires,' and then we separated.

In spite of my boasting, for some reason I couldn't get to sleep. I tossed to and fro, every now and then turning the light on to see what time it was. My bedroom walls were painted dark blue, but by artificial light they looked almost black. They were so shiny and translucent that when I sat up in bed I could see my reflection in them, or at any rate my shadow. I grew tired of this and then it occurred to me that if I had a book I might read myself to sleep – it was one of the recognized remedies for insomnia. But I hadn't: there were two book-ends – soap-stone elephants, I remember, facing each other across an empty space. I gave myself till half-past two, then I got up, put on my dressing-gown and opened my bedroom door. All was in darkness. The library lay at the other end of the long house and to reach it I had to cross the hall. I had no torch and didn't know where the switches were, so my progress was slow. I tried to make as little noise as possible, then I remembered that if Nesta heard me she would think I was Victor Chisholm going his nightly rounds. After this I grew bolder and almost at once found the central switch panel at the foot of the staircase. This lit up the passage to the library. The library door was open and in I went, automatically fumbling for the switch. But no sooner had my hand touched the wall than it fell to my side, for I had a feeling that I was not alone in the room. I don't know what it was based on, but something was already implicit in my vision before it became physically clear to me: a figure at the far end of the room, in the deep alcove of the fireplace, bending, almost crouching over the fire. The figure had its back to me and was so near to the fire as to be almost in it. Whether it made a movement or not I couldn't tell, but a spurt of flame started up against which the figure showed darker than before. I knew it must be Victor Chisholm and I stifled an impulse to say 'Hullo!' – from a confused feeling that like a sleep-walker he ought not to be disturbed; it would startle and humiliate him. But I wanted a book, and my groping fingers found one. I withdrew it from the shelf, but not quite noiselessly, for with the tail of my eye I saw the figure move.

Back in my room I wondered if I ought to have left the hall lights on for Victor's return journey, but at once concluded that as he hadn't turned them on himself, he knew his way well enough not to need them. A sense of achievement possessed me: I had caught my fellow-guest out, and I had got my book. It turned out to be the fourth volume of John Evelyn's Diary; but I hadn't read more than a few sentences before I fell asleep.

When I met Victor Chisholm at breakfast I meant to ask him how he had slept. It was an innocent, conventional inquiry, but somehow I couldn't bring myself to put it. Instead, we congratulated each other on the bright, frosty, late October morning, almost as if we had been responsible for it. Presently the two other men joined us, but none of the ladies of the party, and lacking their conversational stimulus we relapsed into silence over our newspapers.

But I didn't want to keep my adventure to myself, and later in the morning, when I judged that Nesta would not be preoccupied with household management, I waylaid her.

'Your friend Victor Chisholm has been on the tiles again,' I began, and before she could get a word in I told her the story of last night's encounter. Half-way through I was afraid it might fall flat, for, after all, her guest's peculiarities were no news to her; but it didn't. She looked surprised and faintly worried.

'I oughtn't to have told you,' I said with assumed contrition, 'but I thought it would amuse you.'

She made an effort to smile.

'Oh well, it does,' she said, and then her serious look came back. 'But there's one thing that puzzles me.'

'What's that?'

'He told me he had had a very good night.'

'Oh well, he would say that. It's only civil if you're staying in someone's house. I should have said the same if you had asked me, only I thought you would want to hear about Victor.'

Nesta didn't take this up.

'But we know each other much too well,' she said, arguing with herself. 'Victor comes down here – well, he comes pretty often, and he *always* tells me if he's been taking his security measures. I can't understand it.'

Why does she seem so upset? I asked myself. Does she care more for Victor than she admits? Is she distressed by the thought that he should lie to her? Does she suspect him of infidelity?

'Oh, I expect he thought that for once he wouldn't bother you,' I said.

'You're quite sure it was Victor?' she asked, with an effort.

I opened my eyes.

'Who else could it have been?'

'Well, somebody else looking for a book.'

I said I thought this most unlikely. 'Besides, he wasn't looking for a book. He was looking at the fire – I think he stirred it with his foot.'

'Stirred it with his foot?'

'Well, something made a flame jump up.'

Nesta said nothing, but looked more anxious than before.

Hoping to make her say something that would enlighten me, I observed jokingly:

'But he's come to the right place. I saw a row of buckets in the hall and one of those patent fire-extinguishers—'

'Oh, Walter insisted on having them,' said Nesta, hurriedly. 'This is a very old house, you know, and we have to take reasonable precautions. Having a fire-complex doesn't mean there isn't such a thing as having a fire, any more than having persecution mania means there isn't such a thing as persecution.'

Then I remembered something.

'If he doesn't want to be taken for a burglar,' I said, 'why doesn't he turn on the lights?'

'But he does turn them on,' said Nesta, 'just for that reason.'

I shook my head.

'He didn't turn them on last night.'

The problem of Victor's nocturnal ramblings exercised me and made me unsociable. I never enjoy desultory conversation, and our preluncheon chit-chat seemed to me unusually insipid. So when the meal was over I excused myself from playing golf, though I had brought my clubs with me, and announced that I was going to have a siesta as I had slept badly. There was a murmur of sympathy, but Nesta made no comment and no one, least of all Victor, betrayed uneasiness.

In the middle of the afternoon I woke up and had an idea. I strode down to the village to search out the oldest inhabitant. To my surprise I found him, or his equivalent, digging in his front garden. Leaning over the wall I engaged him in conversation; and very soon he told me what I had somehow expected to hear, though, like so many pieces of knowledge that one picks up, it was difficult to act upon, and I rather wished I had never heard it. What chiefly intrigued me was the question: Did Victor know what I knew? It was clear, I thought, that Nesta did. But had she told him?

I did not think that I could ask her, it would seem too like prying; besides if she had wanted to tell me, she would have told me. What I had heard could be held to explain a good many things.

My secret gnawed at me and made the social contacts of the party seem unreal, as though I were a Communist in a Government office, my only accomplice being the head of the Department.

Suddenly, after tea I think it was, the conversation turned my way. 'Is the house haunted, Nesta?' asked one of the visitors, a woman, who like myself was a stranger to the house. 'It ought to be – it wouldn't be complete without a ghost!'

I watched Nesta as she answered carefully, 'No, I'm afraid I must disappoint you – it isn't.' And I watched Victor Chisholm, but he kept what might have been called his poker face – if it had been sinister, which it was not. The speaker wasn't to be satisfied; she returned to the charge more than once, suggesting various phantoms suitable to Monkshood Manor; but Nesta disowned them all, finally suppressing them with a yawn. One by one, on various pretexts, the company disbanded, and Victor Chisholm and I were left alone.

'I once stayed in a country house that was said to be haunted,' I remarked chattily.

'Oh, did you?' he said, with his air of being politely pleased to listen, while he was saving himself up for something in which one had no concern; 'was it fun?'

'Well, not exactly fun,' I said. 'I'll tell you about it if you can bear to hear. The house was an old one, like this, and the land on which it stood had belonged to the Church. Well, after the Dissolution of the Monasteries they pulled the Abbey, or whatever it was, down, and used some of the stones for building this house I'm telling you about. Nobody could stop them. But one of the old monks who had fallen into poverty, as a result of being dissolved, and who remembered the bygone days when they feasted and sang and wassailed and got fat and clapped each other on the back in the way you see in the pictures – he felt sore about it, and on his deathbed he laid a curse on the place and swore that four hundred years later he would come back from wherever he was and set fire to it.'

I watched Victor Chisholm for some sign of uneasiness but he showed none and all he said was:

'Do you think a ghost could do that? I've always understood that it wasn't very easy to set a house on fire. It isn't very easy to light a fire, is it, when it's been laid for the purpose, with paper and sticks and so on.'

This, I thought – and I congratulated myself upon my subtlety – is the voice of reassurance speaking: this is what well-meaning people tell him, and what he tells himself, hoping to calm his fears.

'I'm not up in the subject of ghosts,' I said, 'but they can clank chains and presumably some of them come from a hot place and wouldn't mind handling a burning brand or two. Or kicking one. That fire in the library, for instance—'

'Oh, but surely,' he said – and I saw that I had scared him – 'the library fire is absolutely safe? I – I'm sometimes nervous about fires myself, but I should never bother about that one. There's so much stone flagging around it. Do you really think—'

'I've no idea,' I said, feeling I had the answer to one of my questions. 'But my hostess at the time was certainly apprehensive. I had to worm the story out of her. It's a very usual one, of course, almost the regulation legend, very boring, really.'

'And was the house ever burnt down?' asked Victor.

'I never heard,' I said.

Of course Victor might have been dissembling. He might have known the legend of Monkshood Manor, he might have been afraid of the library fire: neurotic people are notoriously given to lying. But I didn't think so. Yet the alternative was too fantastic. I couldn't believe in it either, and gradually (for logic can sometimes be bluffed) I succeeded in disbelieving both alternatives at once.

Before nightfall I took the precaution of furnishing my blue room with books more interesting than Evelyn's Diary. But I didn't need them. I slept excellently, and so, to judge from discreet inquiries I made in the morning, did the rest of the party.

I couldn't get much out of Nesta. She rather avoided me, and for the first time in my life I felt like a policeman who must be treated with reserve in case he finds out too much. I still persuaded myself that Victor Chisholm had been and had not been in the library in the early hours of Saturday morning: if pressed, I should have said he had been. The third possibility, put forward by Nesta, that another guest had been searching for a book, I dismissed. My theory was that Nesta had a superstitious dread of a fire breaking out at Monkshood Manor and was keeping Victor in ignorance while she availed herself of his services as a night-watchman without warning him of the risk he ran.

Risk? There was no risk: yet I vaguely felt that I ought to do something about it, so I tried to make my social prevail over my private conscience and throw myself into the collective life of a week-end party. I thought about the form my coming Collins would take, and wondered if I ought to apologize for being a dull guest. In the meantime I could search Nesta out and make amends for something that I felt had been slightly critical in my attitude towards her.

My quest took me to the library. Nesta was not there but

someone was – a housemaid on her hands and knees working vigorously at the carpet with a dust-pan and brush.

'Good heavens!' I exclaimed, surprised into speech by the sight of such antiquated cleaning methods; 'haven't you got a vacuum cleaner?'

The maid, who was pretty, looked up and said:

'Yes, but it won't bring these marks out.'

'Really?' I said. 'What sort of marks are they?'

'I don't know,' said the maid. 'But they look like footmarks.'

I bent down: they did look like footmarks, but they had another peculiarity which for some reason I refrained from commenting on. Instead I said, glancing at the fireplace:

'It looks as though someone had been paddling in the ashes.'

'That's what I think,' she said, leaning back to study the marks on the carpet.

'Well, it's clean dirt,' I observed, 'and should come off all right.'

'Yes, it should,' she agreed. 'But it doesn't. It's my belief that it's been *burnt* in.'

'Oh no!' I assured her, but curiosity overcame me, and I, too, got down on my hands and knees, and buried my nose in the carpet.

'Hugo, what are you doing?' said Nesta's voice behind me.

I jumped up guiltily.

'What were you doing?' she repeated almost sternly.

I had an inspiration.

'To tell you the truth,' I said, 'I wanted to know whether this lovely Persian carpet had been dyed with an aniline dye. There's only one way to tell, you know – by licking it. Aniline tastes sour.'

'And does it?' asked Nesta.

'Not in the least.'

'I'm glad of that,' said Nesta, and leading me from the

room she began to tell me the history of the carpet. This gave me an opportunity to praise the house and all its appointments.

'What treasures you have, Nesta,' I wound up. 'I hope they are fully insured.'

'Yes, they are,' she answered, rather dryly. 'But I didn't know you were an expert on carpets, Hugo.'

As soon as I could I returned to the library. The maid had done her work well: hardly a trace of the footmarks remained, and the smell of burning, which I thought I had detected, clinging to them, had quite worn off. You could still see the track they made, away from the fireplace towards the door: but they didn't reach the door or go in a direct line for it; they stopped at a point halfway between, against the inner wall, which was sheathed in books. There was nothing surprising in that: after a few steps the ashes would have been all rubbed off.

And there was another thing I couldn't see, and almost wondered if I had seen it – the mark of the big toe, which showed that the feet had been bare. Victor might have come down in his bare feet, to avoid making a noise; but it was odd, all the same, if not as odd as I had first thought it.

In the afternoon we went a long motor drive in two cars to have tea with a neighbour. As soon as Monkshood Manor was out of sight its problems began to fade, and in the confusion of the two parties joining forces round the tea-table they seemed quite unreal. And even when the house came into view again, stretched cat-like beyond the lawn, I only felt a twinge of my former uneasiness. By Sunday evening a week-end visit seems almost over; the threads with one's temporary residence are snapping; mentally one is already in next week. Before I got into bed I took out my diary and checked up my engagements. They were quite ordinary engagements for luncheon and dinner and so on, but suddenly they seemed extraordinarily desirable. I fixed my mind on them and went to sleep thinking about them.

I even dreamed about them, or one of them. It started as an ordinary dinner party but one of the guests was late and we had to wait for him. 'Who is he?' someone asked, and our host answered, 'I don't know, he will tell us when he comes.' Everyone seemed to accept this answer as reasonable and satisfactory, and we hung about talking and sipping cocktails until our host said, 'I don't think he can be coming after all. We won't wait any longer.' But just as we were sitting down to dinner there was a knock at the door and a voice said, 'May I come in?' And then I saw that we weren't at my friend's house in London, but back again at Monkshood, and the door that was opening was the library door, which was lined with bindings to make it look like bookshelves. For some reason it wasn't at the end of the wall but in the middle; and I said, 'Why is he coming in by that door?' 'Because it's the door he used to use,' somebody answered. The door was a long time opening, and it seemed to be opening by itself with nobody behind it; then came a hand and a sleeve – and a figure wearing a monk's cowl.

I woke with a start and was at once aware of a strong smell. For a moment I thought it was the smell of cooking, and wondered if it could be breakfast-time. If so, the cook had burnt something, for there was a smell of burning too. But it couldn't be breakfast time for not a glimmer of light showed round the window curtains. Actually, as I discovered when I turned on my bedside lamp, it was half-past two – the same hour that I had chosen for my sortie two nights before.

The smell seemed to be growing fainter, and I wondered if it could be an illusion, an effect of auto-suggestion. I opened the door and put my head into the passage and as quickly withdrew it. Not only because the smell was stronger there, but for another reason. The passage was not in darkness, as it had been the other night, for the hall lights had been turned on.

Well, let Victor see to it, I thought, whatever it is; no doubt he's on the prowl: let his be the glory. But curiosity overcame me and I changed my mind.

In the hall the smell was stronger. It seemed to come in waves, but where did it come from? My steps took me to the library. The door was open. A flickering light came through, and a smell strong enough to make my throat smart and my eyes water. I lingered, putting off the moment of going in: then I remembered the fire buckets in the hall and ran back for one. The water had a thick film of dust over it and I had an irrational feeling that it would be less effective so, and that I ought to change it. I did not do so, however, but hurried back and somehow forced myself to go into the room.

There were shadows, of course, and there was smoke, drifting about as smoke does. The two together make a shape that is almost opaque. And the shape was opaque that I saw before I saw anything else, a shape that seemed to rise from its knees beside the fireplace and glide slantwise across my vision towards the inner wall of the library. I might not have noticed it so particularly had it not recalled to me the shape of the late-comer in my dream. Before I could ask myself what it was, or meant, it had disappeared, chased perhaps from my attention by the obligation to act. I had the bucket: where should I begin? The dark mass of the big round library table was between me and the fireplace; beyond it should have been the card-table, but that I could not see. Except on the hearth no flames were visible.

Relief struggling with misgiving, I turned the light on and advanced towards the fireplace, but I stopped half-way, for lying in front of it, beside the overturned card-table, lay a body – Victor's. He was lying face downwards, curiously humped like a snail, under his brown Jaeger dressing-gown, which covered him and the floor around him. And it was from his dressing-gown, which was smouldering in patches, and stuck all over with playing cards, some of which were also alight, that the smell of burning came. Yes, and from Victor himself; for when I tried to lift him up I found beneath him a half-charred log, a couple of feet long, which the pressure of his body had almost extinguished, but not quite, and from which I could not at once release him, so deeply had it burnt into his flesh.

But the Persian carpet, being on the unburnt, underside of the log, was hardly scorched.

Afterwards, the explanation given was that the log had toppled off the fireplace and rolled on to the carpet; and Victor, coming down on a tour of inspection, had tripped over it and died of shock before being burnt. The evidence of shock was very strong, the doctor said. I don't know whether Nesta believed this: shortly afterwards she sold the house. I have since come to believe it, but I didn't at the time. At the time I believed that Victor had met his death defending the house against a fire-raising intruder, who, though defeated in his main object, had got the better of Victor in some peculiarly horrible way; for though one of Victor's felt slippers had caught fire, and was nearly burnt through, the other was intact, while the footprints leading to the wall – though they were fainter than they had been the other time – both showed the mark of a great toe. I pointed this out to the police who shrugged their shoulders. He might have taken his slippers off and put them on again, they said. One thing was certain: Victor had literally embraced his neurosis, and by doing so had rid himself of it for ever.

Eric C. Higgs

BLOOD OF THE KAPU TIKI

Until recently, ERIC C. HIGGS *was something of a mysterious figure to many horror fans, known chiefly as the author of an undisputed classic of '80s horror,* The Happy Man (1985), *a book that achieved a cult status and long fetched sensational prices on the secondhand market when one of the scarce copies came available. After publishing three novels in the 1980s, Higgs disappeared from fiction writing, leaving fans to wonder what had become of him. It is with bittersweet feelings that we offer this brand-new tale marking Eric Higgs's long-awaited return to horror, since he passed away suddenly shortly after sending us the manuscript. We are pleased to be able to present it here for the first time, and we feel sure fans of his other work will enjoy it.*

M ELINA SAT DOWN HARD, feeling as if the wind had been knocked from her lungs. Never had she felt so disoriented, so surprised, so *violated.*

'Divorce,' she said hoarsely, staring at the floor. Her lunch suddenly felt like a rock in her stomach and she wondered if she were going to vomit. 'My God, Kevin ... did you really just say ...'

Her husband brought the expensive lighter's flame to an even more expensive Cohiba Robusto. 'Can it really be this much of a surprise?'

Melina looked up, eyes flashing with sudden heat. 'You'd better believe this is some kind of damned surprise!'

'Oh, come on.' Kevin blew out a plume of smoke. 'Haven't you noticed how, well, how we've been growing apart?'

'Have you ... met someone? Is that it?'

He looked away. 'With my schedule? Are you mad? No way!'

Melina gripped the sofa's armrest so tightly her knuckles turned white. 'Then for God's sake – what is it?'

'Well. You know. People fall in love. And then they drift apart.'

'You said our love was eternal!'

'Oh, please, Melina.' Kevin sat in the brand-new lounge chair with a sigh. The furniture store had only delivered it last week. Melina remembered how happy they'd been when they'd bought it. Hadn't even blinked at the four-thousand dollar price tag. Because the good times were supposedly here. The good times were fat and juicy and ready to roll. Because the big payoff for all the hard work was but an angel's breadth away. 'People say all kind of silly things when they're in love, dear. But then things change.'

'All I know is that I've been busting my tail—'

'Doing what?' He scoffed as he puffed at his cigar. 'You haven't been doing any work for the past year that I'm aware of. A maid comes in every day to clean up this mess, and—'

Melina hitched herself to the edge of the sofa, her brown eyes flashing. 'But that was the deal! I was to put you through school, and when you graduated—'

'You'd do nothing but sit on your butt? And be this suburban . . . well, whatever it is you've become?'

Melina had never loved anyone as much as she'd loved Kevin. But suddenly she hated him. Hated his chiseled surfer-boy looks, his tailor-made suit, even his aromatic cigar. Could she really have been this much of a fool, all along?

'I supported you,' Melina said evenly. 'For years. *Years*, Kevin! First medical school. And then when you had the bright idea of going to law school, I supported you through that—'

'Yes, yes, yes!' Kevin got up from the sofa angrily, went to an ashtray and crushed out the cigar.

'Ten years, Kevin.' Melina's eyes shot daggers into his

broad back. 'Ten years of waitressing and telemarketing and every kind of shit job I could get, just to keep us chugging along—'

Kevin wheeled around. 'And it worked! It worked! Now I'm a lawyer *and* a doctor – and in the one year I've finally been able to practice I've made two-hundred-and-eighty thousand dollars! And that's just the start! Do you have any idea how much money a lawyer who's been trained as a doctor can make in malpractice suits? Next year that two-hundred-and-eighty is going to look like it came off the kiddie table!'

'But just for you, huh? Is that it? Now that the dream is finally here – Melina's out in the cold?'

Kevin regarded his wife evenly. And tried to remember the girl he'd met in Honolulu, back when he didn't have so much as a pot to piss in or a broken window to throw it out of. Hot, she'd been. Hottest Hawaiian babe he'd ever laid eyes on. Hell, hottest damn woman ever to hit the planet. But boy how time had taken its cruel, cruel toll. She was only thirty now. But already looked forty. A hard forty, at that. The lovely olive skin was now an unappealing sort of lackluster brown, the once-slender face had gone puffy, the Hawaiian Tropic Bikini Contest figure had turned downright matronly. Had she been taking lessons in how to become an ugly old frump?

'You won't be out in the cold,' Kevin said in the reason-able tones that his own father, that bastard, had favored for the rolling-out of bad news. 'You're entitled to half of everything I've made to this point. My lawyer will contact your—'

'NO!' Melina flung herself off the sofa and wrapped her arms around Kevin's knees, pressing her face against the lightweight wool of the tailored pants. 'No, Kevin! I won't let you go! You can't do this to me!'

Kevin tried to back up, lip curling with disgust. 'Melina, please—'

'Don't leave me, Kevin!' She knew this was wrong. Knew this was degradation beyond all degrading debasement. Knew that what she should be doing was plunging a kitchen knife into his treacherous heart. But found herself powerless in this last surge of mindless love from her breaking heart. 'Darling, whatever it is you want from me, I'll do it! I want to have your children, I want to start our family! I'll change any way you want! I'll be the wife you want! Just don't leave me!'

Kevin yanked at her shoulders but she tightened her grip and he finally had to shove her away roughly. She hit the floor with a thump.

'Melina! My God! Get a grip!'

She looked up, tears standing on her eyelids. 'Oh, darling,' she cried. 'Darling, please . . .'

Kevin threw on his jacket and headed for the door. Melina pushed herself up, unreasoning love changing to unreasoning hate in the space of a heartbeat. She glared at her husband with eyes that seemed to spit electric sparks. 'Where are you going? Off to your whore?'

'*There's no one else!*' Kevin threw open the door and stared at Melina contemptuously. 'If you must know the truth of it, I'm leaving because I can't stand another minute of your *hog body* and *hog face!*'

Kevin slammed the door.

Melina collapsed to the carpet and let go with a series of great, racking sobs.

Kevin took the key out of the special hiding place in his wallet and slipped it in the bungalow's lock. Opened the door and stepped inside the small living room. There was only one candle and it was inside a red lantern, throwing off a soft and sensuous light. Gentle music with a slow jungle rhythm flowed from hidden speakers.

Alicia sprawled on the sofa, smoking a cigarette, the

moonlight showing that she was in a long white kimono. And nothing else.

'Thought you'd never get here,' Alicia said, smoke drifting from her model's lips. 'I'd just about given up.'

Kevin tried to say hello but the words caught in his throat. He was, as always, awed by her beauty. Had been, ever since she walked into his office six weeks ago. Tall, graceful as a leopard, eyes full of languid secrets. A prize beyond all prizes.

Kevin moved toward her, reaching out.

'Did you tell her, Kevin? Is it done?'

Kevin ignored her question and came to the sofa as if in a trance. He started to take her into his arms—

'Hold on, buster.' Alicia pushed Kevin away ... but not without giving him a heart-stopping glimpse of a full and beautiful bosom just beneath the folds of the kimono. 'You said you were going to tell her tonight.'

Kevin stared at her with eyes emptied of reason. Alicia got up with an impatient sigh and looked down at him, hands on hips.

'Answer me, Kevin. Did you tell her?'

'I ... told her ...'

'And that you're going to file for divorce?'

'Yes.'

'And that you and I are getting married?'

'She knows everything.'

The cross look on Alicia's face held for a moment longer ... and then she smiled. A sexy smile that Kevin found himself falling into, like a swimmer caught in a mighty vortex.

'Well, then.' Alicia pulled the gown off her shoulders and let it drop. Kevin's eyes widened. Nothing he'd seen on the internet had ever come within a million miles of this. No, the hottest porn star in the world wasn't even in the same universe as this. Nothing was.

It seemed like he couldn't take a breath. His heart

thumped and hammered. He wondered if it might explode.

But if it does explode, he thought as he blindly reached for her, *I'll die the happiest son of a bitch on this planet.*

Melina made her way upstairs slowly. She felt a hundred years old, and prayed for the energy for what needed to be done.

But when Melina made it to the bedroom she collapsed on the bed with a moan. Forget about it, she thought. Just concentrate on finding a lawyer who was ten times scarier than Kevin and get him to skin the bastard six ways to Sunday. Then get on with the rest of your life.

But then the drab years of plugging away at the lousy little jobs marched before her eyes. Up in the mornings at five. Then coming home at six to have Kevin tell her yet again that they were a team, that they were building a bright future together. And then scarfing down a cup of instant soup and getting dressed for her evening job. Ten years of it. Never one sick day. Never one vacation. It had made her old before her time.

Melina got off the bed.

It took a good twenty minutes of rummaging in back of the closet, but then she found it. The box Grandma Kalapana had given her on her wedding day. It was dusty and covered with so much grime it was difficult to make out the fearsome little figures carved on the side.

Melina went to the balcony and set the box on the glass table. It looked black and forbidding in the moonlight.

She took a breath . . . reached for the box . . . and with a swift motion opened it.

Inside was a bowl and a vial.

Melina took out the bowl. It was a hideous thing, held aloft by three squat little Polynesian gods, their mouths open with silent screams.

Next, the vial. It was bamboo, very old. Melina opened

the cork carefully . . . and was greeted by a stench that was both horrid and yet somehow cloying.

Melina poured the oily liquid into the bowl. It reflected the moonlight dully. She raised her hands in supplication and looked at the moon.

'Makua kahiko,' she said as she waved her right hand over the bowl, then the left. 'Makua kahiko . . . ho'olono a'u.'

Melina looked into the depths of the oily liquid. It swirled and shimmered like black mercury. And her heart skipped a beat when a dim figure softly came into focus, like the image on a slowly-developing Polaroid.

She closed her eyes. *Kanuna Ôana ana!*

And when Melina looked into the bowl again she saw Kevin. And a blond wahine.

They were on a sofa, naked, the woman's head thrown back with a kind of triumphant joy as Kevin hammered against her like a machine, grimacing with effort . . . and then his eyes rolled back and his mouth widened with a coarse bellow that sounded like he'd been run through with a sword.

Kevin lay on the sofa, smoking, feeling his heart slow down. And watching Alicia dress. She had selected a long Chinese jacket of bright red silk, and as she buttoned it up to her lovely throat he was appreciative of the fact that she wore nothing underneath. This would come in handy when it was time to initiate Round Two in the evening's festivities. But that would be later. Now the edge was off and he was quite content to enjoy her beauty for its own sake.

'I've got a little barbecue going out back.' Alicia brushed a blond hair out of the way and smiled. 'Spicy coconut chicken.'

'Hmmm. And drinks?'

'Lots of drinks. All you want.' She smoothed the dress down and smiled. She was as slim in the hips as she was full in the bust. 'Party's just getting started,' she purred. 'Best party in the world.'

Kevin's heart gave a little skip that let him know Round Two might not be so far off after all. And there was a definite possibility there'd be a Five and Six as well. Kevin got off the sofa and went to the bathroom. Retrieved the shorts and Hawaiian shirt from their customary spot behind the door. It was time to party down. Yes sir, by God, and by all that was holy, it was at long last time for serious partyin' down.

Melina looked up from the bowl and closed her eyes. She had held onto some last vestiges of youth when she looked into the bowl, but now all of her prettiness seemed to be gone. But what had replaced it was not altogether unlovely. A mature sort of beauty now sat upon her face, the sort that spoke of tests endured and won, of passing sorrows and passing joys, and the sure knowledge that she was part of something that would remain until the end of time. It was a powerful beauty.

But it was also dark.

The moon went behind a cloud. Cool wind blew strands of black hair across her face. Melina opened her eyes . . . eyes that were a thousand years old . . . and looked into the bowl.

Kevin strode down the pebble path to the far reaches of Alicia's back yard. Smiled when he saw that things were in full-on 'tiki mode'. There were no electric lights, just the yellow glow of garden torches, throwing the lush foliage into dramatic light and shadow. And of course, the strange, slow, retro music that Alicia loved flowed from hidden speakers.

'See you got some new tikis.' Kevin nodded toward one of the carved Polynesian gods, this one a good six feet tall.

Alicia looked up from the grill with a fashion model's smile. 'You know I can't resist them. They're good luck. And as far as I'm concerned, one can't have enough good luck.'

'Well, it looks like you're about due to win the lottery.' Kevin surveyed the totems – some only a foot tall, others coming up to waist level – and stopped counting at eight. There were still more, half-hidden by the banana trees and elephant ears, their fierce little faces seeming to move and twist in the flickering torch light.

Kevin pulled out a chair. 'Where's this drink you were promising?'

'Right here.' Alicia looked as pleased as a little girl as she fetched the drink tray. It contained a pitcher of some red liquid and two black mugs that looked like miniature statues from Easter Island. 'It's called "Blood of the Kapu Tiki."'

'Ah.'

'Two kinds of rum, lime juice, orange juice, and ... other things.' Alicia finished pouring and garnished the drinks with bright paper umbrellas. Handed one to Kevin. 'Cheers.'

'Cheers, baby. To us.'

'Us. Tiger.'

Kevin raised his eyebrows at the taste. Tart. Delicious. Lethal. His next sip took the drink down to the halfway mark.

Alicia smiled. 'Better watch yourself. These things are deadly.'

'Kiddo, you're talking to a boozer from way back.' Kevin reached for the pitcher.

'Cigar?' Alicia opened a mahogany humidor.

Kevin selected a panatela and lit up, watched with a smile as Alicia went back to the grill. She knew how to treat a man, that was for sure. No nagging, no drag-assing around the house, no moaning about how tired she was after a hard day of work. And always taking care to make sure she never gained so much as an ounce.

Unlike Melina.

Kevin blew out a plume of smoke and sat back with a sigh.

The hidden garden speakers hummed with a mysterious jungle of choruses and exquisite vibraphonic syncopation. One of the tikis looked at him with wide, angry eyes and a mouth full of dagger-like teeth.

Poor Melina, Kevin thought. Her heart was in the right place, but she just didn't have what it took to be the wife of an important man. He was too stupid to understand this when he was twenty-two, but now that ten years had passed he could see how the right wife was crucial to an ambitious man's career. Bill Allingsway, the senior partner, had that sort of wife. Beautiful, smart, able to throw parties that attracted famous politicians and famous artists. And as for the other side of the coin, one only had to consider poor old Sam Kovacks. He'd really blown it with his new wife. Young enough to be his granddaughter, dumb as a hammer, and saddled with a set of enormous fake breasts. It had everyone laughing behind Kovacks' back. And despite all his years at the firm, suddenly the juicy cases weren't coming Kovacks' way anymore.

But there would be no such problem with Alicia. She had it all – in spades. No telling how far he'd go with a woman of such beauty and intelligence at his side.

Governor, may I present my wife . . . Alicia.

Could he imagine introducing Melina to the Governor? That dumpy little Hawaiian broad? Kevin chuckled as he poured himself another drink. Alicia worked the skewered bits of chicken deftly. The smell was delicious.

Melina looked into the black depths of the bowl. The liquid moved in heavy, slow-motion swirls, like heated tar. A bluish mist began to rise.

'Akua kahiko,' Melina whispered as she inhaled the fumes. 'Ha'awi a'u kaulike.'

A small, greasy wave of nausea hit Kevin as suddenly as

bad news. He put the drink down. And the cigar. Rubbed his face. A face that was suddenly clammy with sweat.

'Kevin? You all right?'

He looked up. And for a moment was disoriented. The tall tiki next to Alicia . . . had it really been that close to her? Hadn't it been—

'Kevin?'

'Oh, I . . . I'm just a little woozy.' He stood up. 'It's been a long day. I think I'll just go splash a little water on my face.'

Alicia frowned prettily. 'I shouldn't have made that drink so strong.'

'You made it just fine. I'll be all right.'

Kevin went back to the house. But halfway there stopped and looked back. Alicia was bent over the grill, humming to the slow strains of 'Bali Hai.' Wavering light from the garden torches cast strange patterns on the tikis surrounding her. Almost as if they were . . . studying her, somehow . . .

Something gave his spine an uneasy little squeeze. Kevin shook his head and continued on to the house, looking forward to that splash of cold water.

Melina narrowed her eyes and stared into the terrible little bowl. And wasn't surprised when one of the three little gods that held it up slowly turned its loathsome face to look up at her. Melina stared right back, looking directly into its beady eyes. They began to glow red.

'Ha'awi a'u kaulike.' Melina's words were as soft as a butterfly's wings. 'Ha'awi a'u kaulike.'

Kevin patted the towel against his face. And felt much, much better. It had been a long day. And an especially unpleasant one at that. And come to think of it, he hadn't had anything to eat since Melina's typically lackluster breakfast. He should've gotten something down before tackling that drink and cigar.

'KEVINNNN!!!'

It was Alicia's shout, as loud and desperate as a siren, and Kevin felt the hairs on the back of his neck stand on end as he rushed from the bathroom—

'Kevin!!! *HELP ME!!!*'

This was followed by a terrible, rising shriek as Kevin ran through the house—

'Alicia! My God, what is it?'

Another scream exploded in the night – this one coarse, full of a sickening sort of despair. Kevin burst through the porch's door and out into the yard—

Alicia was nowhere in sight!

Smoke rose from the skewers burning on the grill. The black fronds of banana trees framed the empty barbecue area.

'Alicia!!!' Kevin raced past the grill. '*Alicia, where are you?*'

There was a rustling in the bushes and another scream went off like a cherry bomb. Kevin frantically pushed through palm fronds—

'Alicia! Alicia!'

There was another rustle – this one nearby – and Kevin crashed through the foliage, and—

And—

Kevin stood there, solid as a statue, his chest feeling like a sack of ice, his eyes wide as dinner plates. The sight of the nightmare before him exploded in his brain, a sight that made no sense, a sight he denied over and over even as the image refused to go away—

Alicia was being held by the tikis!

Tikis that had somehow come to a hideous sort of life, like the enchanted apple trees in *The Wizard of Oz*, their strange little hands holding Alicia's arms and legs, their furious wooden eyes looking down upon her with a cold sort of rage, their sharpened mouths opening –

'No!' Kevin screamed. '*No! No! NO!*'

Alicia writhed and squirmed in their wooden grasp, her eyes showing that she was terrified to the point of madness. The tallest of the tikis gave Kevin a slow look . . . a look of contempt and anger . . . and then opened its serrated jaws and clamped down on Alicia's neck like a bear trap snapping closed. Alicia spasmed and screamed but it was a garbled sort of scream, as if it were coming from underwater, and a great fount of crimson shot from her mouth.

The detective made another note on his pad. 'So the neighbors called it in?'

'Yes, sir. They said the owner is a Ms Alicia Ralley, but we haven't found her yet. When we looked out back all we found was – ' The young patrol officer shifted uneasily. '– well, just a lot of blood. All by the barbecue area. And the guy was out there, too – the one we've got cuffed in back of the car.'

The detective glanced at the patrol car, where the blond man sat in the back seat, slowly rocking back and forth and moaning. He'd seen guys like this before. Guys that had lost their minds. It's something you never forget. Mostly because of the eyes – big, round fruitcake eyes, like they were wild things that had been suddenly caged. Eyes that had seen something no amount of counseling or therapy would ever make them un-see.

'He say anything?' The detective asked. But already knew the answer.

'Well . . . he was kind of babbling.'

'Uh-huh. He give you any trouble?'

'Not at first.' By the patrol officer's wide-eyed look, the detective judged this to be one of his first crime scenes. 'When we got here we just found him sitting on the ground and hugging one of these wooden Hawaiian sculptures and crying like a baby. He came with us willingly enough . . . but man, when we tried to make him let that statue go, he really went crazy.'

'Yeah?'

'Yes, sir, it took me and Phil and – I mean, Officers Harkins and Bartleby – it took all three of us to get him to pry it loose. He started screaming like a wild animal when we got it out of his hands. But then he quieted down once we got him inside the cruiser.'

'This thing here?' The wooden statue was lying on the ground. It was about three feet long, as big around as a paint can.

'Yes, sir.'

'Any I.D. on the man?'

'None yet. But we haven't finished searching the house. Harkins and Bartleby are still out back looking for the woman, but honestly, it doesn't look she's anywhere around. Want me to help them or continue searching the house?'

'I want you to put in a call to the Mobile Crime Lab. I want floodlights and every officer not involved on an active call out here. We're going to search every inch of this place until we find Ms Ralley.'

'Yes, sir!'

The detective watched the patrol officer hurry back to his vehicle to place the call. Then sighed. It was shaping up to be one of those complicated nights. He took out a cigarette and lighted up. But stopped short of throwing the match on the ground. The Hawaiian statue the man had been cradling was there, looking up at him with its blank eyes. He'd seen these things increasingly of late – 'tikis', they were called. Sergeant Grumman had a few in his backyard by his pool. And he'd even seen a couple for sale at Home Depot. Funny things.

But . . . this one was different. It didn't seem to have the usual angry sort of scowl. No, this one had a mouth that was opened in something like surprise. And the eyes weren't so much angry as . . . horrified.

The top part was especially strange. Usually these things

had a carving of a totem-like band or even a kind of Polyne-sian crown. But not this one. There were long, wavy lines instead . . .

Like the flowing hair of a blonde woman.

Elizabeth Jenkins

ON NO ACCOUNT, MY LOVE

ELIZABETH JENKINS (1905-2010) *was a writer best known for her nonfiction work, which includes biographies of Lady Caroline Lamb, Jane Austen, and Queen Elizabeth I. Of her thirteen novels, the most famous is* The Tortoise and the Hare (1954), *a finely drawn, perceptive story of a marriage threatened with ruin by the intrusion of another woman. Yet another author who was not known for horror fiction, Jenkins nonetheless explored the darkest recesses of human nature in her novel* Harriet (1934), *inspired by a real-life Victorian murder case and republished by Valancourt. 'On No Account, My Love', apparently Jenkins's only ghost story, was first published in the third volume of Lady Cynthia Asquith's famous* Ghost Book *series. It is a tale whose slow and leisurely build-up leaves the reader perhaps unprepared for the story's chilling implications, which are not made evident until the very end.*

M Y COUSIN HERO IS BEAUTIFUL but unmindful of the fact. Though her husband has done well in his profession it has needed ceaseless energy on Hero's part to keep up the domestic standard she thinks worthy of him and the children; therefore, capable and high-spirited though she is, she bears the stamp of care. Her beauty is the last thing in her mind, though sometimes when she fixes you with her keen blue eyes, intent on discovering just how misguided you have been so that she may put you right, the loveliness of her face, sharp as a cameo, astonishes even someone who knows her as well as I do.

Decisiveness is one of Hero's leading qualities, and a passionate conviction that she is right: not from any virtue of her own, but because she knows what the right is, and has joined herself to it. In the present degenerate state of society there is a great deal that is wrong, and against everything of the sort Hero is dauntlessly embattled. Her upright carriage, small as she is, and her great eyes filled with stern resolve give her rather the look of being posted on the ramparts. Her affection takes the form of a protective, almost proprietary interest in the ones she loves; she cannot help knowing what is best for them; she only wishes, for their sake, that they could see the facts as clearly as she does.

Her kindness to me is of a critical sort, for I am, though so nearly related, entirely outside the strain of heredity that distinguishes my cousin. I am vague, unpractical, and, as she does not disguise from me, often downright silly in the management of my affairs. At the same time, there are matters into which I fancy that I can see farther than she can.

These characteristics and the chiselled features and blue eyes that go with them, of which Hero is the present embodiment, have appeared in my mother's family for four generations. They missed me, but my mother had them, so had two of her sisters. In all three, the look of blazing moral energy was tinged with a faint terror and desperation, as if they had been called on to sustain some ordeal like that of the Boy on the Burning Deck. It was not open to them to save themselves by failure, and they could see the flames licking up the ground in front of them. In the generation before my mother and her sisters, photographs of my great-aunts showed more faces with the unmistakable stamp of beauty, intensity and care; and behind these again, the *fons et origo* of all this, my great-grandmother. Hers was the mould of the family face and her descendants were startlingly like her; yet there was a great difference between them. Their beautiful faces, in early youth even, were strained and anxious; her expression, though intense, was confident: they were oppressed and she was triumphant.

She was one of those people whose personality makes such a strong impression that it lasts a long while after death.

Great-grandmother, with her strictness, her sternness, her domineering will, was an alarming story to us in our childhood though she had died long before we were born. As we grew up, I felt how much I should have disliked and shrunk from her. In Hero, her idea aroused a passionate resentment. Hero used to say, she would just have liked to see her trying it on with *her*. Indeed, she and great-grandmother would have been worthy of each other's steel.

No one knew where she came from; her name was or was said to be Seymour, but she had been adopted by two maiden ladies and if she knew in what circumstances she never said. She was proposed to, at the then late age of twenty-nine, by a gentleman of modest means. We have her written reply in which she barely puts down her thanks for the honour of his regard before she says: 'I must tell you that I have no fortune and no prospect of any.' This letter amused my father for he said that when he proposed to my mother she immediately exclaimed: 'Oh! But I am much older than you think I am.' Our great-grandfather, like my father after him, paid no heed to these disclaimers. Miss Seymour became Mrs Standish and went to live in Derbyshire in a town that was rapidly developing as a health resort. Her husband died early, leaving her with several young children and little else beside the house they lived in. This was one in a crescent on the hillside, at what was then the top of the town. At that time the graceful curve of its façade stood out white against the murky violet of the hills, now the whole hillside has been engulfed in a tide of building development. The expansion was beginning in the 1860s and it gave Mrs Standish the opportunity of supporting her family by a girls' boarding school. She made a really remarkable success of this project; before long she acquired the houses on each side of her own and these considerable premises were filled to overflowing with her young family, her employees and the girls under her care. The whole household was welded together under her vigilant and energetic rule. The domestic conditions were those of almost supernormal cleanliness, neatness, economy and punctuality, at the cost of many a red-armed servant girl crying on the back stairs, and the teaching was carried on with such gusto, the drilling in grammar and dates and tables and maps and principal exports had the stimulus of a round game, but a game slightly nightmarish in quality, a game played with tigers. The school throughout its long life, for it passed from hand to hand, till Magnall's Questions gave way to the Examinations of the Joint Board, preserved intact its original tradition of thoroughness, enthusiasm and clear handwriting. The relentless driving that produced it had, one must suppose, a good effect on the average pupil but it bore hardly on the two extremes; it burdened the dull and in the intelligent and highly strung it induced a morbid conscientiousness. Mrs Standish's own descendants were among the latter. An enlightened policy of child-care would have soothed and kept them back; Mrs Standish goaded them on till their talents were unnaturally burnished and their nervous systems a wreck. As Mama she had been formidable, as Grandmama she was a holy terror, and it was from that phase of her rule that the stories came of her severe discipline, the preposterous tales of what she exacted and what she wouldn't allow, that made such an impression on the rest of us who had never seen her. One of her daughters was in love with a young man who sought her hand. They had met at choir practice but great-grandmother objected to his principles and forbade the match. She knew best, naturally. Our great-aunt developed what was called brain-fever and lay in bed for weeks. It was summer and the day of the school fête when parents came to a great tea-drinking, inspected needlework and listened to songs, recitations and piano pieces afterwards. Downstairs all was gaiety and commotion, white frocks, striped awnings, geraniums and strawberries on a fleet of glass plates. No one could be spared to watch the invalid, except my mother, a child of five, who was left in her aunt's bedroom, perched on a high stool from where she could see the figure in the white bed with a bandage over its eyes, moving its head on the pillow very slightly but all the time. The child was told to come downstairs at once and tell somebody if the patient started to get out of bed. The white curtains were drawn across the sunny window, the walls were in shadow; the dreadful bandage round the head made it look like something on an ancient tomb near to where the little girls sat in church. From far below came up the sounds of the party, too far away to be of any help. The child sat transfixed in an agony of fright lest the terrible figure should begin to rise. My mother said she thought that if that had happened, she would have gone out of her mind with fear.

The story used to fill me with indignation, for my mother communicated her sufferings to me in a way I never forgot, and I laid them, and a great deal of nervous unhappiness, at my great-grandmother's door. My mother, feeling sometimes that she had given an unfair impression, would say in contrite tones: 'She had, I think, a wonderful way of giving pleasure by small things: these dolls that were kept in the drawing-room! They had their own tea-set and a trunk for their extra dresses and hats: we used to be allowed to play with them on special occasions. I have never forgotten the excitement and delight of seeing them put down on the yellow hearthrug.'

'When everything was more or less horrid, I suppose anything that wasn't did seem wonderful,' I suggested. My mother said, it was not *that*, exactly. 'So much of what she did was excellent; it was only . . .' My mother broke off and sighed. 'Only!' cried Hero, sparkling with ire. 'I should think it was, indeed! *Only* that she was an abominable old tyrant who made people's lives a misery!' My mother succeeded thoroughly in making us understand the harsh side of the régime but she could not with all her efforts induce us to see that there had been a part of it that was worth having.

The school after four generations had been honourably wound up; the later phases of its existence had no distinctive interest for me, but whenever I met someone who had had, or heard of, first-hand experience of its early days, there was always brought to light some new detail of my great-grandmother's reign; of hot afternoons when thirsty children were not allowed to go for drinks of water because, said Mrs Standish with inexorable logic, drinking was drinking, and if you did not learn to control a desire for water, where would you be when wine and spirits were within your reach? And of festivals of delicious things, religiously kept: gooseberry pies and cream at Whitsun, hot rolls for breakfast on Sunday mornings and two or three times a term, a Sweet Saturday, when everyone was allowed to choose sweets and order sixpenny-worth of them, and they were brought in to the big schoolroom in great baskets. No doubt the child of today, devouring chocolate and ice cream at all hours, has never had a gastronomic sensation like that produced by a single brandy ball under Mrs Standish's aegis.

Of the three houses occupied by her, one was now a private hotel, one empty and for sale and the third in the possession of some very old friends. They asked me to visit them on my way back from a journey in the north. I was especially pleased to go; I wanted to see with my own eyes the houses of which I had heard so much, and besides this, our friends were in the middle of a very interesting experience. They had newly acquired a cook-housekeeper, a Mrs Garnish, who, it turned out, was a medium and received messages in automatic writing every night. Mrs Garnish went to bed with a pencil and sheets of paper beside her, and in the morning the latter were covered with regular handwriting, a little different from her own. The lines were even but they sometimes went at an angle across the paper and sometimes were written right off it so that the end of a line would be lost. Nonetheless a great body of communication was received, and it was of absorbing interest to our friends, for the greater part of it appeared to come from their own relations who were dead, and some from friends and connections whom they themselves could barely remember except by name. There was no doubting the good faith of the medium, and whatever might be the explanation of it, they were witnessing a very singular phenomenon. On a few occasions when clairvoyants had read cards for me they had asked me whether I were mediumistic, and when told no, they had said I should develop the faculty later. As they had never read my future with any marked success, and as the development they foretold had showed no signs of taking place, I had almost forgotten it. I remembered it again as I came down from Yorkshire into Derbyshire and leaning in a corner of the railway carriage, gazing at the wonderful landscape as we wound among dales and streams, I felt a stir of excitement, wondering if any messages would come for me during the night that I was under what had once been my great-grandmother's roof.

The crescent no longer stood out against the hills, for buildings had encroached around and far above it, and at close quarters the façade was seen to be cracked and darkened and patched with boards announcing hotels and offices. Inside however was all the space and gracefulness of its period. I walked in through a vestibule with inner doors whose panels of milky glass were scattered with clear glass stars and edged with strips of glass in ruby, amber, emerald, sapphire and violet. There were gothic-pointed windows on each side of the front door and embrasures for statues or plants. I was so much moved by all this that I barely noticed Mrs Garnish as she let me in and yet I knew it was she: short and square with a face of glistening pallor, pince-nez, a quiet smile and the most respectable clothes, ending in stockings of clerical-grey and black strapped shoes.

Our friends with sympathetic kindness had got the key of the empty house from the house agent, for they thought I should be able to imagine the original scene more clearly from empty rooms than from their own, filled with modern comforts. After lunch therefore on a bright afternoon in April, I let myself into the middle of the three houses, the one that had been my great-grandmother's home. The functional nature of the premises and her restricted income by all accounts saved her from the over-furnishing and over-ornamentation of the late Victorian era. Her rooms had been almost as elegantly bare as if she had furnished them in the previous century. The only rich objects in view had been the lofty gilt pier glasses already over the chimney-pieces when she had taken the house. Two of these were still there on the first floor; one was enclosed and separated into three by gilt Ionic columns, the other reared a gilt trophy of musical instruments, from which fringed gold scarves drooped in festoons on each side of the glass. The mirrors themselves were filled with watery gleams and shadows, for they were opposite the great sash windows through whose panes the girls had looked at the roofs of the town below or up at the great marbled expanse of the northern sky. I walked slowly across dusty boards, everything I had ever heard about the rooms coming back to me; I wondered in which of the three drawing-rooms it was that my mother had played with dolls on the yellow rug, where the round table had stood that was covered with a magenta velvet cloth, on which of the chimney-pieces there had been the famous pair of emerald glass baskets. These objects had remained in many minds with a brilliance accentuated by the extent of drab serge and plain drugget around them. I climbed the front staircase till the stairs grew almost as narrow and steep as those of a church tower and found myself in a row of small bedrooms whose sash windows, filled with a pale blaze of sky, were so immediately in front of one on opening the door, one felt about to fall through them. So high up, a strong breeze was rattling the frames. I looked about the empty walls and wondered if this room or one like it had been the scene of my great-aunt's brain fever, but for once the memory did not appal me; it now took on the proportion of a part in a much larger whole. After a long while I let myself out of the house and returned to the next door one through a pair of glass doors identical with those through which I had just emerged. Indoors I saw that it had become dusk, and an electric light was burning in the hall outside the drawing-room door. On a space of wall just beside it, was an enlarged photograph in an oval frame of Mrs Standish taken in advanced years. I had seen similar ones but never one that showed the face so well. The hair drooped smoothly under lace, the features in their symmetry and their sharpness were what I had often seen, but the eyes were sunken and tired; the hands rested on her lap palms upward, the back of one curved in the palm of the other. There was no suggestion of a posed portrait; this was a moment's pause in the day of a busy woman, who had sat still for a minute that someone might take her photograph. As I stood looking at it I felt growing in me, unexpected and unsought, a feeling of sympathy, of admiration, of affection even for my great-grandmother. I saw, for the first time objectively, what a creature of spirit and style she had been, of what buoyancy of intellect. I imagined her *obiter dicta*, so many of which had come down to us, uttered in that voice I knew so well but louder, more resonant, with a twang like that of a harpsichord. Looking at the photograph with its saffron and mulberry gloss, I pored over the expression, calm and positive and a little fatigued, and I remembered all the good things said about her which I had so perversely disregarded: how splendidly capable she was with a child in the throes of croup, how unfailingly she remembered birthdays and would think of special treats for anyone who had been left out, how she had said that to be one of a family was a blessing, and that brothers and sisters must endure anything rather than quarrel. As I stood in the quiet hall, noises in different parts of the house came to my ears, a waft of radio music from behind the drawing-room door, and a sound of saucepans from the regions at the back. I thought with a rising excitement of Mrs Garnish. The idea of being able to get into touch with my great-grandmother gave me a thrill of interest keener than any book or picture had ever evoked in me. I felt sure that some contact was possible, was waiting for me, and as I went into the lighted drawing-room I was so rapt with the thought, I could barely see what was in front of me.

In the course of the evening I told our friends what my hopes were. They were sympathetic but non-committal. Then we dropped this matter and spent an evening full of news and reminiscence. My bedroom was one of the lofty ones, but curtained, carpeted, warmed, with books, bedside lamp and a large soft eiderdown. I gave one glance through the panes before getting to bed. The sky was quite black and the harsh lights from the streets and the noise of traffic and nocturnal shouting deprived the scene of any visual depth or any charm. I suffered a reaction from my previous mood: I felt that everything I cared about was lost and went to my comfortable bed in a prosaic frame of mind.

Next day I was to leave by a train shortly after twelve, and in the course of the morning when we had the breakfast-room to ourselves, my hostess handed me a sheet of paper, saying something on it might refer to me. I left the room with it in my hand but my eagerness would not let me mount the stairs with it and I carried it into the glassed-in vestibule to examine it by one of the gothic windows. It was a sheet from an exercise book, blue-lined. The pencilled writing did not keep to the lines but it was regular and firm and had been crossed, almost at right-angles, by more writing, which made the whole thing difficult to read. The writing parallel with the lines seemed to be about a Colonel Mortimer-Fisher who had had three sons but all were with him now. They were working for those left behind, and sent messages of a hopeful and joyous nature to various groups of initials. My heart sank as I made all this out: I suddenly remembered all I had ever heard of the trite, depressing clichés of spirit communication; here was an example. I felt that even those who had known Colonel Mortimer-Fisher and his sons and held them dear could hardly be stirred by this. In a moment of disappointment and self-contempt I turned the paper round to bring the diagonally written lines straight. Their writing though less black was a good deal larger.

Elizabeth Elizabeth Elizabeth Elizabeth, I read, and the repetition of my name made my heart stop beating. No dangerous for you very dangerous very very dangerous on no account my love.

I stood quite still, I have no idea for how long. Then I crossed the vestibule and the hall, both of them sunny and empty, and made my way, hesitating, to the semi-basement kitchen to say a word and a goodbye to Mrs Garnish. The door stood open and a large clock ticked on the narrow shelf high above what had once been a range, its cavern now occupied by a gas cooker. The light came over a stone wall and slanted through the top row of panes in a broad, clear shaft. A row of green plants stood under it on the deep sill. At the scrubbed white table Mrs Garnish was sitting in a mid-day pause. A bright blue canister was before her, a small brown teapot and a large white cup and saucer. She sat motionless with her eyes closed but her head, instead of being sunk forward as another person's would have been, was upright, even raised a little. Her greenish-pale face glistened. Nothing moved but the jerking hands of the clock.

It came over me that I had no business there, that I had already been told as much. I came upstairs again to objects that looked like cardboard, to mechanical words and auto-matic actions.

I came back unable to say much to anyone about my visit. Hero, whom I met a couple of days afterwards, was struck by my unusual silence. When she had satisfied herself that I was not sickening for anything, she looked at me anxiously but without saying more. She is now turning over in her mind whether I had better go abroad for a little.

J. B. Priestley

UNDERGROUND

J. B. PRIESTLEY (1894-1984) *was a defining British cultural figure of the twentieth century, from his wartime BBC broadcasts to his best-selling and award-winning fiction to his extremely popular plays, required reading even today in British schools and still frequently performed and adapted for TV and film. Priestley did not write widely in the genres of horror or weird fiction, but his novel* Benighted (1927), *basis for the James Whale film* The Old Dark House (1932), *and his collection of strange stories* The Other Place (1953) *(both available from Valancourt) will appeal to fans of the genre. 'Underground', first published in the* Christmas number of The Illustrated London News *in 1974, is the story of a not-very-nice-guy whose journey in the London Underground becomes quite literally a hellish experience. Eight of Priestley's books spanning a variety of genres, from adventure to science fiction to fantasy, are available from Valancourt, and his finest novel,* Bright Day (1944), *is forthcoming.*

R AY AGGARSTONE TOOK THE NORTHERN LINE from Leicester Square. It was some time since he had gone anywhere by Underground. Either he had used his car or had taken taxis for shorter journeys. But now that he was almost ready for what he liked to call, to himself but not to anybody else, the *Big Getaway,* he had sold his car for just over four hundred quid. Just showed you how useful it could be to chat somebody up, in this case that stupid sod who was always in the Saloon bar of the King's Arms. While waiting on the crowded platform at Leicester Square, Ray told himself once again that he was careful as well as very clever. For instance, after that car deal and with a few drinks inside them, some fellows would have boasted about the Brazilian

setup and the flight to Rio, but not Ray – not on your life!
He had told this stupid sod exactly the same story he had
told his mother and his wife, Cherry, now waiting for him
somewhere near the end of this Northern Line. 'Going to
France, old man – Nice actually – where I've bought into a
very promising property deal. Smart work, if I may say so.'

But of course he hadn't shown him the letters he'd con-
cocted to show his Mum and Cherry, now ready to part with
eight thousand between them, about all they had. They
were both so excited about his plan for them to join him at
Nice within the next two or three weeks, like a pair of idiotic
kids, they left *business* entirely to him, Mum's clever handsome son, Cherry's dominating, fascinating if occasionally
unfaithful husband. Serve them right when he vanished
with the two cheques he was going to collect – the silly cows!

No train yet but more people arriving on the platform.
He changed his place, bumping and shoving a bit, if only to
show these types what he thought about them. A run-down
lot in a running-down country! He could never come back
of course, not after those two women finally decided he'd
robbed them blind, but he didn't want to anyhow. He'd had
it here all right – finish! He couldn't blame Rita and Karl for
sneering and jeering, even though now and again they got
his goat, specially Karl. But that was early on, before they
began to talk business.

The train came along, already more than half full. And
because he hadn't stood near the platform edge, though he
pushed and shoved as hard as anybody, perhaps a bit harder
than most, of course he didn't get a seat – not a hope! So
there he was, standing and swaying, wedged in with a lot
of fat arses, smelly underclothes and bad breath. Looking
around, disgusted, he couldn't imagine now what had made
him come down here when he might have hired a car, travelled in comfort and also impressed Mum and Cherry. So, to
stop cursing himself, he began thinking about Rita and Karl

again. After all he'd be meeting them in Rio in two or three days, and he began to wonder how things would work over there. Every time Karl, who was her husband all right, had gone to Manchester or Leeds and had stayed the night, he'd had Rita, a hot brunette if there ever was one, who'd start moaning if a finger touched a tit. Did Karl know, just guess, not care – or what? Anyhow, what Karl, a real businessman in the German-Swedish style, did know was that his friend, smart Ray Aggarstone, would be shortly financing most of the deal they'd worked out. Moreover, there must be plenty of hot moaning brunettes in Brazil.

Tottenham Court Road and people, dreary bloody people, pushing their way out and pushing their way in. And off again – sway, rattle, bang, bang, rattle, sway. A long thin woman, loaded with parcels, dug an elbow into his ribs, and he used his own elbow, with some force, to knock it away. She glared at him over her parcels, but all he did was to raise his eyebrows at her. After a moment or two she was able to move away a few inches. It was then that a curious thing happened. Through the gap she had left between them he saw for the first time a small figure sitting down. It had the face of an old-looking boy or a rather young-looking dwarf. He stared at this creature, who then met his stare with a widening of the eyes, odd eyes, yellowish. Next, the little oddity closed his eyes and moved his head slowly from side to side, almost as if he was giving a 'No-no-no' signal. As soon as the eyes opened again, Ray gave them a hard scowling look. But now there was no sign of recognition in them. It was just as if Ray was no longer there at all. The boy-or-dwarf might have been looking *through him*. A silly idea. Ray began to think how he would deal with Mum and Cherry.

At Euston there was a lot more pushing out and shoving in, twerps on the move. The little monster had gone, and in his place was a fat suet-faced woman who stared angrily at anything or nothing, just to prove she had a right to a seat.

Rattling and swaying on again, Ray told himself how he ought to deal with Mum and Cherry this time. Very different, he decided, from last time when he'd been all solemn, very much the business man, explaining again why Cherry had to stay with Mum, now that he'd got rid of their flat, and why he was staying in an hotel to be near the two Frenchmen who'd agreed to let him buy into the big property development just outside Nice. This time, everything being settled now they were giving him their cheques, there'd be no point in going on with the solemn business thing. It would have to be all merry chit-chat about Nice and the Riviera, how they'd be joining him down there quite soon, how he'd be arranging their flights, booking a posh double-bedded room with bath for Cherry and him, with a good single nearby for Mum, and at least one balcony the three could use for breakfast – all that bullshit. Yes, there he'd be, egging them on, the stupid cows, maybe taking them out to a pub if Mum hadn't got anything in to drink.

Somebody touched his arm. This was deliberate. A woman was smiling at him. She was an oldish woman, white-haired but with a plump red-cheeked face and bright blue eyes; and he'd seen her before somewhere. 'You're Ray Aggarstone, aren't you?' she said, smiling away.

It seemed as if he hadn't time to think before he heard himself saying, 'No, I'm not.' He said it sharply too, as if really telling her to mind her own dam' business.

It wiped the smile off her face and narrowed and darkened her eyes, almost turning her into another person. 'I think you *are* Ray Aggarstone, y'know,' she said; and though the train was making a lot of noise, somehow she managed to say it quietly. 'And you must remember me. I'm an old friend of your mother's.'

She must have been too, he realised now. But he hadn't to be bothered with her, when he was busy with his own thoughts and plans. He shook his head at her. 'Got this all wrong.' And he had to shout because the train might have been grinding its way through rocks, the noise it was making. 'I don't know you. And you don't know me.'

'Yes, I do. Or I did do, once,' she went on steadily. 'She thought the world of you, Ray. Her only son – so good-looking, so clever!'

He found a snarl coming out of him this time. 'Do you mind! Just turn it up!' And he looked away, to get rid of her. But when he turned his head again, she was still there, though not quite so close, having managed to back away from him a little. And now she seemed a lot older and was giving him a long sad look. He couldn't return it – he suddenly felt he had nothing to return it with, not even a scowl – so he looked away again and was relieved to find the train was stopping at Camden Town. This time not many got in, but then not many got out, so he was still forced to stand, even though he'd a bit more space round him. And this suited him all right because if there was one thing he didn't like it was being jammed among all these idiotic, bloody disgusting people, staring old cows, smelly bitches and stupid buggers of all ages and sizes. When he got to Brazil and the money was rolling in, as Karl swore it would, he'd work it so that there was no more of this horrible caper. The only people allowed near him would be the ones he could enjoy seeing, hearing, smelling and touching.

As the train started rattling and banging off again, he started thinking again. Working out how he'd deal with Cherry and his mother, chatting them up about life on the Riviera, breakfasts on balconies, drinks to welcome the wonderful new life, laughs and hugs and kisses and all that female crap, he realised he'd overdone it, not for them but for himself. For what he'd gone and done, if only for a minute or two, was to go soft and feel a bit sorry for both of them, considering that he was about to skin them down to their last fifty quid each. No time for that tonight! He'd got to be as sensible and hard as he'd been when he worked out the plan. Serve 'em right for not having more sense! He'd to look after himself, so they could look after themselves – and women always managed somehow. And he began to remember and light up every grievance he'd ever had against the pair of 'em. He'd deal with them the way he'd planned, pretending to be as silly as they were, and when they laughed then he'd laugh too, even, just for a private giggle, bringing out and flourishing his wallet, which already had in it his Air France ticket to Rio.

It was just past Chalk Farm when the man tapped him on the shoulder. He was a tall man, so tall he had to bend over Ray, and he had very sharp grey eyes and a long chin.

'Better get out at Hampstead,' the man said, almost in Ray's ear.

'Can't do,' Ray told him briskly. 'Going as far as Hendon Central. Unless of course I have to change. Is that it?'

'You might say that's it.' A solemn reply.

This sounded idiotic to Ray. 'I don't know what you're talking about.' This tall fellow didn't look a chump, but then, like so many people now, he might be round the bend.

Two women pushed past them, getting ready for Belsize Park. The man waited but then he tapped Ray on the shoulder again and bent closer to his ear. 'Just a last word. Most people think this line's at its deepest at Hampstead. What they don't know – and I don't suppose you do – is that there's a second line, starting at Hampstead, that goes deeper still – on and on, deeper and deeper –'

'Oh – come off it!' Ray was impatient now. This was obviously a crackpot.

'I'm not on it.' The man gave a short crackpot's laugh. 'But you may be *if* you don't get out at Hampstead and then take a taxi or a bus – *and go back.*'

'That's enough,' Ray told him. 'I'll mind my own business and you mind yours.'

'No, it's not as simple as that,' said the tall man quite mildly. 'You're part of my business now. That's why I'm telling you – not asking you, *telling* you – to forget Hendon Central and get out at Hampstead—'

Ray lost his temper. 'And I'm *telling* you – not asking you – to piss off.'

The train was slowing up. Belsize Park now. There were sufficient people getting out to push between Ray and the tall man, but then there was quite a gap between them now. Only a few got on, and Ray saw that he could have a seat at last if he wanted one. But somehow he didn't. Perhaps he felt he might go soft again if he sat down. Better to keep on standing and be hard and tough. The tall man, easily seen, had moved down and was now near the far door, ready to get out at Hampstead, where the big daft sod thought every-body ought to get out. All these mental hospitals and yet a crackpot pest like this was allowed to wander around loose, making a bloody nuisance of himself! Anyhow, as soon as the train pulled up at Hampstead, out the chap went, fol-lowed by nearly everybody else. This left the carriage almost empty. Ray could have taken as many seats as he wanted now, but he didn't make a move, not for the moment trusting himself to let go of the strap he was clinging to, for he had to admit that he felt a bit faint, probably because of all the clat-tering and swaying and what so many stinking people had done to the air had combined to make him feel faint.

This was an unusually long wait. He closed his eyes, just for a few moments, and when he opened them again he was both surprised and alarmed to discover that he had the whole long carriage to himself. Nobody else at all in sight. Had they shouted, 'Hampstead – all change!' and he'd missed it? Even dim as he felt, he was about to make for the door when, with an unpleasant jerk, the train started again. Then two things, equally unpleasant, happened together. There were several loud bangs and the lights went out. Badly shaken, there in the dark with the train obviously gathering speed, he made up his mind he would get out at the next stop, which would be Golders Green, and find a taxi to take him up to Mum's place. The lights came on again, and though they seemed bright enough at first, after the dark, he soon realized that in fact they were much lower than they'd been before. Ten to one some power-cut frigging nonsense!

Then quite suddenly – and it came like a hammer-blow at the heart – he *knew* that this train was going nowhere near Golders Green. At the same time he felt that it wasn't moving like all the others, which went more or less level or climbed a bit to rush out into the open air. No, it was *going down and down*. And what had that tall crackpot said? Something about a second line going deeper still – *on and on, deeper and deeper*—? He tried to forget this but he couldn't, and he began to wish there was somebody else with him who could explain what was happening. The train went rattling on, faster now than the usual underground train. There was nothing to be seen of course, and with this poor lighting he could hardly catch a glimpse of his own reflection. He tried cursing and blinding, to stop himself feeling frightened; but it didn't work.

However, bringing a flood of relief, something happened he never remembered seeing before on an underground train. Some sort of conductor chap, wearing a dark uniform, had come through a door at the far end of the carriage and was now walking towards him – that is, if you could call this slow shuffle a walk. Enjoying his relief, Ray took a seat at last and began rehearsing the indignant questions he would ask. 'Now look here,' he called out, 'what the hell's the idea—?' But there he stopped, terrified. He was staring at something out of a nightmare. The man hadn't a face, just eyes like a couple of blackcurrants, and nothing else – no mouth, no nose, no ears. In his terror Ray huddled into his seat and shut his eyes tight, hoping feverishly that the lard-faced monster wouldn't stop, even to put a finger on him, but would go shuffling past him. And this indeed he did, so that when Ray risked opening his eyes he was alone again. That was something, and what happened next was better still. At last the train was slowing down. There must be a station soon – certainly not Golders Green – but whatever the station was, however far it might be from Hendon Central, it was where he would get out of this nightmare train.

He caught glimpses of an enormous packed platform. As soon as the train stopped he reached the door, but even then it was too late. He was swept back by a solid mass of people, who pushed and shoved like maniacs and closed round him so that he couldn't move and felt he could hardly breathe. And what people! All the faces he'd ever looked away from, disgust blotting out compassion, seemed to be here, and the train was already moving again. He felt he was hemmed in by ulcers, abscesses, half-blind eyes, rotting noses, gangrenous mouths and chins. And how far, how long? Even out of the depths of his nausea, he'd have to say something.

He put his question to the face nearest to him, a twisted slobbery caricature of a face, but all he got in reply was a senseless gabble.

'No use asking him,' a voice said over his shoulder. 'He's forgotten how to talk. What you want to know?' The voice belonged to a bull of a man with a face like a volcanic eruption.

'Where – ' and it was a shaky question, 'where are we going?'

'Where we going?' the bull roared. 'We're not going anywhere, you silly sod.' Now he roared louder still. 'Time to push around, shove about, all you bastards!'

Ray found at his elbow an old creature whose nose and chin nearly met: she could have been a witch out of an ancient fairy tale. 'I'll tell you where you're *not* going, young man,' she said, cackling and spitting. '*He-he-he!* You're not going to Rio in Brazil. Not now and not ever. *He-he-he!*'

His heart turning into ice-water, he understood at last that he might never know anything again except this underground journey to nowhere, wedged beyond any chance of escape among these malicious jeering monstrosities . . .

. . . 'Full name's Raymond Geoffrey Aggarstone, but liked to call himself just *Ray,*' said the first man. 'Got that? Okay. Now – effects. Silver cigarette case, inscribed *Darling Ray from his loving Cherry* . . . Posh lighter . . . Diary, gold pencil, three fivers and four pound notes in small notecase in one inside pocket . . .'

'Not too fast,' said the second man. 'And what about trousers pockets – keys and change and all that?'

'Come to them in a minute, chum,' said the first man. 'And if I'm going too fast, why ask for more? . . . Wallet in right inside pocket . . . Contains credit cards, two letters, and something from Air France—'

'Hold it! Yes, sir?' But this query was addressed to the new arrival. He was a tall man, with a long chin and sharp grey eyes, and he was obviously top brass authority, not the kind of bloke to be asked what he was doing there and where was his warrant card.

'I'll take the two letters,' this tall man said pleasantly but with assured authority. 'Not needed for the next of kin. I must look at that Air France booking too. Thank you!' He examined it, took out a pen and made an alteration. 'Yes, as I thought. There's a mistake here. Should have been Nice not Rio. Here you are, ready for the next of kin, but I'll keep the two letters, they'd only bewilder a couple of miserable women.' He gave the two men a sombre look. 'You know, this is a world where the guilty all too often go unpunished and the innocent are increasingly victimised, robbed, ruined, maimed or murdered.'

'That's true enough, sir,' said the first man. 'As I've said more than once to the wife and kids.'

'Well, now and again,' the tall man told him, 'we have the chance to change that. Just now and again. By the way, what are the facts here?'

'Found unconscious in the Northern Line train at Hampstead, sir. Major heart attack. Never recovered consciousness. In fact, died in the ambulance, sir. Finish!'

'Thank you! Possibly *finish* – possibly not. We don't know, do we? Goodnight!' And he left them so quickly, he might almost have vanished, a trick some of these top blokes seem to have mastered.

James Purdy

MR EVENING

JAMES PURDY (1914-2009), *like many Valancourt authors, achieved widespread critical acclaim and admiration from his fellow writers (he has counted Tennessee Williams, Gore Vidal, and Jonathan Franzen among his many fans), but rarely received the wider popular attention his works deserved. His books, often both savagely funny and horrifyingly violent, as well as open and unapologetic in their treatment of gay themes, sometimes elicited controversy: major U. S. publishers refused to touch two of his early books, which had to be published abroad, and as recently as 1990 one of his books was suppressed by police in Germany. Purdy's work often mixed high camp with Gothic grotesquerie, as in his novels* In a Shallow Grave *(1976) and* Narrow Rooms *(1978), both forthcoming from Valancourt, and his tale 'Mr Evening', first published in 1968, is no exception. Described by one critic as 'a darkly whimsical exercise in bloodless gothic horror', it's a delectably insidious tale, the horror of which only becomes evident as it reaches its climax.*

'YOU WERE ASKING THE OTHER DAY, Pearl, what that very tall young Mr Evening – the one who goes past the house so often – does for a living, and I think I've found out for you,' Mrs Owens addressed her younger sister from her chair loaded with hand-sewn cushions.

Mrs Owens continued to gaze out the big front window, its heavy shutter pulled back now in daylight to allow her a full view of the street.

She had paused long enough to allow Pearl's curiosity to whet itself while her own attention strayed to the faces of passersby. Indeed Mrs Owens's only two occupations now were correcting the endless inventory of her heirlooms and observing those who passed her window, protected from the street by massive wrought-iron bars.

'Mr Evening is in and out of his rooming house frequently enough to be up to a good deal, if you ask me, Grace,' Pearl finally broke through her sister's silence.

Coming out of her reverie, Mrs Owens smiled. 'We've always known he was busy, of course.' She took a piece of newsprint from her lap, and closed her eyes briefly in the descending rays of the January sun. 'But now at last we know what he's busy at.' She waved the clipping gently.

'Ah, don't start so, child.' Mrs Owens almost laughed. 'Pray look at this, would you,' and she handed the younger woman a somewhat lengthy 'notice' clipped neatly from the *Wall Street Journal.*

While Pearl put on thick glasses to study the fine print, Mrs Owens went on as much for herself as her sister: 'Mr Evening has always given me a special feeling.' She touched her lavaliere. 'He's far too young to be as idle as he looks, and on the other hand, as you've pointed out, he's clearly busier than those who make a profession of daily responsibility.'

'It's means, Grace,' Pearl said, blinking over her reading, but making no comment on it, which was a kind of desperate plea, it turned out, for information concerning a certain scarce china cup, circa 1910. 'He has means,' Pearl repeated.

'Means?' Mrs Owens showed annoyance. 'Well, I should hope he has, in his predicament.' She hinted at even further knowledge concerning him, but with a note of displeasure creeping into her tone at Pearl's somewhat offhand, bored manner.

'I've telephoned him to appear, of course.' Mrs Owens had decided against any further "preparation" for her sister, and threw the whole completed plan at her now in one fling. 'On Thursday, naturally.'

Putting down the 'notice' Pearl waited for Mrs Owens

to make some elaboration on so unusual a decision, but no elaboration came.

'But you've never sold anything, let alone shown to any-body!' Pearl cried, after some moments of deeply troubled cogitation.

'Who spoke of selling!' Mrs Owens tightened an earring. 'And as to showing, as you say, I haven't thought that far . . . But don't you see, poor darling' – here Mrs Owens's voice boomed in what was perhaps less self-defense than self-explanation – 'I've not met anybody in half a century who wants heirlooms so bad as he.' She tapped the clipping. 'He's worded everything here with one thought only in mind – my seeing it.'

Pearl withdrew into incomprehension.

'Don't you see this has to be the case!' Here she touched the 'notice' with her fingers again. 'Who else has the things he's enumerated here? He's obviously investigated what I have, and he could have inserted this in the want ads only in the hope it would catch my eye.'

'But you're certainly not going to invite someone to the house who merely wants what you have!' Pearl found her-self for the first time in her life not only going against her sister in opinion, but voicing something akin to disapproval.

'Why, you yourself said only the other night that what we needed was company!' Mrs Owens put these words adroitly now in her sister's mouth, where they could never have been.

'But Mr Evening!' Pearl protested against his coming, ignoring or forgetting the fact she had been quoted as having said something she never in the first place had thought.

'Don't we need somebody to tell us about heirlooms! I mean *our* heirlooms, of course. Haven't you said as much yourself time after time?'

Mrs Owens was trying to get her sister to go along with her, to admit complicity, so to speak, in what she herself had

brought about, and now she found that Pearl put her mind
and temper against even consideration.

'Someone told me only recently' – Pearl now hinted at a
side to her own life perhaps unknown to Mrs Owens – 'that
the young man you speak of, Mr Evening, can hardly carry
on a conversation.'

Mrs Owens paused. She had not been inactive in making
her own investigations concerning their caller-to-be, and
one of the things she had discovered, in addition to his being
a Southerner, was that he did not or would not 'talk' very
much.

'We don't need a conversationalist – at least not about
them,' Mrs Owens nearly snapped, by *them* meaning the heirlooms. 'What we need is an appreciator, and the *muter* the
better, say I.'

'But if that's all you want him for!' – Pearl refused to be
won – 'why, he'll smell out your plan. He'll see you're only
showing him what he can never hope to buy or have.'

A look of deep disappointment tinged with spleen crossed
Mrs Owens's still-beautiful face.

'Let him *smell* out our plan, then, as you put it,' Mrs Owens
chided in the wake of her sister's opposition, 'we won't care!
If he can't talk, don't you see, so much the better. We'll have
a session of "looking" from him, and his "appreciation" will
perk us up. We'll see him taking in everything, dear love, and
it will review our own lifelong success . . . Don't be so down
on it now . . . And mind you, we won't be here quite forever,'
she ended, and a certain hard majestical note in her voice
was not lost on the younger woman. 'The fact,' Mrs Owens
summed it all up, 'that we've nothing to give him needn't
spoil for us the probability he's got something to give us.'

Pearl said no more then, and Mrs Owens spoke under her
breath: 'I haven't a particle of a doubt that I'm in the right
about him, and if it should turn out I'm wrong, I'll shoulder
all the blame.'

Whatever particle of a doubt there may have been in Mrs Owens's own mind, there was considerably more of doubt and apprehension in Mr Evening's as he weighed, in his rooming house, the rash decision he had made to visit formidable Mrs Owens in – one could not say her business establishment, since she had none – but her background of accumulation of heirlooms, which vague world was, he could only admit, also his own. Because he had never known or understood people well, and he was the most insignificant of 'collectors', he was at a loss as to why Mrs Owens should feel he had anything to give her, and since her 'legend' was too well known to him, he knew she, likewise, had nothing at all to give him, except, and this was why he was going, the 'look-in' which his visit would give him. Whatever risk there was in going to see her, and there appeared to be some, he felt, from 'warnings' of a queer kind from those who had dealt with her, it was worth something just to get inside, even though again he had been informed by those in the business it would be doubtful if he would be allowed to mention 'purchase' and in the end it was also doubtful he would be allowed even a close peek.

On the other hand, if Mrs Owens wanted him to tell her something – this crossed his mind as he went toward her huge pillared house, though he could not imagine even vaguely what he could have to tell her, and if she was mad enough to think him capable of entertaining her, for after all she was a lonely ancient lady on the threshold of death, he would disabuse her of all such expectations almost as soon as they had met. He was uneasy with old women, he sup- posed, though in his work he spent more time with them than with other people, and he wanted, he finally said out loud to himself, that hand-painted china cup, 1910, no matter what it might cost him. He fancied she might yield it to him at some atrocious illegal price. It was no more improbable, after all, than that she had invited him in the first place. Mrs

Owens never invited anybody, that is, from the outside, and the inside people in her life had all died or were incapacitated from paying calls. Yes, he had been summoned, and he could hope at least therefore that what everybody else told him was at least thinkable – purchase, and if that was not in store for him, then the other improbable thing, 'viewing.'

But Mr Evening could not pretend. If his getting the piece of china or even more improbably other larger heirlooms, kept from daylight as well as human eyes, locked away in the floors above her living room, if possession meant long hours of currying favor, talking and laughing and dining and killing the evening, then no thank you, never. His inability to pretend, he supposed, had kept him from rising in the antique trade, for although he had a kind of business of his own here in Brooklyn, his own private income was what kept him afloat, and what he owned in heirlooms, though remarkable for a young dealer, did not make him a figure in the trade. His inconspicuous position in the business made his being summoned by Mrs Owens all the more inexplicable and even astonishing. Mr Evening was, however, too unversed both in people and the niceties of his own profession to be either sufficiently impressed or frightened.

Meanwhile Pearl, moments before Mr Evening's arrival gazing out of the corner of her eye at her sister, saw with final and uncomfortable consternation the telltale look of anticipation on the older woman's face which demonstrated that she 'wanted' Mr Evening with almost the same inexplicable maniacal whim which she had once long ago demonstrated toward a certain impossible-to-find Spanish medieval chair, and how she had got hold of the latter still remained a mystery to the world of dealers.

'Shall we without further ado, then, strike a bargain?' Mrs Owens intoned, looking past Mr Evening, who had arrived on a bad snowy January night.

He had been reduced to more than his customary kind of silent social incommunicativeness by finally seeing Mrs Owens in the flesh, a woman who while reputed to be so old, looked unaccountably beautiful, whose clothes were floral in their charm, wafting sachets of woody scent to his nostrils, and whose voice sounded like fine chimes.

'Of course I don't mean there's to be a sale! Even youthful you couldn't have come here thinking that.' She dismissed at once any business with a pronounced flourish of white hands. 'Nothing's for sale, and won't be even should we die.' She faced him with a lessening of defiance, but he stirred uncomfortably.

'Whatever you may think, whatever you may have been told' – she went now to deal with the improbable fact of their meeting, – 'let me say that I can't resist their being admired' (she meant the heirlooms, of course). She unfolded the piece of newsprint of his 'notice'. 'I could tell immediately by your way of putting things' – she touched the paper – 'that you knew all about them. Or better, I knew you knew all about them by the way you left things undescribed. I knew you could admire, without stint or reservation.' She finished with a kind of low bow.

'I'm relieved' – he began to look about the large high room – 'that you're not curious then to know who I am, to know about me, that is, as I'm afraid I wouldn't be able to satisfy your curiosity on that score. That is to say, there's almost nothing to tell about me, and you already know what my vocation is.'

She allowed this speech to die in silence, as she did with an occasional intruding sound of traffic which unaccountably reached her parlor, but then at his helpless sinking look, she said in an attempt, perhaps, to comfort, 'I don't have to be curious about anything that holds me, Mr Evening. It always unfolds itself, in any case.

'For instance,' she went on, her face taking on a mock-wrathful look, 'people sometimes try to remind me that I was once a famous actress, which though being a fact, is irrelevant, and, more, now meaningless, for even in those remote days, when let's say I was on the stage, even then, Mr Evening, these' – and she indicated with a flourish of those commanding white hands the munificent surroundings – 'these were everything!'

'One is really only strictly curious about people one never intends to meet, I think, Mr Evening,' Mrs Owens said.

She now rose and stood for a moment, so that the imposition of her height over him, seated in his low easy chair, was emphasized, then walking over to a tiny beautiful peachwood table, she looked at something on it. His own attention, still occupied with her presence, did not move for a moment to what she was bestowing a long, calm glance on. She made no motion to touch the object on the table before her. Though his vision clouded a bit, he looked directly at it now, and saw what it was, and saw there could be no mistake about it. It was the pale rose shell-like 1910 hand-painted china cup.

'You don't need to bring it to me!' he cried, and even she was startled by such an outburst. Mr Evening had gone as white as chalk.

He searched in vain in his pockets for a handkerchief, and noting his distress, Mrs Owens handed him one from the folds of her own dress.

'I won't ever beg of you,' he said, wiping his brow with the handkerchief. 'I would offer anything for the cup, of course, but I can't beg.'

'What will you do then, Mr Evening?' She came to within a few inches of him.

He sat before her, his head slightly tilted forward, his palms upturned like one who wishes to determine if rain is beginning.

'Don't answer' – she spoke in loud, gay tones – 'for nobody expects you to do anything, beg, bargain, implore, steal. Whatever you are, or were, Mr Evening – I catch from your accent you are Southern – you were never an actor, thank fortune. It's one of the reasons you're here, you are so much yourself.'

'Now, mark me.' Mrs Owens strode past his chair to a heavy gold-brocaded curtain, her voice almost menacing in its depth of resonance. 'I've not allowed you to look at this cup in order to tempt you. I merely wanted you to know I'd read your "notice", which you wrote, in any case, only for me. Furthermore, as you know, I'm not bargaining with you in any received sense of the word. You and I are beyond bargaining with one another. Money will never be mentioned between us, papers, or signatures – all that goes without saying. But I do want something,' and she turned from the curtain and directed her luminous gray eyes to his face. 'You're not like anybody else, Mr Evening, and it's this quality of yours which has, I won't say won me, you're beyond winning anybody, but which has brought an essential part of myself back to me by your being just what you are and wanting so deeply what you want!'

Holding her handkerchief entirely over his face now so that he spoke to her as from under a sheet, he mumbled, 'I don't like company, Mrs Owens.' His interruption had the effect of freezing her to the curtain before her. 'And company, I'm afraid, includes you and your sister. I can't come and talk, and I don't like supper parties. If I did, if I liked them, that is, I'd prefer you.'

'What extraordinary candor!' Mrs Owens was at a loss where to walk, at what to look. 'And how gloriously rude!' She considered everything quickly. 'Good, very good, Mr Evening . . . But *good* won't carry us far enough!' she cried, and her voice rose in a great swell of volume until she saw with satisfaction that he moved under her strength. The handkerchief fell away, and his face, very flushed, but with the eyes closed, bent in her direction.

'You don't have to talk' – Mrs Owens dismissed this as
if with loathing of that idea that he might – 'and you don't
have to listen. You can snore in your chair if you like. But
if you come, say, once a week, that will more than do for
a start. You could consider this house as a kind of waiting
room, let's say, for a day that's sure and bound to come for
all, and especially us . . . You'd wait here, say, on Thursday,
and we could offer you the room where you are now, and
food, which you would be entitled to spurn, and all you
would need do is let time pass. I could allow you to see, very
gradually' – she looked hurriedly in the direction of the cup
– 'a few things here and there, not many at a visit, of course,
it might easily unhinge you in your expectant state' – she
laughed – 'and certainly I could show you nothing for quite
a while from up there,' and she moved her head toward the
floors above. 'But in the end, if you kept it up, the visits, I
mean, I can assure you your waiting would "pay off", as they
say out there . . . I can't be any more specific.' She brought
her explanation of the bargain to an abrupt close, and indicated with a sweeping gesture he might stand and depart.

Thursday, then, set aside by Mrs Owens for Mr Evening
to begin attendance on the heirlooms, loomed up for the
two of them as a kind of fateful, even direful, mark on the
calendar; in fact, both the mistress of the heirlooms and
her viewer were ill with anticipation. Mr Evening's dislike
of company and being entertained vied with his passion for
'viewing'. On the other hand, Mrs Owens, watched over by a
saddened and anguished Pearl, felt the hours and days speed
precipitously to an encounter which she now could not
understand her ever having arranged or wanted. Never had
she lived through such a week, and her fingers, usually white
and still as they rested on her satin cushions, were almost
raw from a violent pulling on and off of her rings.

At last Thursday, 8:30 P.M., came, finding Mrs Owens

with one glass of wine – all she ever allowed herself, with barely a teaspoon of it tasted. Nine-thirty struck, ten, no Mr Evening. Her lips, barely touched with an uncommon kind of rouge, moved in a bitter self-deprecatory smile. She rose and walked deliberately to a small ebony cabinet, and took out her smelling bottle, which she had not touched for months. Opening it, she found it had considerably weakened in strength, but she took it with her back to her chair, sniffing its dilute fumes from time to time.

Then about a quarter past eleven, when she had finished with hope, having struck the silk and mohair of her chair several castigating blows, the miracle, Mr Evening, ushered in by Giles (who rare for him showed some animation), appeared in his heavy black country coat. Mrs Owens, not so much frosty from his lateness as incredulous that she was seeing him, barely nodded. Having refused her supper, she had opened a large gilt book of Flaxman etchings, and was occupying herself with these, while Pearl, seated at a little table of her own in the furthest reaches of the room, was dining on some tender bits of fish soaked in a sauce into which she dipped a muffin.

Mr Evening, ignored by both ladies, had sat down. He had not been drinking, Mrs Owens's first impression, but his cheeks were beet-red from cold, and he looked, she saw with uneasy observation, more handsome and much younger than on his first call.

'I hate snow intensely.' Mrs Owens studied his pants cuffs heavy with flakes. 'Yet going south somewhere' – it was not clear to whom she was speaking from this time on – 'that would be now too much in the way of preparation merely to avoid winter wet ... At one time traveling itself was home to me, of course,' she continued, and her hands fell on a massive yellowed ivory paper-opener with a larger than customary blade. 'One was put up in those days, not hurled over landscape like an electric particle. One wore *clothes,*

one "appeared" at dinner, which was an occasion, one conversed, *listened,* or merely sat with eyes averted, one rose,
was looked after, watched over, if you will, one was often
more at home *going* in those days than when one remained
home, or reached one's destination.'

Mrs Owens stopped, mortified by a yawn from Mr
Evening. Reduced to a kind of quivering dumbness, Mrs
Owens could only restrain herself, remembering the 'agreement'.

A butler appeared wearing green goggles and at a nearly
imperceptible nod from Mrs Owens picked up a minuscule
marble-topped gold inlaid table, and placed it within a comfortable arm's reach of Mr Evening. Later, another servant
brought something steaming under silver receptacles from
the kitchen.

'Unlike the flock of crows in flight today' – Mrs Owens's
voice seemed to come across footlights – 'I can remember *all*
my traveling.' She turned the pages of Flaxman with critical
quickness. 'And that means in my case the globe, all of it,
when it was largely inaccessible, and certainly infrequently
commented or written upon by tradespeople and typists.'
She concentrated a moment in silence as if remembering
perhaps how old she was and how far off her travel had
been. 'I didn't miss a country, however unrecommended or
unlisted by some guide or hotel bursar. There's no point in
going now or leaving one's front door when every dot on
the map has been ground to dust by somebody's heavy foot.
When everybody is *en route,* stay home! . . . Pearl, my dear,
you're not looking at your plate!'

Pearl, who had finished her fish, was touching with nearsighted uncertainty the linen tablecloth with a gleaming
fork. 'Wear your glasses, dear child, for heaven's sweet sake,
or you'll stab yourself!'

Mr Evening had closed his eyes. He appeared like one who
must impress upon himself not to touch food in a strange

house. But the china on his table was stunning, though obviously brand-new and therefore not 'anything'. At last, however, against his better judgment, he lifted one of the cups, then set it down noiselessly. Immediately the butler poured him coffee. Against his will, he drank a tablespoon or so, for after the wet and cold he needed at least a taste of something hot. It was an unbelievable brew, heady, clear, fresh. Mrs Owens immediately noted the pleasure on his face, and a kind of shiver ran through her. Her table, ever nonpareil, might win him, she saw, where nothing in her other 'offerings' tonight had reached him.

'After travel was lost to me,' Mrs Owens went on in the manner of someone who is dictating memoirs to a machine, 'the church failed likewise to hold me. Even then' (one felt she referred to the early years of another century), 'they had let in every kind of speaker. The church had begun to offer thought and problems instead of merging and repose . . . So it went out of my life along with going abroad . . . Then my eyes are not, well, not so bad as Pearl's, who is blind without glasses, but reading tires me more and more, though I see the natural world of objects better perhaps now than ever before. Besides, I've read more than most, for I've had nothing in life but time. I've read, in sum, everything, and if there's a real author, I've been through him often more than twice.'

Mr Evening now tried a slice of baked Alaska, and it won him. His beginning the meal backwards was hardly intentional, but he had looked so snowy the butler had poured the coffee first, and the coffee had suggested to the kitchen the dessert course instead of the entrée.

Noting that Mr Evening did not touch his wine, Mrs Owens thought a moment, then began again, 'Drinking has never been a consolation to me either. Life might have been more endurable, perhaps, especially in this epoch,' and she looked at her glass, down scarcely two ounces. 'Therefore spirits hardly needed to join travel in the things I've eliminated ...' Gazing upwards, she brought out, 'The human face, perhaps strangely enough, is really all that has been left to me,' and after a moment's consultation with herself, she looked obliquely at Mr Evening, who halted conveying his fork, full of meringue, to his mouth. 'I need the human face, let's say.' She talked into the thick pages of the Flax-man drawings. 'I can't stare at my servants, though outsiders have praised their fetching appeal. (I can't look at what I've acquired, I've memorized it too well.) No, I'm talking about the unnegotiable human face. Somebody,' she said, looking nowhere now in particular, 'has that, of course, while, on the other hand, I have what he wants badly, and so shall we say we are, if not a match, confederates of a sort.'

Time had passed, if not swiftly, steadily. Morning itself was advancing. Mr Evening, during the entire visit, having opened his mouth chiefly to partake of food whose taste alone invited him, since he had already dined, took up his napkin, wiped his handsome red lips on it, though it was, he saw, an indignity to soil such a piece of linen, and rose. Both Mrs Owens and her sister had long since dozed or pretended to doze by the carefully tended log fire. He said good night therefore to stone ears, and went out the door.

It was the fifth Thursday of his visits to Mrs Owens that the change which he had feared and suspected from the start, and which he was somehow incapable of averting, came about.

Mrs Owens and her sister had ignored him more and more on the occasion of his 'calls', and an onlooker, not in on the agreement, might have thought his presence was either distasteful to the ladies, or that he was too insignificant – an impecunious relative, perhaps – to merit the bestowal of a glance or word.

The spell of the pretense of indifference, of not recogniz-ing one another, ended haphazardly one hour when Pearl, without any preface of warning, said in a loud voice that strong light was being allowed to reach and ruin the ingrain carpet on the third floor.

Before Mrs Owens could take in the information or issue a command as to what might be done, if she intended indeed to do anything about protecting the carpet from light, she heard a certain flurry from the direction of the visitor, and turning saw what the mention of this special carpet had done to the face of Mr Evening. He bore an expression of greed, passionate covetousness, one might even say a deranged, demented wish for immediate ownership. Indeed his countenance was so arresting in its eloquence that Mrs Owens found herself, going against her own protocol, saying, 'Are you quite all right, sir?' But before she had the words out of her mouth he had come over to her chair without waiting her permission.

'Did you say ingrain carpet?' he asked with great abruptness.

When Mrs Owens, too astonished at his tone and movement, did not reply, she heard Mr Evening's peremptory: 'Show it to me at once!'

'If you have not taken leave of your senses, Mr Evening,' Mrs Owens began, bringing forth from the folds of her red cashmere dress an enormous gold chain, which she pressed, 'would you be so kind, I might even say, so decent, as to remember our agreement, if you cannot remember who I am, and in whose house you are visiting.'

Then, quickly, in a voice of annihilating anger, loud enough to be heard on a passing steamship: 'You've not waited long enough, spoilsport!'

Standing before her, jaws apart, an expression close to that of an idiot who has been slapped into brief attention, he could only stutter something inaudible.

Alarmed by her own outburst, Mrs Owens hastened to add, 'It's not ready to be shown, my dear, special friend.'

Mrs Owens took his hands now in hers, and kissed them gently.

Kneeling before her, not letting go her chill handclasp, looking up into her furrowed rouged cheeks, 'Allow me one glimpse,' he beseeched.

She extricated her hands from his and touched his forehead.

'Quite out of the question.' She seemed almost to flirt now, and her voice had gone up an octave. 'But the day will come' – she motioned for him to seat himself again – 'before one perhaps is expecting it. You have only hope ahead of you, dear Mr Evening.'

Obeying her, he seated himself again, and his look of crestfallen abject submissiveness, coupled with fear, comforted and strengthened Mrs Owens so that she was able to smile tentatively.

'No one who does not live here, you see, can see the carpet.' She was almost apologetic for her tirade, certainly she was consoling.

He bent his head.

Then they heard the wind from the northeast, and felt the huge shutter on the front of the house struggle as if for life. The snow followed soon after, hard as hail.

Tenting him to the quick, Mrs Owens studied Mr Evening's incipient immobility, and after waiting to see whether it would pass, and as she suspected, noted that it did not, she rang for the night servant, gave the latter cursory instructions, and then sat studying her guest until the servant returned with a tiny decanter and a sliver of handsome glass, setting these by Mr Evening, who lightly caressed both vessels.

'Alas, Mr Evening, they're only new,' Mrs Owens said.

He did not remember more until someone put a lap robe over his knees, and he knew the night had advanced into the glimmerings of dawn, and that he therefore must have slept upright in the chair all those hours, fortified by nips from the brandy, which, unlike the glass that contained it, was ancient.

When morning had well advanced, he found he could not rise. A new attendant, with coal-black sideburns and ashen cheeks, assisted him to the bathroom, helped him bathe and then held him securely under the armpits while he urinated a stream largely blood. He stared into the bowl but regarded the crimson pool there without particular interest or alarm.

Then he was back in the chair again, the snow still pelted the shutters, and the east wind raved like lunatics helpless without sedation.

Although he was certain Mrs Owens passed from time to time in the adjoining room – who could fail to recognize her tread, as dominating and certain as her resonant voice – she did not enter that day either to look at him or inquire. Occasionally he heard, to his acute distress, dishes being moved and, so it seemed, placed in straw.

Once or twice he thought he heard her clap her hands, an anachronism so imperial he found himself giggling convulsively. He also heard a parrot screech, and then almost immediately caught the sound of its cage being taken up and the cries of the bird retreating further and further into total silence.

Some time later he was served food so highly seasoned, so copiously sprinkled with herbs and spices that added to his disinclination to partake of food, he could not identify a morsel of what he tasted.

Then Giles reappeared, with a sterling-silver basin, a gleaming tray of verbena soap, and improbably enough, looking up at him, his own straight razor, for if it was one thing in the world of manhood he had mastered, it was to shave beautifully with a razor, an accomplishment he had learned from his captain in military school.

'How did they get my own things fetched here, Giles?'

he inquired, with no real interest in having his question answered.

'We've had to bring everything, under the circumstances,' Giles replied in a hollow vestryman's voice.

Mr Evening lay back then, while he felt the servant's hands tuck a blanket about his slippers and thighs.

'Mrs Owens thinks it's because your blood is thinner than we Northerners that the snow affects you in this way.' Giles offered a tentative explanation of the young man's plight.

Suddenly from directly overhead, Mr Evening heard carpenters, loud as if in the room with him, sawing and hammering. He stirred uncomfortably in his stocking feet.

In the hall directly in line with his chair, though separated by a kind of heavy partition, Mrs Owens and two gentlemen of vaguely familiar voices were doing a loud inventory of 'effects'.

Preparations for an auction must be in progress, Mr Evening decided. He now heard with incipient unease and at the same time a kind of feeble ecstasy the names of every rare heirloom in the trade, but these great objects' names were loudly hawked, checked, callously enumerated, and the whole proceedings were carried off with a kind of rage and contempt in the voice of the auctioneer so that one had the impression the most priceless and rarest treasures worthy finally of finding a home only in the Louvre were being noted here prior to their being carted out in boxes and tossed into the bonfire. At one point in the inventory he let out a great cry of 'Stop it!'

The partition in the wall opened, and Mrs Owens stood staring at him from about ten feet away; then after a look of what was meant perhaps to be total unrecognition or bilious displeasure, she closed the sliding panel fast, and the inventory was again in progress, louder, if anything, than before, the tone of the hawker's voice more rasping and vicious.

Following a long nap, he remembered two strangers,

dressed in overalls, enter with a gleaming gold tape; they stooped down, grunting and querulous, and made meticulous if furtive movements of measuring him from head to toe, his sitting posture requiring them, evidently, to check their results more than once.

Was it now Friday night, or had the weekend already passed, and were we arrived at Monday?

The snow had continued unabated, so far as his memory served, though the wind was weaker, or more fitful, and the shutters nearly silent. He supposed all kinds of people had called on him at his lodgings. Then Giles appeared again, after Mr Evening had passed more indistinct hours in his chair, and the servant helped him into the toilet, where he passed thick clots of blood, and on his return to his chair, Mr Evening found himself face to face with his own large steamer trunk and a pair of valises.

While he kept his eyes averted from the phenomenal appearance of his luggage, Giles combed and cut his long chestnut hair, trimmed the shagginess of his eyebrows, and massaged the back of his neck. Mr Evening did not ask him if there was any reason or occasion for tonsorial attention, but at last he did inquire, more for breaking the lugubrious silence than for getting any pertinent answer, 'What was the carpentering upstairs for, Giles?'

The servant hesitated, stammered, and in his confusion came near nipping Mr Evening's ear with the barber's shears, but at last answered the question in a loud whisper: 'They're remodeling the bed.'

The room in which he had sat these past days, however many, four, six, a fortnight, perhaps, the room which had been Mrs Owens's and her sister's on those first Thursday nights of his visits, was now only his alone, and the two women had passed on to other quarters in a house whose chambers were, like its heirlooms, difficult, perhaps impossible, to number.

Limited to a kind of speechless listlessness – he assumed he must be very ill, though he did not wonder why no doctor came – and passing several hours without attendance, suddenly, in pique at being neglected, he employed Mrs Owens's own queer custom and clapped his hands peremptorily. A dark-skinned youth with severe bruises about his temples appeared and, without inquiry or greeting, adjusted Mr Evening's feet on a stool, poured him a drink of something red with a bitter taste, and, while he waited for the sick man to drink, made a gesture of inquiry as to whether Mr Evening wished to relieve himself.

More indistinct hours swam slowly into blurred unremembrance. At last the hammering, pounding, moving of furniture, together with the suffocating fumes of turpentine and paint, all ceased to molest him.

Mrs Owens, improbably, appeared again, accompanied by Pearl.

'I am glad to see you better, Mr Evening, needless to say,' Mrs Owens began icily, and one could see at once that she appeared some years younger, perhaps strong sunlight – now pouring in – flattered her, or could it be, he wondered, she had had recourse to plastic surgery during his illness, at any rate, she was much younger, while her voice was harsher, harder, more actresslike than ever before.

'Because of your splendid recovery, we are therefore ready to move you into your room,' Mrs Owens went on, 'where, I'm glad to report, you'll find more than one ingrain carpet spread out for you to rest your eyes on ... The bed,' she added after a careful pause, 'I do hope will meet with your approval' (here he attempted to say something contradictory, but she indicated she would not allow it), 'for its refashioning has cost all of us here some pains to make over.' Here he felt she would have used the word *heirloom*, but prevented herself from doing so. She said only, in conclusion, 'You're over, do you realize, six foot six in your stocking feet!'

She studied him closely. 'We couldn't let you lie with your legs hanging out of the bedclothes!'

'Now, sir' – Mrs Owens folded her arms – 'can you move, do you suppose, to the next floor, provided someone, of course, assists you?'

The next thing he remembered was being helped up the interminable winding staircase by a brace of servants, while Mrs Owens and Pearl brought up the rear, Mrs Owens talking away: 'Those of us who are Northerners, Mr Evening, have of course the blood from birth to take these terribly snowy days, Boreas and his blasts, the sight of Orion climbing the winter night, but our friends of Southern birth must be more careful. That is why we take such good care of you. You should have come, in any case, from the beginning and not kept picking away at a mere Thursday call,' she ended on a scolding note.

The servants deposited Mr Evening on a large horsehair sofa which in turn faced the longest bed he had ever set eyes on, counting any, he was certain, he had ever stared at in museums. And now it must be confessed that Mr Evening, for all the length of him, had never from early youth slept in the kind of bed that his height and build required, for after coming into his fortune, he had continued to live in lodging houses which did not provide anything adequate for his physical measurements. Here at Mrs Owens's, where his living was all unchosen by him, he now saw the bed perfectly suited for his frame.

A tiny screen was thrown up around the horsehair sofa, and while Mrs Owens and Pearl waited as if for a performance to begin, Cole, a Norwegian, as it turned out, quietly got Mr Evening's old business clothes off, and clad him in gleaming green and shell silk pajamas, and in a lightning single stride across the room carried the invalid to the bed, propped him up in a layer of cushions and pillows so that he looked as a matter of fact more seated now than when he had spent those days and nights in the big chair downstairs.

Although food had been brought for all of them, seated in different sections of the immense room, that is for Pearl, Mrs Owens, and Mr Evening, only Pearl partook of any. Mr Evening, sunk in cushions, looked nowhere in particular, certainly not at his food. Mrs Owens, ignoring her own repast (some sort of roast game), produced from the folds of her organdy gown a jewel-studded lorgnette, and began reading aloud in droning monotone a list of rare antiques, finally naming with emphasis a certain ormolu clock, which caused Mr Evening to cry out, 'If you please, read no more while I am dining!', although he had not touched a morsel.

Mrs Owens put down the paper, waved it against her like a fan, and having put away her lorgnette came over to the counterpane of the bed.

She bent over him like a physician and he closed his eyes. The scent which came from her bosom was altogether like that of a garden by the sea.

'Our whole life together, certainly,' she began, like one talking in her sleep, 'was to have been an enumeration of effects. I construed it so at any rate ... I had thought,' she went on, 'that you would be attentive ... I procured these special glasses' – she touched the lorgnette briefly – 'and if I may be allowed an explanation, I thought I would read to you since I no longer read to myself, and may I confess it, while I lifted my eyes occasionally from the paper, I hoped to rest them by letting them light on your fine features ... If you are to deprive me of that pleasure, dear Mr Evening, say so, and new arrangements and new preparations can be made.'

She pressed her hand now on the bed, as if to test its quality.

'I do not think even so poor an observer and so indifferent a guest as yourself can be unaware of the stupendous animation, movement, preparation, the entire metamorphosis indeed which your coming here has entailed. Mark me, I am willing to do more for you, but if I am to be deprived of the simple and may I say sole pleasure left to me, reading a list of precious heirlooms and at the same time resting my eyes from time to time on you, then say so, then excuse me, pray, and allow me to depart from my own house.'

Never one endowed with power over language, Mr Evening, at this, the most dramatic moment in his life, could only seize Mrs Owens's pliant bejeweled hand in his rough, chapped one, hold her finger to his face, and cry, 'No!'

'No what?' she said, withdrawing her hand, a tiny indication of pleasure, however, moving her lips.

Raising himself up from the hillock of cushions, he got out, 'What about the things I was doing out there,' and he pointed haphazardly in the direction of where he thought his shop might possibly lie.

Mrs Owens shook her head. 'Whatever you did out there, Mr Evening' – she looked down at him – 'or, rather, amend that, sir, to this; you are now doing whatever and more than you could have ever done elsewhere . . . This is your home!' she cried, and as if beside herself, 'Your work is here, and only here!'

'Am I as ill as everything points to?' He turned to Pearl, who continued to dine.

Pearl looked to her sister for instructions.

'I don't know how you could be so self-centered as to talk about a minor upset of the urinary tract as illness' – Mrs Owens raised her voice – 'especially when we have prepared a list like this' – she tapped with her lorgnette on the inventory of antiques – 'which you can't be ass enough not to know will one day be yours!'

Mrs Owens stood up and fixed him with her gaze.

Mr Evening's eyes fell then like dropping balls to the floor, where the unobtainable ingrain carpets, unobserved by him till then, rested beneath them like live breathing things. He wept shamelessly and Mrs Owens restrained what might have been a grin.

He dried his eyes slowly on the napkin which she had proffered him.

'If you would have at least the decency to pretend to drink your coffee, you would see your cup,' she said.

'Yes,' she sighed, as she studied Mr Evening's disoriented features as he now caught sight of the 1910 hand-painted cup within his very fingertip, unobserved by him earlier, as had been the ingrain carpets. 'Yes,' Mrs Owens continued, 'while I have gained back my eyesight, as it were' – she raised her lorgnette briefly – 'others are to all practical purposes sand-blind . . . Pearl' – she turned to her sister – 'you may be excused from the room.'

'My dear Mr Evening,' Mrs Owens said, her voice materially altered once Pearl had disappeared.

He had put down the 1910 cup, perhaps because it seemed unthinkable to drink out of anything so irreplaceable, and so delicate that a mere touch of his lips might snap it.

'You can't possibly now go out of my life.' Mrs Owens half-stretched out her hand to him.

He supposed she had false teeth, they were too splendid for real, yet all of her suddenly was splendid, and from her person again came a succession of wild fragrance, honey-suckle, jasmine, flowers without names, one perfume succeeding another in enervating succession, as various as all her priceless heirlooms.

'Winter, even to a Southerner, dear Mr Evening, can offer some tender recompense, and for me, whose blood, if I may be allowed to mention it again, is incapable of thinning.' Here she turned down the bedclothes clear to his feet. The length of his feet and the beautiful architecture of his bare instep caused her for a moment to hesitate.

'I'm certain,' she kept her words steady, placing an icy hand under the top of his pajamas, and letting it rest, as if in permanent location on his breast, 'that you are handsome to the eye all over.'

His teeth chattered briefly, as he felt her head come down on him so precipitously, but she seemed content merely to rest on his bare chest. He supposed he would catch an awful cold from it all, but he did not move, hearing her say, 'And after I'm gone, all – all of it will be yours, and all I ask in return, Mr Evening, is that all days be Thursday from now on.'

He lay there without understanding how it had occurred, whether a servant had entered or her hands with the quickness of hummingbirds had done the trick, but there he was naked as he had come into the world, stretched out in the bed that was his exact length at last and which allowed him to see just what an unusually tall young man he was indeed.

John Keir Cross

MOTHERING SUNDAY

JOHN KEIR CROSS (1914-1967) *was best known for his radio and TV work for the BBC, which included adaptations of classic horror stories by writers like M. R. James, Ambrose Bierce, and Bram Stoker, and he also wrote a number of science fiction and fantasy novels for young readers. His major contribution to the horror genre is the volume* The Other Passenger (1944), *a collection of eighteen tales ranging from traditional ghost stories to contes cruels, black humor, tales of dark fantasy and surreal nightmare, and arguably the finest horror story about a ventriloquist and his dummy ever written, 'The Glass Eye' (later adapted for one of the best episodes of the* Alfred Hitchcock Presents *television series). Keir Cross also edited several important anthologies of horror stories (cited by Ramsey Campbell as a major influence on his own career), including* Best Black Magic Stories (1960), *in which the following tale first appeared.*

'THERE IS SOMETHING,' said Mrs Carpenter with finality, ' – there is something quite dreadful about that boy.'

Her small, screwed, selfish eyes probed over the farmyard to where the children were playing in the first soft fall of the snow.

Apart from them a little, watching the game with a curious detached avidity, was the boy she had referred to: very pale, very thin, an angular white rag of a child at that distance, with a head that seemed almost bald so nearly white itself was the growth of scruffed hair on it. His black eyes, like buttons, were intent on the activities of the Gaywood children as they rolled and scuffled; his hands, dangling down by his sides, were sticklike and frigid.

'He gives me the creeps, the positive creeps,' Mrs Car-

penter went on. 'I'm peculiarly sensitive to people, Mr Bell
– quite peculiarly. I am aware of the auras we all carry about
with us. You, for instance, are very comfortable and san-
guine, I'd suggest: a person to whom one might cheerfully
confess one's sins . . . but that boy, that boy now: I'd say of
that boy—'

She hesitated with a small grimace, sipping her sherry.
Andrew Bell watched her with a smile, curling himself in the
warmth of the great farm kitchen.

'You'd say of him what, Mrs Carpenter?'

'That he'll come to a bad end – something quite remarka-
bly beastly, which even the Sunday papers will hardly dare to
print. One likes to be charitable – as I think you'll agree, Miss
Patillo? – but such deep instincts are not to be laughingly
tossed aside, oh no. I remember, many years ago, meeting a
man at Bournemouth, in a delightful hotel I found there and
which I must recollect to recommend to you, Miss Patillo
– I remember meeting a man who positively made me contract, but *contract*, the instant he came into the room.' (The
vision of Mrs Carpenter contracting occupied Andrew quite
unpleasantly for a moment.) 'He was extremely handsome
– the younger and more gullible guests were quite "mad
about him", as the foolish fashionable phrase then had it; but
I knew at once that his heart was arid – and the heart is all,
Miss Patillo, as you will learn. I was aware of a black halo
about his head.'

'Like a gramophone record,' thought Andrew. 'What un-
imaginable music might it have played?'

'Two days later,' said Mrs Carpenter, leaning forward portentously and lowering her voice, ' – two days later, Mr Bell,
that man was arrested for a singularly brutal murder. It was
one of those trunk cases, in Notting Hill or Paddington – as
they always are, of course: I can hardly ever bear to set out
on a journey from Paddington – certainly, if ever I must, I
avoid the left-luggage office.'

'And has Master Moore, the boy there,' asked Andrew solemnly, ' – has he a black halo?'

Mrs Carpenter leaned more closely still, spoke more portentously still.

'He has none, Mr Bell – just none; and that is what is wrong. That boy has no halo, no aura. Shall I tell you that I firmly believe that if one could bear to look at those dreadful hands of his one would find no life-line on them? When was he born, do you know? – what month?'

'I do, as a matter of fact,' said Andrew quietly. 'In September, eleven years ago.' And Mrs Carpenter barked triumphantly.

'September! I might have known. An appalling month, Miss Patillo. That man in Bournemouth was a September birth – I asked especially when I learned the truth about him . . . What about the boy's mother, Mr Bell? – did you know her, by any chance?'

'Very well,' said Andrew, setting his own sherry glass down. 'Very well indeed. She was—' But he hesitated for a long serious moment.

'She was what?'

'Nothing. It is very difficult to say. She loved the boy very much, very much. But she is dead now.'

'And the father?' Mrs Carpenter spoke more quietly herself, impressed by something in Andrew's tone.

'I . . . did not know the father,' he said, after another brief pause. And then a curious silence fell on the little group by the window, and all three, in their different ways, looked out again towards the children. The boy still stood apart from the others, quite motionless. He was a waxy small figure in the puffs and swirls of the falling snow, some flakes of it clinging to his round head, making it seem whiter than ever. The others, shouting, their voices drifting in flat echoes over the fields, were rolling a gigantic snowball, its track a winding green serpent. One of the Gaywood girls, with a laugh, suddenly scooped up a handful of the snow and threw it at their silent companion. But still he did not move – only smiled in a forlorn way as the snow struck his cheek, adhering to it strangely.

'The lovely snow,' murmured Patsy Patillo. 'How nice to have it for our Christmas visit. So good for the children. And it makes Paul's farm look like a Christmas card,' – with a flurried little smile of self-consciousness.

'Is the father dead too?' asked Mrs Carpenter, ignoring the girl's remark. And this time Andrew's pause was so long that she looked at him sharply and made as if to repeat the question.

'I think so,' he said at last. 'I . . . think so.'

'Why does Paul Gaywood have him to stay here? Where does he live? – the boy, I mean. I'm sure he can't be good for the others.' The inexorable voice was now almost petulant.

'Paul has old loyalties, Mrs Carpenter,' said Andrew patiently. 'He was very fond of Viola – Viola Moore, the boy's mother. He was – as we all were in the old days – he was sorry for her. He feels that the boy is lonely. He's at school somewhere in Switzerland. Viola had a little money and was able to put it in trust for the boy. Paul has him for the holidays – at least,' and again he paused strangely, 'at least for the Christmas holidays.'

Now, as they watched, the children abandoned the snowball and ran towards the other end of the field where some neighbouring youngsters had appeared and were building a snowman. Stiffly, as if, almost, he were unaccustomed to walking, the gaunt small boy who was the subject of the speculation limped after them. The falling snow intensified – the gusts of it hid the little figure from sight as he plodded on towards the far-off shouting voices.

Mrs Carpenter shivered melodramatically.

'Well,' she said, with finality again, 'there's *something* very

strange about it all, and that I will insist. Some day I may
know the truth – and whatever it is it will be unpleasant.'

She stirred and expanded, with a pronouncement that
she proposed to go to lie down before Paul returned from
superintending the milking and could give some attention
to his guests. And a moment later she had swept from the
room, which strangely seemed to sigh, almost, and relax;
and Andrew, settling himself in his seat again, smiled very
oddly, Patsy thought.

'She won't,' he murmured. 'She never will, Patsy – know
the truth, I mean.'

'Is it unpleasant?' asked the girl.

'I don't know. In fact, I'm not even sure that I know the
truth myself . . . I wonder why Paul ever invited that abominable woman down? If I'd known I might have refused his
invitation – except,' and he stretched out his hand to touch
hers, ' – except that I knew you'd be here, Patsy, and that
would have made me face anything.'

'I suspect his old loyalties again,' said Patsy with a smile,
returning the pressure of his hand. 'Mrs Carpenter was an
aunt of his wife's, I think. At least we must bear with her,
darling – we shall steal away as often as we can. But tell me,'
and her tone changed, ' – you were so serious, Andrew, so
very serious. Is the story of that boy so strange? – I've heard
of Viola Moore before somewhere—'

'The story,' said Andrew, his thin face contracting in
a frown, 'the story, Patsy, is hardly a story at all. It's a kind
of dream, I think – or even a parable. It's absurd – all quite
absurd: it's only something half-formed and a speculation
in the night . . . I know nothing, you know – just nothing.
Except, perhaps, that prayers are answered sometimes
– sometimes. I'm not sure that I wouldn't go even further
and say that prayers are answered . . . always. Pour me more
sherry, darling.'

She did, then took his hand again. Outside, the first

dusk was settling, the thickening snow falling through it in increasing gusts. They sat on in the gloom, the rising flicker of the great fire sending their shadows high against the old walls and crooked beams of the ancient place. And Andrew's voice was very quiet through the silence. Patsy listened, half in a dream herself. And Mrs Carpenter, far away, mountainous beneath her eiderdown, snored on and on . . .

That year (said Andrew) there was also snow at Christmas. I'd gone down for the vacation to Korder's place in Berkshire. I was barely out of adolescence, I suppose – there was something immensely exciting about being the guest of so famous a man, with so many other nearly-famous people there also.

The house was huge – a magnificent place; but even it seemed crowded there were so many of us. Korder used to love to surround himself with young people. I should think that we were all on the best side of twenty-five – except for Korder himself, of course, and . . . Viola.

You said you thought you had heard of Viola Moore. She's forgotten now, but in those times she was quite celebrated in a strange, insubstantial way. She painted – curious, tenuous watercolours that had about them something of the forlorn air she always somehow wore herself. It's the one word, the only word – forlorn . . . as you even must have seen it in the boy out there.

Viola was – what? Thirty-seven – thirty-eight . . . perhaps even over forty. She wore clothes that were tragically out-of-date – loose, straight-waisted; somehow out of the late 'twenties, one might guess, or the early 'thirties, from pictures one had seen – old snapshots of lost aunts. There was an indescribable essence of those faded days all round and through her – in tangible things like the clothes and the way she did her hair, but more subtly still as a kind of . . . aura, almost, but in a different way from Mrs Carpenter's.

She was oddly out of place among us all – and yet, you know ... and yet, although one would never have expected it, from her whole appearance and flavour – and yet she threw herself into all our activities with an almost bitter intensity – yes, almost bitter. She was queerly ... *hungry,* I'd nearly say – hungry to be one of us, to be part of us, to ... to how shall I put it? – to salvage something.

In a group like that, all young, all still self-consciously a little bohemian, in the old word, since we were most of us just embarking on our various artistic careers, there was naturally a great deal of amorous pairing off – encouraged, of course, by Korder: it was, I think, in his old age, why he loved to have so many of us round him. He used to sit back in his musty corner with a great glass of brandy, watching us through a queer edged smile: you would suddenly, in the midst of a swift grapple with someone or other, find him regarding you from the shadows of a stairway or a hidden window-embrasure. I suppose, looking back now, that it's all very dated itself and rather unpleasant even; but it was quite delirious and wonderful at the time, you know – we were emancipated and venturesome – we wore Mrs Carpenter's black haloes, if some of us, as I see now, had to sit up o' nights painting over their pristine white.

But the snow, the snow. We arrived at the house in snow, driving and plunging through great drifts of it, some of us hours late and with immense adventures to recount. And it still fell for almost a week after we had assembled – we were cut off from the village absolutely. There was much foraging in old store-cupboards for food, and someone found some yeast and we made our own bread – a great deal of that kind of thing. But Korder had a gigantic and subtle cellar, so we didn't need to eat so very much – not in the overall mood.

And through it all went Viola, always avid, with wilder suggestions for games and subjects for conversation than anyone else – almost drugged, you might think, almost fever-

ish from the pervading young vicarious boisterousness of it
all. And Korder always sitting back and watching – watching
her particularly, I thought: always watching her, with that
quiet damnable smile of his . . .

He was the devil, that old man – and I don't mean the
ancient mountebank with a tail and a smell of sulphur, but
the real Devil, the evil that is abroad. Yet in another sense
perhaps I do mean the goat with the cloven hooves – as an
expression of it all, as the Goat only ever was, of course, even
back in the Middle Ages. The Church has its rituals – so has
the Church that is no Church.

We none of us knew his age. Behind that awful freshness
of his long classical face there was another face, which we
only occasionally glimpsed – and comprehended according
to our capacities. But we are back to Mrs Carpenter and her
auras again: it was his aura that was almost the full curse
of him – an essence he somehow exuded that almost *was*
a smell. One hears of the odour of sanctity, whatever that
might mean; but his was the odour of unsanctity – of unholi-
ness – of the decay in that bleak corner of the Cosmos, wherever it is, to which God sweeps away His rubbish.

You know how he made his money – at least one way;
from those impossible sentimental novels he wrote under
some absurd name and which brought him a fortune from
the hidden callow lechery in them. He wrote only two books
as himself, both printed privately and circulated only among
friends. I read one and was offered the other; but I couldn't
stomach it – I was beginning to grow up.

It was whispered, among other things, that he did indeed
study necromancy, was a conjurer in the old sense. There
was one room, certainly, in that house – like Bluebeard's –
that we were never permitted to enter. And sometimes,
you know, as we rambled past it, there was a queer high
whining out of it, a kind of breathless incantation of some

wicked sort – and a true smell of brimstone after all beneath the black door. Mummery, of course; but it was hideously impressive when you knew him – it was easy in those times to see it all as some kind of gesture, something abandoned and lost and magnificent. We were susceptible – on the brink of the larger romance; which is not love, you know, my dearest Patsy, but hate. Growing up is losing hate and finding love – it is only the older men whose thoughts turn lightly in the spring, not the younger. And Korder had never grown up, for all his age.

But the mummery . . . So pointless, you know – a kind of parlour magic after all, that might easily be contrived with hidden wires and a simple chemical or two. But always with an edge of silly small cruelty to it that was also pointless – childish; yet gave pain.

For instance: In the huge drawing-room where we used to foregather there was a large crooked porcelain vase on an ebony pedestal. An antique of some kind, one supposed – at least old, quite incalculably old; but with its age adding somehow no grace to it, but increasing its unpleasantness. Its *shape* was unpleasant in some way indefinable – like Mrs Carpenter's shape: what simple Chesterton called 'the wrong shape'. Across it were crude intaglio designs of an unequivocal obscenity, and round the belly of the thing an inscription of some sort in an unknown language.

Somehow the conversation had centred on it that evening. Esther Colebrook had asked what the inscription meant – I remember her leaning forward to the fire a little, that dark lovely delicate face of hers and the fall of her hair. And Korder smiled.

'It is forbidden to ask, dear Esther,' he said, in his low, slightly mocking voice. 'It is in the language which cannot be taught – one knows its meaning when the time comes, without translation.'

'And when does the time come?' asked Esther.

'When one is ready. Therefore, be ready to be ready.'

He smiled again, sipping his brandy. And now came the mummery, you see. He said slyly:

'There is a curious legend about that vase. It is probably why it has survived so long in this house of mine, when it might shatter to pieces in any other. It is said that it will stand so, quite intact, until the end of time itself, no matter what blows may be directed against it. But if once – if *once* – it is so much as caressed by a virgin, Esther, then it will break in a thousand fragments.'

We laughed: and Esther rose solemnly at once and laid her finger on the ugly rim of the thing.

'You see?' said Korder.

And we laughed again. One or two of the others went over in the spirit of it all – one girl, I remember, as an extension of the whole absurd joke, took up a heavy iron poker and struck the vase as hard as she could, and it only rocked a little on its pedestal.

Then Viola, with an incredible childish coyness on that pale face of hers, minced across the room from where she had been sitting all alone, as always, in a dark corner. I don't think I shall ever forget that little mincing way she walked, like a seaside girl on an eternal esplanade, or the gleam of her dyed hair in the fireshine, the spindly legs thrust out from that sacklike frock of hers that was far too short.

She put out her hand with the immense home-made jewellery on it – and even then, you know, I saw her poor finger-nails bitten down to the quick.

The vase seemed to crumple and collapse, almost before her fingers reached it. The jagged pieces of it rocked and slithered across the floor about her feet.

There was a gale of laughter – and she was trying to laugh too, you know. She cried out, again with that edge of awful dated coyness, and blushing so painfully, and laughing and blushing and stamping her foot pettishly:

'It's a liar – oh, such a whopping liar, Mr Korder! It's a fibber – oh, such a fibber!'

...You know, dearest Patsy, I couldn't laugh, suddenly. There was something in me which couldn't laugh after all. The green field had come off like a lid, as Auden says somewhere. I suppose, because I couldn't laugh, that I was the one who escaped from it all – from all that callow bleak world of ours – before any of the others. Where are they now, I wonder? I've lost touch except with one or two. Guy Mitcham the sculptor, of course – trying to be a pale shadow of old dead Korder himself these days. And Geoffrey Glaspell, who is a monument of respectability at Motspur Park or somewhere like that – but there are strange tales. And Esther, who died last year, you know – do you remember? – those appalling circumstances of it all? ... but it was never her fault, never for a moment. One tries to forget – or remember: one remains younger than one thinks ... or grows older than one thinks.

It was that same Guy Mitcham, the sculptor, who built the snowman, I remember. At least, we all helped, but it was Mitcham who added the expert finishing touches. The snow had gone crisp and hard in the bitter frosts, it was like a crust over the great lawns and gardens, weighting the trees down, hanging pendulously at all the eaves. There was a terrible waiting stillness in the air, before the thaw we knew must come soon. It was as if the whole great process of the world had come to a little deathly pause that icy Sunday, the very quick of things had been mortally chilled for a moment ... How strange it is, my dear, that I should find myself talking like this in this friendly room with you! – as if I were writing an elaborate pastiche of a style out of those past days themselves. This is not what I am – you know that. I am that comfortable person Mrs Carpenter described, to whom you might cheerfully confess your sins – except that you have none, sweet heart, and I would not like to have hers confessed to me. But you see, as I remember it all, I find myself changing very strangely, under the spell. Let me finish and rid myself – there's little enough left; and I shall be simple Andrew again – we shall go out into that good snow, among the children. You will recognise me for the man you know.

... Our snowman was huge and absurd on the lawn there, before the big blind house. It had begun as a romp – even we, you know, shut up there for so long, had begun to feel the need for exercise. Some of the girls had wrapped themselves up and started a snow-fight, and there was a sudden kind of fleeting young healthiness in each one of us – we streamed out to join them. We bombarded each other as we saw Paul's children doing outside there a moment ago – the whole spell was broken – something died in that house for a moment. But it crept back again. I can remember Korder standing quietly watching us through the french windows with a glass of his eternal brandy in his hand. He was wrapped about the shoulders in a black shawl, his face very white among the shadows – and for once he was not smiling. But we went on, in the sudden release we all felt.

I remember that Esther had started to roll a gigantic snowball – I remember that Viola, even Viola, had joined with her, and they were both laughing as it crunched over the lawn and grew so vast that they could no longer move it – tilted it over on its side so that it rocked for a moment, then settled, as hard and smooth as a marble boulder.

Glaspell shouted: 'A snowman – we'll make a snowman!' – and in a moment, still in the mood of it all, we had set to rolling another ball, smaller, to heave on top of the first, and were scooping up the snow with our hands and making the thing shapely in the old traditional way. It was to conform, you know, as snowmen always have conformed, as the one the children are building across the field out there will conform: the classical squat pyramid, with pebbles for buttons, and the round face on top with nuts of coal for eyes, and an old pipe in the mouth, and a hat found from somewhere, and a broom beneath the bulge of the arm ... and it was almost done, it grew very quickly with so many of us at work on it, adding touches here and there and moulding the primitive legs and the fat paunch. But suddenly Mitcham, in his quick deft professional way, gave it a face, a real face ... and everything changed, and I remember Korder smiling at us again and raising his glass a little in a ghostly toast as he looked out at us through the window.

We still laughed, you know, but now it was a different kind of joke. We saw the sudden possibilities, with the snow so sculpturally hard. We helped Guy Mitcham as he shouted orders, like students in his *atelier*. His face was flushed as he went to work, there was a real momentary artist's excitement in him. I remember the grey cold evening as the snowman grew before us there, the Snow Man, no longer the snowman. I remember its completion to every last naked masculine detail, and the face a travesty of some old Greek statue almost, yet with a hint in it – a hint, I suppose as a kind of jest from Mitcham at the very end – of ... Korder's face.

Someone – it was Esther – had garlanded some laurel leaves, and we set them over the shoulders and round the brow. It stood immensely there, in the first moonlight now; and we were suddenly silent and tired. But Viola, before we went in – and I shall never forget – Viola suddenly laughed again and skipped forward with her long furs dangling; and she went up on an impossible tiptoe and pecked forward with her sharp cold nose. She kissed it on the hollow mouth.

'Watch out!' cried Glaspell. 'He'll melt beneath your passion, Viola – he'll crumple like the vase!'

And she said, giggling, in that voice ... God forgive me, Patsy! – she said: 'He's such a pretty boy – yum-yum! He's such a pretty big cold boy, and needing comfort in the snow. He's such a pretty boy – yum-yum!'

She skipped back to join us. She took my arm as we went in to where Korder had the drinks waiting for us.

We were the last to enter and so I closed the door behind us and made to lock it.

'No, no,' cried Viola playfully, tapping me on the arm. 'No, no, Mr Bell – don't lock the door. He may want to come in in the night.'

Andrew, in his story-telling, paused, he suddenly paused. Outside they heard the boisterous banging of doors as Paul Gaywood came in from the milking parlour. They heard him shout something to one of the men, then his steps in the hallway outside the kitchen. Andrew abruptly rose.

'That's all, Patsy – that's all. I know nothing. I told you it was as insubstantial as a dream. Except that as I lay awake that night, in that house, I heard – oh, I thought I heard ... God knows! *They* were the most insubstantial of all: those large soft shufflings along the corridor, icy in the darkness. They stopped outside her room, beyond mine. And there was one small soft scream, of pain, I think, or dreadful pleasure. But I dreamed that too.

'I said – long ago, when I began, my dear – I said, do you remember? that all prayers are always answered. They are. But God forgive me, it is why I never pray!'

They went across the snow in the yard and over the meadow. Paul, discovering them in the dusky kitchen, had bustled them into clothes and rubber boots to find the children and bring them in to supper. 'You need air,' he had cried. 'You're so pale, the pair of you, sitting there! Damned city lives you lead!'

He strode out ahead, his red farmer's face uplifted happily as he breathed in the crisp evening. Andrew and Patsy followed arm in arm, both very quiet, she shivering a little. Behind, awakened from her doze, enormous in her furs and galoshes, Mrs Carpenter plunged and floundered like a galleon in a white sea.

'It was someone in that house, of course,' Andrew was saying in a whisper, so that Patsy had to strain a little more closely to hear him. 'It was someone nearer death than life. It must have been. It was Korder – I dreamed that it *must* have been Korder somehow. Yet was it? – for as I lay there, there was one thing that I did hear that I knew was no dream: from that locked room of his downstairs the high-pitched dreadful whine of one of his beastly mummeries, some kind of unholy incantation . . .'

Paul beckoned them forward. There were distant voices beyond the rim of the small hollow they now were mounting. The snow gusted round them as they trudged. Mrs Carpenter, behind, called out puffily:

'One forgets, of course, how inexpert one is in the face of such natural phenomena as snow. One has become too civilised, perhaps.'

She slipped and nearly fell, assembled herself with a shrill self-conscious laugh, and thrust on through the drifts again.

'I only saw Viola once again – years later,' said Andrew. 'I went to call on her in a studio I heard she'd rented in Camden Town. Her boy was three, four perhaps. She had nearly died in the bearing of him that old September. She was still very ill. She knew, quite plainly, that she hadn't much longer – I could tell: she knew. She sat shivering in shawls, talking to me about a thousand things but the one thing. Her eyes were always on that boy, who sat very quietly beside the empty fireplace. From first to last he said nothing, only sat there so calmly, unmoving in all the cold.

'I didn't stay long – I couldn't. I knew as I left that I would never see Viola again. I knew also that I would never, in all my life, see anything like the dreadful, hungry, overwhelming love in that square pale face in its frame of dyed bobbed hair as she looked and looked and only looked at him: her boy.

'And I cursed old dead Korder's memory, with his mummery, his black, white magic. And yet I didn't. And yet I did.'

They were over the rim of the hollow. Paul had stopped, very strangely. Before them, in the gusting snow, the children had all fallen silent. They stood back in a wide ring from the snowman they had made, looking towards it even fearfully a little.

The boy with white hair stood close to it, peering up into the blank round face, his small black eyes, like nuts of coal, all bright with tears. Even as they gazed he spread his spindly arms and clasped them tightly round the squat effigy, and buried his thin face almost ferociously in the icy breast, his lonely shoulders shaking.

Mrs Carpenter loomed forward, gasping.

'Look at him – just look at him, Mr Bell,' she puffed. 'I told you – he gives me the creeps, that boy. What normal child would behave so? One may not care for him particularly, but someone had better get him away from that thing quickly – he'll catch his death of cold.'

The small unloved and loveless thing still clung there tightly to the snowman.

'He'll catch,' whispered Andrew to the trembling Patsy beside him, an immense and helpless sadness in his tone, 'he'll catch – he's caught – his life of cold.'

Simon Raven

THE BOTTLE OF 1912

Like James Purdy, SIMON RAVEN (1927-2001) *was something of a literary outsider and iconoclast, whose works, many of them unabashedly gay-themed, often featured a wicked sense of humour. But although best known for his novels satirizing the English upper class, a persistent interest in horror and the supernatural runs through Raven's work, from his innovative vampire novel* Doctors Wear Scarlet (1960), *hailed by Karl Edward Wagner as one of the thirteen best supernatural horror novels of all time, to his macabre short fiction, collected in* Remember Your Grammar and Other Haunted Stories (1997). *'The Bottle of 1912', a short, poignant tale, written in Raven's trademark elegant style, first appeared in* 1961. *Raven's classic first novel,* The Feathers of Death (1959) *is available from Valancourt, and his* Doctors Wear Scarlet *is forthcoming.*

I N THE SPRING OF 1947 I RETURNED, you might say, from the dead. Never mind what I had been doing. I suppose you would call me a spy; I had penetrated into a world so remote that it was a long time before I learned of the end of the war, and even longer before my task was done and I could make my way back, by slow and careful stages, to the Headquarters in Delhi. Here they were in the fever which precedes departure, for India would be independent in a few months; and besides being thus preoccupied, they were rather embarrassed to see me.

'We didn't expect to see *you* again,' said Stetson accusingly; 'we gave *you* up last summer.'

'It all took longer than we thought.'

'Evidently. How long will it take you to make out your report?'

'A week . . . ten days. And then I suppose I can go home?'

'Yes,' said Stetson, 'you can go home.'

'By the way,' I said, 'you should have all my mail here. I gave this as my holding address.'

'We did have it. But we sent it off to your next of kin when we ceased to expect you back. A married sister in Kent, I think?'

'That's right.'

'You'll just have to wait a few days longer for your bills. After all, you've waited some years already . . .'

Yes, I thought: four years. Ever since 1943 when I left England, reported to Stetson, and went off into the hills. A few days more would hardly matter. But I should like to have read those letters from my sister; to have heard the news of her husband and my little nephew and the farm in Kent. And there was another thing – something that had not really occurred to me in the mountains but was obvious now that I was back in the familiar world: my sister would think I was dead. Or at best missing. In 1946 she would have received the parcel with my mail in it, along with a polite letter from Stetson '. . . Very much regret . . . has failed to report back . . . must reluctantly conclude . . .'; so that for all I knew there was a tablet bearing my name on the church wall by now. How awkward it was coming back from the dead. No wonder Stetson had been so put out. But it would be easier with my sister: I would not shock her with a cable but would send her a long, soothing letter. She wouldn't have time to reply, but that didn't matter. She would have been prepared . . . and gently. I would tell her to keep my mail and to expect me in about ten days – I should be flown home, Stetson said – and that I should warn her as soon as I reached London.

So I wrote to my sister; then I settled to my report for Stetson; and nine days later I left by air for home.

And so now at last I was to see them all again – the only family I had. My sister Anne, Richard her husband, my nephew (and my godson) Robin. Robin had been five when I left in 1943, a merry, bubbling infant; now he would be nine, gravely dressed in grey shorts and knee-stockings, rather reserved I anticipated, in his smart prep. school blazer. Very different from the trusting baby who had trotted round the room in his blue pyjamas on my last night at home.

'Robin can stay up a little longer,' Anne had said. 'This is a special occasion.'

'Yes,' said Richard; 'we must have a bottle of the 1912.'

On any special occasion, grave or gay, Richard would open a bottle or two of the famous 1912. There had been, Richard would say, no year to equal it. If only his father had realized soon enough and bought more ... I remembered how, on that distant evening in 1943, he had said:

'I've only a dozen left now. But I shall save a bottle for the day you come back.'

'When *will* uncle Jonathan come back?' asked Robin.

'Quite soon,' I said.

'How soon is quite soon?'

'When the war's over. The time will pass very quickly.'

'Sometimes it does,' said Robin reflectively, 'sometimes not. What makes the time go slow and then suddenly fast?'

'You'll be busy,' I said, 'busy learning things at school. Time always goes fast for busy people.'

'Will *you* be busy, Uncle Jonathan?'

'I expect so.'

'So the time will go fast for both of us till Uncle Jonathan comes home again. Robin is very glad,' said Robin.

Then he gave me a hug and a kiss and was taken away to bed by Anne.

'The government is going to take this place over as a hospital,' Richard had said later, gently tilting the decanter of 1912 over my glass. 'I'm not really too upset. It's very difficult for Anne just now with no servants and Robin at a demanding age. It's next August they're coming, I think.'

'Where will you live?'

'I'm having a sort of flat done up over the stables. It wasn't easy to arrange – the work permits and so on were endless – but they agreed finally because I shall still be farming the land. It'll be quite comfortable and I shall still be living more or less in my own home. And if things go well after the war, perhaps we can move back.'

'Government concerns are like women. Easy to get into a house, impossible to get out.'

Richard laughed.

'We want no cynicism from departing heroes,' he said.

Then Anne rejoined us.

'Robin is asleep,' she said. 'He put Uncle Jonathan before Mummy and Daddy in his prayers tonight. Afterwards he told me it was just this once, because Uncle Jonathan was going away to the war.'

And two big tears had rolled slowly down her cheeks.

This, then, was the family to which I was returning after so long. My sister Anne, her gentle husband with his cherished acres of Kentish soil, and my nephew Robin – now, I must suppose, an unknown quantity. And, of course, the last bottle of 1912. How wonderful it would be to sit with them all again, above the stables or perhaps in the old house itself, hearing Richard's quiet voice tell of the crops or the summer's cricket, persuading Robin to take me back into his life and to talk of his school and his friends, and drinking the noblest of all wines from Anne's beautiful glass. I was not ashamed that I thought almost as much of the wine as of the people I loved, for the bottle of wine had become a symbol to me as the years went on. It was the symbol of my return; when it appeared, cradled in Richard's careful hands, it would be a sign that the years of pain were finally done and that at last and for ever I was home. What more seemly offering to the returning soldier and what more fitting object for his thoughts? Wine, that maketh glad the heart of a man.

My aeroplane was punctual, but in London I came up against a mild difficulty. I had promised in my letter from Delhi to warn Anne as soon as I reached England. Enquiring from the telephone exchange, I found that Richard's house was now listed as ——— Hospital, and that they had no number for Richard himself, whom I must presume was still living with Anne above the stables. That Richard should not be listed was really natural enough, because at the time when he had the stables done up to live in, neither love nor money could procure private telephones and this, according to the exchange, was still the case. But how to warn Anne? I toyed with the idea of ringing the Hospital and asking them to take over a message, but did not fancy talking to some sniffish Matron who would make me feel she was being put upon. In the end I dictated a wire, incurring some expense by making it elaborately plain in the address that the recipient lived in an annexe of the Hospital. I should be arriving by train, I told Anne, at nine-thirty that night.

There was no one to meet me at the station (no petrol? Had that wretched wire misfired after all my trouble?), so I took a taxi to the gate of the park where, having only a small case, I yielded to a sentimental impulse and paid off the driver. I would walk up the drive, I thought, at once delaying and giving spice to the arrival I had dreamed of so often. Although it had been dark some time, there was a fair three-quarter moon and I could relish the familiar trees and hedges. At first I was surprised to find myself walking, not on gravel, but on concrete; then I remembered that government hospitals have money to spend. I hoped they had not spent too much, for I cared little for alteration, let it be a cause that was never so excellent. On the whole I was reassured. There were two or three shapeless huts in the fields on either side, but perhaps Richard would find them useful when the hospital left or be able to remove them. And as I approached the house, I saw that its low and graceful front, long and white and welcoming, was the same as ever; save for a couple of ambulances parked at the bottom of the steps nothing indicated disturbance or even change. Inside of course ... But I could hear about that later. Now I must go to my family. To the bottle of 1912. I turned along a wall, went through a door, stepped into the stable yard. And there to greet me, with his head sticking out of a window above the stables, was my nephew Robin.

'Uncle Jonathan,' he called, 'uncle Jonathan.'

'Robin,' I said, 'oh, Robin.'

'I knew you were coming,' he called.

'You had my telegram all right?'

'I knew you were coming. Go through that door in front of you and up the stairs. I'm in the first room at the top.'

I opened the door and, with some difficulty, picked my way up the narrow and uncarpeted stairway. War-time work, I thought; shoddy. But there was nothing shoddy or uncomfortable about the room in which I found my nephew. There was a polished table and a bright fire. Robin himself was standing near the window, behind a beautifully covered sofa which I remembered from the house in the old days. He had grown up splendidly, my godson. Straight fair hair, a round, honest face with a clear if slightly pale complexion. Bright eyes. A sound, well-proportioned build, suggesting that he was ten or eleven rather than nine. Robin had always been big for his age. He made a handsome figure standing there behind the sofa in his blue pyjamas, allowed to wait up – how else on such a night – to welcome his uncle home.

'I've waited so long for you to come,' he said, 'to welcome you back from the war. And then today they told me you were coming.'

'I took a lot of trouble to address the telegram right,' I said.

Then I waited for him to come to me. He did not move. Boys of nine dislike demonstration, I thought, they don't want to be kissed and mauled about even by mothers and long-lost uncles. He is shy, reserved, as I knew he would be. Let him come in his own time.

'Where are Mummy and Daddy?' I asked.

'I always knew you were all right,' he said; 'I knew you would come back.'

I could wait no longer.

'Then come and shake hands with me, Robin. Let me have a look at you.'

Still he did not move.

'I knew you would come back. The wine is ready for you.'

He pointed to a small side table. On it stood a decanter, gleaming, purple, imperial, and by it one of Anne's most beautiful glasses, into which some wine had already been poured.

'The 1912?' I asked. 'The last bottle?'

'Yes, Uncle Jonathan. The last bottle. Now you must drink.'

'But where are Mummy and Daddy? I must wait for them.'

'They don't want you to wait, Uncle Jonathan.'

'Then surely you will drink with me, Robin? You are a big chap now. A small glass won't harm you.'

'No, thank you, Uncle Jonathan. But you must drink.'

So I lifted the full glass that stood on the table and raised it in front of my face.

'To you, Robin,' I said, 'to my nephew and godson, who has grown into such a fine boy.'

'Thank you, Uncle Jonathan,' he said.

I sipped the wine. For a moment the magnificent flavour, first deep and distant, then rich, then subtly apologetic for its richness, bringing the assurance that life was good and God was merciful, was there as it always had been. Then I was alone in a cold, bare room, with only the moon to shine on the cracked and filthy glass in my hand and with a taste of vinegar and ashes on my tongue.

At the reception desk of the hospital they gave me my bundle of letters, the letters which had followed me to Delhi and had been sent back to my next of kin in Kent. There were only a few from Anne and Richard, and one scrawl in capitals from Robin, at the bottom of the pile. Above these was the buff envelope, and the sheets of thin war-time paper inside it, which told how they had all three been killed, in the late summer of 1943, when a braking ambulance skidded off the gravel drive and crashed into them where they stood by the park gate.

Ethel Lina White

'WITH WHAT MEASURE YE METE . . .'

ETHEL LINA WHITE (1876-1944) *was an extremely popular and influential author of crime novels, including* Some Must Watch *(1933), famously filmed as* The Spiral Staircase, *and* The Wheel Spins *(1936), basis for the Hitchcock film* The Lady Vanishes. *White was not a horror author, though she flirts with the supernatural in some of her works, such as* Wax *(1935), republished by Valancourt, which features deadly doings in a creepy wax museum that seem at first to be attributable to supernatural causes. 'With What Measure Ye Mete . . .', a rare foray for White into the horror genre, first appeared in the periodical* Black and White *in 1906.*

Extract from the Diary of Desmond Clay

17 November: Had a most extraordinary and startling experience two days ago – so utterly inexplicable that I have not written it up till today. Took car on Friday at Kennington Gate to Streatham. Felt pretty much the same as usual. Passed Brixton Station, and remember looking at the clock. Time was 4.45. Next thing I knew was that I was near Streatham Common, taking the turning to the left. On consulting watch, found it was 5.25. The intervening time is an absolute blank. Try as I will, I cannot piece it together. It is impossible to conclude that I fell asleep, as I had evidently got out of the car at Streatham Hill Station, as I originally intended. Am worried and perplexed at this strange lapse, and, at first recurrence, shall consult a specialist. Saw Enid; she grows dearer every day. A compensation, I suppose, for my past bitter experience of treachery and

pain. However, *de mortuis* – for I hear Mrs Laflèche is dead; something sudden. Forty minutes wiped clean out – sponged away from my memory. Wish I could remember – or else forget all about it.

When Iris Devine married Syd Laflèche with his £12,000 a year, the world said she was a lucky girl. It made the identical remark seven years later, when she became his widow – but with a sympathising accent this time. Yet, regarding the affair from its purely commercial aspect, it was not without its points. Iris had given youth, a moderate portion of good looks, and little else beside, in exchange for a gentleman of agreeable characteristics, very shady antecedents, and an unimpeachable banking account. The flaw in the transaction was the fact that Iris was not a free asset. Yet this item had been quickly discounted by the girl. Born of a struggling theatrical family, her life had been played out, to a considerable degree, in the fierce glow of limelight, which had dried up the dews of youth too soon. The fact that the path that led to her union with Laflèche was paved by a human heart, only made the way for her feet softer.

Yet among the many parts she had played she did not look forward to dismissing her quondam lover. However, she counted on Desmond's gentleness and lack of emotion, feeling she would score heavily through his hatred of a scene. There would be no disagreeable reproaches, she argued – Desmond would not forget that he was a gentleman.

But in this she was mistaken. Desmond *did* forget, and when he passed out of Iris's life as a personal element it was to remain there as a vaguely disquieting memory.

Then the great Wheel of Change snatched her up and whirled her through a cycle of prosperity, excitement, and disillusionment, finally shaking her off and dropping her suddenly into the Kennington Road one foggy November day, just at four o'clock. The fog was creeping on with the

stealthy advance of a foe – swelling and darkening in the
shadows, and gathering in the corners, only to shrink back
before the glow of the street lights. The cars whirled by in an
intermittent procession, their red eyes gleaming through the
mist. Iris watched them with fascination. They represented
her old life – the car and omnibus era. Seven years of car-
riages and motors had ousted them from a willing memory,
but today they seemed to regain their old ascendancy. Each
name revived old recollections – the struggle to capture this,
the easy conquest of that.

Suddenly yielding to an impulse, Iris hailed the next
car, and climbing the narrow stair with difficulty, as the car
lurched on, she groped along the shaking platform on the
top and dropped heavily into the nearest seat.

'Free!' she cried, and then laughed out again into the chill
air. 'Free!'

The mean houses slid by, yellow patches gleaming
through the fan-lights. Iris hailed them with delight. She
held up her muff, to ward off the damp air, and laughed
again, as the soft fur caressed her face. The six brief weeks of
widowhood had found her stunned; today, for the first time,
she realised her position, and her liberty.

She nodded familiarly to a beer-palace, resplendent with
flaring lights. 'Seven years' penal servitude,' she whispered.
'Free!'

'All fares.' The man came to take her ticket. Iris had not
troubled to notice the destination of the car.

'All the way,' she said, recklessly, and then the woman
of wealth, suddenly smitten by habit, found herself keenly
counting the coppers that the man gave her for change. That
made her laugh again, and she gripped her hands tightly
in an ecstasy. 'Free! Seven years' hard!' Then she frowned
slightly. 'Now, am I really free, or – ticket-of-leave?' The
thought amused her, and she toyed with it.

'Ticket-of-leave! Then I must be really good, for a bit, or

else – back again! And it may be a life-sentence next time. Oh, lucky woman! Free!'

But the car refused to run to this tune now, and it whirred along rapping out in uneven jerks: 'Ticket of leave! Ticket of leave!'

Iris laid back dreamily, soothed by the sway of the motion. Imperceptibly, her thoughts slipped away to the crime that held the sentence.

Suddenly, a thick curtain of blue shot down, blotting out the grey world, and spreading over the fog. It hung there for a fraction of a second, and then split in two pieces, and half was the calm turquoise sky, and half the restless, heaving sea. The tide of Memory, in sweeping round the world, had, in a momentary back-wash, left Iris stranded high and dry on the recollection of her parting scene with Desmond.

Well she remembered it! The bold cliff, the winding path, and Desmond swinging along by the foam, hurrying to meet her. She shuddered when she saw the light in his eyes, for she knew it was hers to darken it, hers to kill the faith, and banish the joy – hers to murder youth, and imperil her soul – and all in the sacred name of Mammon! She felt so utterly sorry for herself, that she thought he must be sorry, too, and she could hardly understand it, when she saw the joy in the boy's eyes fade to bewilderment, and then as the baleful light broke through the cloud of doubt, a storm of anger, fierce, ungovernable rage, that blotted the calm face. Iris hardly recognised his voice, though she shrank beneath his reproaches, and bent her head to the tempest, praying for the lull. It seemed to Iris that he raved on interminably, but only one sentence stayed with her.

'It's a monstrous thing you've done, inhuman! To win my heart, and then trample on it. Oh, I know, it has been done before. And it will be done again. But it is no small thing. It is murder! I tell you, it is murder! You have killed the best part of me. I can feel it. And you can't do it with impunity.

There will be a reckoning, I tell you – you must ...' The voice dragged incoherently, and then Desmond pulled himself together. He had remembered the fact on which Iris had counted, that he was a gentleman, to whom were barred the rights of primeval man. His face flamed, and in shame-faced manner, he apologised humbly for his tirade. The anger had faded from his face, and only dull pain was there. The victory was with Iris. Raising his hat, he left her, and she watched him go into the setting sun, his white-clad form cutting the purple of the heather. Even as he went, she wanted him. She wanted one last look, one smile, even if grudged; in short, she wanted a conscience-salve.

She bent her brows, and tightened her mouth under the strain of will-force, and tugged at his consciousness – willing him to look back once more. Desmond had never proved unresponsive to that mute appeal, and even now his head turned involuntarily and their eyes met.

Iris cried out in a sudden panic of terror. For the first time, she saw Murder look out of a man's eyes, and the sight rooted her to the spot, panic-stricken.

She saw his profile sharply outlined against the blue, and then the car jolted over the points, and slithered on to another track. For one minute, the Past still tore desperately at her skirts. The next second the shutter of grey had slammed down, and she was again in the grip of the Present.

Only the profile had not vanished. She found that she was still looking at it, and with a thrill, suddenly awoke to the fact that Desmond was on the same car.

Where and when he had got on, she did not know. Leaning forward, she scanned his face with interest. Just the same old Desmond, in every respect. He sat forward, looking in front of him, with a dreamy unconscious smile on his face – absolutely oblivious to his surroundings. Iris's glance was almost a caress, as she scanned each feature. Nothing changed! The calm brow – the clear eyes – the dear mouth!

A man who was clearly under petticoat government. Dame
Fashion had a thrall in him, as was evident in every detail
of his well-groomed appearance, starting from the crown
of his hat, down to the tips of his fashionable boots, while a
point was scored with every detail of his costume. And Mrs
Grundy plainly had him under her thumb, and had stamped
his whole appearance with the Seal of Conventionality.

Iris studied his face yet longer, and then she almost
laughed at the gentleness and well-bred repose imprinted
thereon. Yet, for one brief moment, she had been afraid of
this man, and had thought she had seen the ugly spectre of
murder peeping from his eyes.

The car glided on. Desmond still smiled absently at the
mist. At last, Iris grew impatient. She wished he would turn
and notice her. Desmond was sitting three seats in front, to
the left. A stout policeman by her side hedged her in with the
majesty of the Law, while across the gangway to her left sat
a portly City man. They seemed to represent obstacles, and
she grew yet more restless. She found herself counting the
roses that clustered on the hat of a girl who sat in front. Five
roses of a pinky-mauve shade. And the girl had red hair. Iris
shuddered.

Then she remembered her old powers. Should she *will*
him to once look at her? She set her hat – whose white strings
alone marked her widowhood – straight and pondered. She
knew that during the past seven years Dame Fortune had
only ripened and embellished her charms, though, perhaps,
at the last, as if suddenly repenting of her lavish generosity,
with a dash of feminine spite, she had pecked out a few lines
in the smooth face.

Iris struggled hard with the temptation. *Ought* she to try
to revive the old fascination? Once, Desmond had suffered
bitterly through her action. His face seemed quite tranquil
now. True, there were lines round mouth and eyes, but Iris
was unskilled in reading emotions, and placed them as a trib-

ute to time. If the old game of the Candle and the Moth were to be revived, would the end this time be the total extinction of the Moth?

The woman wavered, and then the love of admiration proved too strong, and the fierce flame of Vanity licked up the last scruples in a glow of desire. Iris had always met a lover's advances halfway, and if he showed no desire to even approach the line of demarcation, then she sallied forth alone, to reveal to him his destination. And she longed for Desmond's other wing. So, with a soulful look in her blue eyes, she leaned forward – her pretty, white chin nestling among her dark furs, calling to Desmond – calling, calling.

And he heard. Seven years of disuse had not blunted her old powers. Desmond slowly, reluctantly, fell under the spell, and, in the old way, he turned his head, and looked at her.

The calm blue eyes looked at her quietly. Then, a sudden chill seized Iris, as, to her amazement, she saw the red lamp of murder kindle in them. She watched the light grow and blaze, as though fed by a Devil's torch, and then Desmond rose from his seat, and came towards her – his head thrust forward, his lower lip hanging, and his whole body bent, and moving with a curious undulating slope.

She gripped her seat in alarm, and then the groundlessness of her fears reassured her. The policeman's warm cape caressed her, and the red calico faces of the roses looked at her cheerfully. The City man turned the leaves of his paper with a brisk rustle. This was no isolated spot, where murder stalks unchallenged. The absolute safety of her position filled her with a sense of comfort.

Desmond came yet closer; she could see his fingers quivering and wrapping themselves round each other, with an undefined sense of coming horror. She watched them with fascination, as they twisted and curled, but even as she looked, they shot out, and she felt her throat held in a bony grip.

One minute of shock, and then the terror died away before the comforting assurance that help was at hand. The policeman coughed noisily, and a man behind broke out into a whistle. The fingers pressed tighter.

A slight singing began in Iris's ears, yet to her amazement *nothing happened.* She cast her eyes desperately round the car, and saw, to her bewilderment, that no one had stirred. It was as though everyone was quite unconscious of what had befallen. Iris reeled before this stunning fact. She could not grasp its significance. A wave of utter incredulity swamped her whole being. Even while the murderous fingers were tightening each minute, even while the man was swaying above her, in the force of his convulsive fury, the everyday world read calmly on, while a tragedy was being enacted.

Indignation ran hot through her veins. Then it was met by a returning current of so icy a horror, that she collapsed into a powerless heap.

Still in his seat, two yards away, was Desmond – looking dreamily into space, his eyes absolutely unconscious. She took in every detail of his form and costume; she noted that his tie was grey crêpe de Chine, and that he wore violets in his buttonhole. And yet, standing over her, glowering with inhuman ferocity, was the other Desmond.

Iris looked, and something caught her strained sight. It was something bright, that glittered and swayed in circles and hoops – something as fine as spun glass, and as dazzling as silver – something like a silken cord. She saw with a thrill that this thread united the two Desmonds.

A jumbled mass of psychological facts heaped themselves up in the woman's brain. Articles she had read on astral bodies, sub-consciousness, second personalities, all blended together, but the one terrible truth seemed to stand out clearly. The injured personality, the spiritual part of Desmond, that she had wounded so mortally, had suddenly remembered its slumbering wrongs, and had slipped out of its corporeal envelope, to avenge its violated individuality. And stinging her brain like a hornet was the thought that she alone had called forth this Minister of Vengeance.

Broad iron bands seemed now to fasten round Iris's head, as the grip pressed more closely. She could feel the blood foaming like a mill-stream through her veins, seeking to find an outlet, and driven back by the encircling hoops.

The pity of her position filled her with anguish. She felt that she was in the thrall of some monstrous nightmare. She struggled to cry out, and tell the people on the car of her danger. The scream 'Murder!' rose to her blue lips, but the cruel hands pressed it back, and sent it down to echo in the depths of her hopeless heart – 'Murder!' With the strong arms near – with the kind faces round her – 'Murder!' And to Iris the horror and pity culminated in the knowledge that Desmond sat and dreamed on, all unconscious of the price that was being paid as Blood Penalty for slaughtered Truth and Faith. His sensitive mouth was set in a smile. His whole being was a mute protest against violence of word or act.

Now the lights began to dance around her, till they joined with the street-lamps in a cluster of golden bulbs. Faster they went, round and round, till a circle was formed, and lamp melted into lamp in a fiery ring. Round and round it spun. Then it suddenly swooped up into the air, while Iris felt herself sinking down – down. She saw the ring grow smaller and smaller, till it flickered to a star – dwindled to a pin-prick – and went out.

Iris now became conscious of a strange conflict that was raging within her. She could feel her reeling brain sending down agonised signals to her heart, which sent back an answering 'thud'. It seemed as if it were holding the fortress against the assaults of Death. The beats grew feebler each minute, like the blows from the picks of entombed miners. The roar of a great sea sounded in Iris's ears. The signals from the brain, running down the jangled nerves, grew more desperate and despairing, but the answering 'thud' was weaker.

Then suddenly something almost imperceptible broke through the roar. It was so faint, so far away, that it seemed like the very last vibration of sound. The sense, rather than the words, fell on Iris's ears, 'Lady – seems – ill.'

They were the very last echoes that reached her from the Finite World. The last heart-beat was followed by silence, and she slipped away into the Infinite.

The next minute, the car seemed to break up, like the pieces of a kaleidoscope. Instead of a compact whole of quietly ranked people, forms passed hurriedly to and fro, pushing each other in excited confusion. Only one was unmoved, a man, who remained in his seat, wrapped in dreamy abstraction.

The forms clustered round, and drew closer to the centre. Then they parted, and Something was borne down the steep stairs. The car went on.

But the man on the seat never stirred.

Robert Westall

BEELZEBUB

ROBERT WESTALL (1929-1993) *was the multi-award-winning author of over forty books for young readers. He is the only author to have won the Carnegie Medal twice, for* The Machine Gunners (1975) *and* The Scarecrows (1981), *while* Blitzcat (1989) *won the Smarties Prize and was named by the American Library Association as one of the best books for young adults in the past 25 years. Westall also wrote extensively in the field of the supernatural and has been called the best writer of traditional British ghost stories since M. R. James. Valancourt has previously published his collection* Antique Dust (1989), *his only book written specifically for adults, featuring tales centred on an antique dealer's encounters with the supernatural, as well as his novella* The Stones of Muncaster Cathedral (1991), *and an original collection,* Spectral Shadows, *which comprises three short novels of the supernatural. Another original Westall collection focusing on his World War II-themed tales, some of them supernatural, is forthcoming from Valancourt. Following the enthusiastic response to Westall's 'The Creatures in the House' in* The Valancourt Book of Horror Stories, Volume 2, *we're pleased to present another of the author's seldom-seen tales, a story the manages the difficult feat of being both chilling and extremely funny.*

THE REGISTER OFFICE STANDS like a red-brick Gibraltar amidst the wild ways of Polborough. Five granite steps lead up to doors of solid oak.

It needs those doors. Polborough has always been wild. The inhabitants have that feckless energy and ingenuity that invariably leads to disaster. They do not have the restraining influence of a cathedral, like their western neighbour, Peterborough. They have done too well, too quickly, out of a network of Thatcherite light industry.

Their latest money-making scheme is night-clubs, famed across the Midlands, which disgorge maddened hordes of the drunken young from as far away as Birmingham on to the streets at 2 A.M. Massive streetlights are a growth industry, while the Polborough police huddle together in their fives and tens and hope that real murder is not taking place. Every year the town's fifty-foot Christmas tree is snapped in half by some drunk trying to climb it. Rape is endemic.

Of course, the Register Office suffers. Every Monday morning its windowsills are lined with crushed lager cans, and polystyrene containers full of curry and rainwater. Unmentionable graffiti sprout like mushrooms. The deep shadowy back porch is littered with the debris of sexual passion.

All this is removed by the caretaker before the public can see it. Under the eagle eye of Mrs Parsons, the senior registrar of births, deaths and marriages. (She is convinced she is *senior* registrar; she is the oldest, has been there the longest.)

The Register Office is lucky to have Mrs Parsons, as she is the first to point out. The superintendent is a Mr Brooks, a worried-looking man nearing forty, who has young children at home who always seem to be ailing, and a wife who rings him several times a day to report their symptoms. He does his job, but anyone can see his mind isn't really on it. Mrs Parsons's enduring memory is of him standing with his hand on her door-handle, dark hair dishevelled, spectacles awry and military raincoat unbuttoned, saying:

'I must get home on time tonight, Mrs Parsons. Will you see to things?'

Mrs Parsons had the time and energy to see to everything, having reached that comfortable stage of life when her children were off her hands, and her husband cowed domestically to a mere fetcher-and-carrier. A woman of solid muscular frame, she swam thirty lengths of the baths every Saturday afternoon, and played badminton regularly. Her cheeks were rosy; her red hair, cut sensibly short, seemed to bristle with energy and she found time not only to be church-warden (*senior* churchwarden) of her parish church, but also organist and head of the Sunday School. She held the theory that most people's troubles were of their own making, and could soon be sorted out by a person with sense.

She ran the Register Office as she ran her parish church. Even in this time of cutbacks, the parquet floor shone like glass. She did fresh flower arrangements twice a week. The smell of wax polish and flowers amounted to an odour of sanctity. The wedding room was freshly painted and cur-tained to Mrs Parsons's taste. And if her fellow registrars grumbled that their own ceilings were peeling and their chairs uncomfortable, Mrs Parsons told them that in times of financial stringency, sacrifices had to be made.

She had installed a receptionist of so dire an aspect as to cow even such wild inhabitants of Polborough as dared to marry or breed or lose their loved ones. Outrageous requests to use the toilet (reserved for staff only) or the telephone (to contact the undertakers) were crushed instantly.

Of course, even Mrs Parsons could not entirely stem that frenzied flood of desire and delusion that was Polbor-ough. She could not stop forty-year-old divorcees, seven months' pregnant, from getting married in long white wedding-dresses, attended by children of a previous union playing bridesmaid in shocking-pink mini-skirts. She could not stop bridegrooms turning up in ragged jeans and train-ers. Or two trampoline champions getting married in their England tracksuits. She could not even stop the proud and pugilistic father of twins registering them as Sugar Ray and Frankie Bruno Rafferty. Or the man who wished to register his son as Thomas H. Lacey.

'What does the "H" stand for?'

'Nothing. Just "H".'

'You can't call somebody just "H".'

'What about Harry H. Corbett then?'

The worst day had been when a prisoner on remand in the local jail came in to get married, accompanied by two warders. Afterwards, of course, the family demanded to have wedding photographs taken on the five steps of the Register Office, just like everybody else. And of course you couldn't expect a man to be photographed in handcuffs on his own wedding day . . . and would the warders, who had been so very kind, like to be in the photograph? In the back row?

No sooner had the large group posed than a car drew up at the kerb. The family closed ranks as tight as a rugby scrum, and the bridegroom was into the car and off before the warders could struggle clear. Only the bride, screeching in marital frustration, had offered any pursuit . . .

Of course, Mrs Parsons was not directly involved. Had she been in charge it would never have happened. But it was she whom the gutter press rang up afterwards, avid for a sensation. She told them coldly that they could purchase copies of the marriage entry, like any other member of the public, and with that, in spite of all their bribes and pleadings, they had to be content.

The frost of Mrs Parsons's disapproval of this incident had not really melted when, one unusually warm afternoon at the end of October, the woman with the baby turned up. Mrs Parsons was not at her best on warm afternoons when there was little business. Her vigorous lifestyle finally caught up with her, and she tended to fall asleep at her desk, which reminded her unpleasantly of her age and her mortality. She would start awake suddenly, with a sense of the world gone awry, and some opportunity missed. It was the nearest she ever got to a sense of guilt.

Mrs Parsons, called to the waiting room by the receptionist's buzzer, summed up the woman at a glance. Dusty black dress, down-at-heel black court-shoes, no tights. And

Mrs Parsons could *smell* the woman, even through the familiar reassuring odour of wax polish and flowers. An earthy
smoky smell that followed Mrs Parsons's clicking protesting
heels up the polished parquet; that settled comfortably in
Mrs Parsons's spotless client's armchair.

The woman had the chaotic voluptuousness of an overgrown cottage garden. Long luxuriant black hair, greasy and
held back by an elastic band. Large shapely breasts that must
never have known a bra. A broad band of filthy lace petticoat
that showed as she crossed her curvaceous but overheavy
white legs. A strappy handbag over her shoulder that was no
more than a bulging home-made sack of leather. A face full
of lovely curves that was somehow both sly and not quite all
there.

But it was the baby that really caught Mrs Parsons's attention. The woman was holding it with its face turned away
from Mrs Parsons. It looked all of six weeks old and very
well grown, but definitely ... slightly ... coloured. The odd
thing was that Mrs Parsons got the impression it was slightly
coloured *green.*

Must be a trick of the light, Mrs Parsons thought. The
curtains she had selected for her own personal office were a
deep tasteful restful green, and the sun was shining on them
pretty strongly, and green light was being gently reflected on
to the ceiling. But if the light made the child look green, why
did it not make the mother look green as well? Mrs Parsons
shook herself free of such distressing fancies, blaming the
warmth of the afternoon. Took a firm grip on herself and
launched into that registrar's litany of questions that she
knew even better by heart than her church's Matins or Even-
song.

'Have you come to register a birth?'

'O' course!' The woman looked at her child, affronted, as
if to make sure it was still there.

'No, no,' said Mrs Parsons hastily. 'But I have to make sure you haven't come in to register a death, haven't I? I mean . . . someone might come in with their child to register someone else's death, mightn't they?'

The woman looked at Mrs Parsons, as if she thought Mrs Parsons might be slightly mad. Then she said, in a thick Fenland accent:

'"Tis birth for this one, though it might be death for some.'

Mrs Parsons had a strong and furious impulse to ask her what the devil she meant; and then an equally strong impulse to draw back from venturing into such a quagmire. The woman's accent was so strong, she might have misheard her. Or it might be some weird old Fenland saying. Stick to the business in hand! At least she now knew she was registering a birth. She drew the relevant draft form towards her and poised her regulation black Biro.

'Are you the baby's mother?'

'O' course!' Again the woman seemed deeply affronted. She gripped her child with a fierce possessiveness. Again, Mrs Parsons felt the need to explain.

'We have to ask, you see. It's our rules. You might have been some other relative . . .' Then she thought wearily, oh, why bother? She'd never felt the need to justify herself before. What was the matter with her this afternoon? The heat? Or that earthy smoky smell that filled the room and seemed to stir long-forgotten memories from her girlhood, when her world was far less hygienic and well organised than it was now.

'What date was the baby born?'

'Six weeks come Friday.'

What a peculiar way of putting it! Didn't they have calendars where she came from? But, on second glance, probably not. There were tiny bits of dried grass clinging to the woman's bare instep, and what looked like a smudge of cow-dung. Mrs Parsons consulted her own calendar and said briskly, 'That would be the twenty-third of September then?'

'If 'ee say so,' said the woman. 'I'd a ruther it had been All Hallows' Eve, but beggars can't be choosers.' She said it resentfully, as if she'd been cheated.

Why All Hallows, for heaven's sake? Again, Mrs Parsons nearly asked the woman, and then drew back. Get involved in that swamp, you might never get out. Best stick to the road you know.

'Whereabouts was the baby born?'

'Our place.'

Yes, of course, it would be. No nice clean hygienic hospital for this one. Probably in the straw of a byre, among the chickens, if not the pigs.

'And where is "our place"?' asked Mrs Parsons, her voice turning to saccharine over steel.

'Our house. Coveny Lane, Witchford.'

Mrs Parsons looked up sharply. That sounded like a joke, a country joke against a townie. And indeed the woman had a slight irritating smile, hovering round her generous lips. But she said:

'It *was* born there! That's where us were all born!'

But just to make sure, Mrs Parsons went across to consult the relevant ordnance survey map, one of several pinned on her walls. When you dealt with so many idiots, you had to make sure. But indeed, there in the distant Fenland village of Witchford was Coveny Lane. Only there were several small buildings marked in Coveny Lane . . .

'What's your house called?'

'Just our house.'

'What do other people call it?'

Again the woman looked at Mrs Parsons, as if she thought Mrs Parsons slightly insane. 'They do call it Smith's place, I suppose.'

Now Mrs Parsons felt better, as her Biro flew across the form. 'Smith's Place sounds quite historical,' she said pleasantly. 'Is it old?'

'Old enough. The roof do leak. But we do call all the houses "Smith's place" or "Jeffrey's place" or "Policeman's place". 'Tain't a proper name.'

A wave of exasperation flowed through Mrs Parsons. 'I don't suppose it's got a *number*,' she asked. 'To help the postman?'

'Us don't need no number. Postie do know where we do live. Us never gets no letters anyway, 'cept bills an' us saves those to light the fire with.'

So Smith's Place it would have to be. Mrs Parsons just hoped that the General Register Office in London never found out, and sent her the printed reprimand the registrars termed a 'yellow peril'.

'Is the baby a girl or a boy?'

The woman just smiled. The smile came from deep inside her like water slowly oozing up round your feet when you stand in a wet field. As if there was some huge joke that Mrs Parsons would never, never be told.

'Oh, come, my good woman, you must *know*!'

'Oh, he'm *male* all right. Just like his father afore him, and haven't I got cause to know it! But cold as clay his father was, in the dark o' night.' Her slow smile *invited* questions now.

Mrs Parsons said 'Male' briskly, and wrote it down. Then said, equally briskly, 'In what name and surname is the baby to be brought up?'

That was the official form of words, properly to be used. Mrs Parsons knew that some of the other, lesser registrars just said, 'What are you going to call the baby?' She sometimes felt tempted to use those words herself, when the atmosphere was cosy. But it was far from cosy now.

'He's a Smith,' said the woman. 'We'm all Smiths, allus were. Allus have been.'

'And the Christian name?' It just slipped out; Mrs Parsons could've kicked herself. Lots of people weren't Christian these days; they might be atheists or humanists and might object. But she was so anxious to get this registration over . . . and the heat . . . and the smell.

'No, us aren't *Christians*,' said the woman starkly. 'Not Christians, not any of us, never.'

But the awful thing was the child. The child suddenly raising its head from the mother's black shoulder, and turning slowly and looking at the registrar. Black black eyes that were full of steady hate, a hate as cold and desolating as a fen-pool.

Mrs Parsons's mind fled into a flurry of panic, like a terrified hamster on its wheel. Dear God, babies can't lift their heads at six weeks, nor focus their eyes. They can't understand what you say and they can't *hate*, I can't bear it . . .

After what seemed forever, the child turned away from her and clawed with one tiny green-tinted hand at the mother's black-clad breast. The woman opened her dress with the utmost casualness. The breast was disturbing in its opulence, then it vanished behind the short black hair on the child's head, and there was the ferocious sound of sucking. Mrs Parsons saw the mother wince.

'I'm sorry . . . I'd rather you didn't do that in here,' said Mrs Parsons with much less than her normal certainty. 'It's . . . against regulations.'

'Would 'ee ruther 'ee looked at 'ee then?' asked the woman. ''Tis the only thing that will pacify him, once he's angered.'

The two women stared at each other a long silent time. Duty told Mrs Parsons there were things that should be reported here; the child must be much older than the regulation six weeks' time limit for reporting a birth. Much too big and strong for six weeks, she could see that now. There should be an investigation; the woman had uttered a perjury . . .

But where was the evidence? The child had been born in some hovel, doubtless without benefit of doctor or midwife; born with the help of some wretched old crone who would only back up the mother's lies, like the Fen people always did. The police would be helpless; townie police in the Fen country.

That was what she told herself. But the truth was that she couldn't hold the woman's gaze, so full of untold knowledge. So she dropped her eyes to her form again.

'And the other name? The forename?'

'Beelzebub,' said the woman.

'My dear woman!' Mrs Parsons knew she shouldn't be protesting. Parents had the right to call their children anything they liked. Much worse even than Sugar Ray and Frankie Bruno. Glasnost Graham had threatened before now, and Perestroika Peters been narrowly averted. She had in her desk an official list of approved names, which showed the approved spellings. But that could only be offered as a guide when requested. It could never be used as a weapon, a coercion. But 'Beelzebub'! The name of a devil out of the Bible ... the woman must have got into a muddle. If she wanted a biblical name, there were lots of nice ones like 'Benjamin' or 'Nathaniel' or even good old Victorian ones like 'Ebenezer' or 'Hezekiah'.

'You can't burden a child with "Beelzebub"!' said Mrs Parsons, her sense of duty overwhelmed by her feelings.

And then, to her horror, as in a dream, she saw the child's head lift and begin to turn towards her again. She could not look away. Again the eyes pierced her very soul with their awful black hate.

'Write!' said the child, in a dreadful, old man's voice.

To support her reeling mind, she leaned forward and clutched the edges of her desk hard. And felt a tiny tickle slide across the skin of her chest. And knew it must be the little silver cross she wore night and day, under her clothes usually. It had slipped from her blouse and was dangling free. Some stray beam of sunlight must have caught the cross, for she saw a flicker of light touch the child's face.

The child flinched, as if burnt, and buried its head in the refuge of its mother's breast again.

Mrs Parsons's mind wriggled vigorously back into reality, as her body wriggled into its foundation garment every morning. Oh, this was all nonsense! Warm afternoon nonsense! She was passing through that awkward time of life; she must go to the doctor and get something! The child must merely have burped and it had sounded like the word 'write'. And its greenness was just the greenness of the light and its size and strength merely . . .

Anyway, her own legal duty was clear. She must write on the form what the mother had told her, and that was the end of it. Her responsibility ended there. So bitterly she wrote the name 'Beelzebub'.

And yet something inside told her she should not have written it. It was another crack in the precious wall of civilisation that held back chaos. There had been so many cracks recently. So many young people not bothering to get married and living in sin . . . a quarter of all the nation's children being born out of wedlock. Those horrible men being tolerated for days on the roofs of prisons, waving their arms and looking like devils from the Pit. Those who should have been on guard were sleeping at their posts, and one day there would be a terrible price to pay . . .

It made her voice a little sharp, a little shrill, as she asked the next statutory question.

'What is the father's full name?'

The woman giggled, a dreadful sound. 'We do just call him "Old Luke".'

'I can't just put down "Old Luke".' It was almost a squeak of outrage. 'The people at General Register Office would never stand for that.'

She glared at the woman, who glared back.

'His full name do be Lucifer. But we do just call him "Old Luke". We don't never see him, you know. Just – he sometimes comes to us, after the dancing, in the dark of night. 'Tis like a dream . . . only you do know he's been, in the morning, you do know that all right! I couldn't sit down for days after . . . and you do know it's he, because he do be as cold as clay.'

Mrs Parsons shuddered, mainly with pity, but not entirely. The customs they still lived by, on the Fen! Who knew? They kept themselves to themselves. Even the police didn't know, let alone the vicars who were supposed to care for their moral welfare. It was a *disgrace,* in this last decade of the twentieth century. This poor young ninny, voluptuous and not quite all there . . . a sitting target for any unscrupulous man after an orgy of drink . . . this pathetic story of Old Luke Lucifer . . . and now she would have the burden of the child, or expect the state to carry the burden of them both, more likely. And most likely it would grow up as much an idiot and a burden to itself as she was . . .

Nevertheless, in accordance with her duties, Mrs Parsons wrote down the father's name.

Luke Lucifer.

And again she knew she shouldn't have done it. There was another crack in the dyke now. In the official records of the nation, in the archives of St Catherine's House, there would be a black lie.

Old Luke Lucifer.

But she had to ask the next question.

'Whereabouts was the father born?'

The woman smiled; an incredulous smile, as at Mrs Parsons's ignorance.

'Why, in the Heavens, before he was cast down!'

Mrs Parsons broke out in a sweat all over, from the small of her back to the palms of her hands. But she controlled herself. She must expect such sweats at her time of life; even if it was not simply caused by the increasing temperature of the room.

But this was the thing she dreaded most. This appalling

way even apparently quite sensible people had of leaping suddenly into the totally nonsensical. Even some vicars . . . there had been a visiting preacher two Sundays ago who had gone on and on about the Second Coming. Rubbish about the Blessed being placed on the right hand, and the Damned on the left, while at the same time the Blessed were being lifted up into the air . . . it had made her head whirl, like some spiritual Spaghetti Junction. She had spoken to the preacher quite severely afterwards, saying that in future she would tolerate only sermons about sensible subjects like Inner City Welfare Work, or the Ordination of Woman . . .

'Place of father's birth unknown,' she said out loud, putting a vicious line through the space left for it on the draft form, so great was her exasperation.

She heard the child mutter ominously at its mother's breast, breaking the sound of sucking. But she swept straight on to the next question, even though she knew the answer would be gibberish. She *must* get this business over, and the awful woman out of her Register Office, back to the swamp of ignorance she'd emerged from. It would be like a Cleansing of the Temple.

'What is the father's occupation?'

'He do go about the world, workin' his Will.'

'Commercial Traveller,' wrote Mrs Parsons, with vicious spite.

Again the child rumbled, horrible noises as from a nether pit. Could it sense what she was writing? Or did its nose just need wiping?

She was nearly there now. Only a few more questions, and those were easier, more practical.

'What is your full name?'

'Joan Smith. Us do be all Smiths.' The woman's voice had gone tight; the child's feeding sounded ferocious.

'And what is *your* occupation?'

'I do find things for people, when they've mislaid them. I

do charm warts, and mix a cure for the Old Johnny. I can blast a man's crops. I do a lot o' they, afore the village shows . . .'

'Herbal healer,' cut in Mrs Parsons shortly. 'And I think you said that you too were born in Coveny Lane, Witchford?'

'That be right.' The woman sounded not only in pain, but miffed at being rushed like this.

Now for the crunch question. Though as the years passed, sadly it became less and less of a crunch. It was the test of whether the child was illegitimate . . . an 'illy' as they called it in the office.

'What was your maiden name?'

'I told 'ee. Smith I was, and Smith I am and Smith I shall be. Though I don't be no maiden no more.' That came out as a thick snigger.

'So you have never married?'

'Course not.'

'Then I cannot enter the father's name on the birth certificate. Not unless he comes to see me himself.' At this point, Mrs Parsons looked up, putting on her most authoritative official face.

But not for long.

The child fed on. But a trickle of blood descended from the mother's breast, staining deep dark brown into her open black dress.

Mrs Parsons was not, at bottom, uncaring. Her cry of distress for the other woman was loud enough to bring her colleagues running. They gathered in a semi-circle, staring in horror and offering suggestions of cotton-wool and calamine lotion, Savlon and the office first-aid kit.

But the look on the Fen-woman's face held them at bay; she crouched in her chair in the corner like a wild beast protecting her cub.

'Let I be! Let I be! I be all right!'

Mr Brooks looked in, looked harassed, and suggested

that an ambulance be summoned. When the suggestion was rejected by all, he fled back to his own office, overwhelmed by such female mystery.

And that led Mrs Parsons to say, 'Leave it to me, ladies. I can handle it.'

When they had all been got rid of, the woman deigned to snatch a large lump of cotton-wool soaked in calamine that Mrs Parsons offered her. She dabbed with it, inside her poor black dress. It seemed to renew some bridge between the pair of them. Mrs Parsons returned to her seat and took charge again.

'Now you do understand? I cannot enter the father's name on the birth certificate unless he comes and asks for it to be put on, himself?'

'He do want his name on.'

'I think you know him better than you make out.' Mrs Parsons smiled a little, as the certainty of her own authority returned.

'Oh, I do know him all right. And his ways.'

Mrs Parsons smiled again, thinking of some great hulking Fen-man, coming cowed into this stronghold of stately authority, sober for once, maybe in his best suit, ill at ease off his own crude ground.

The woman looked at her, almost with pity. ''Ee wouldn't smile if 'ee saw him, missus. 'Ee've seen the son, at six week. Do 'ee really want to see the father?'

And the child on her knee slowly turned its head again and stared at Mrs Parsons, with the pools of hate set in his pale green face. As if in response, the sun went in, outside the window, and the fetid smell grew stronger and more rancid in the over-warm room. Like the smell from the lair of some wild beast.

Mrs Parsons found her own hand clutching the tiny silver cross round her neck.

'Aye,' said the woman. 'That toy in yer hand will scare

the young 'un. For a bit. But it won't scare the old 'un, if he comes for yer.'

'I have to do my duty,' said Mrs Parsons, keeping the tremble out of her voice with difficulty.

''Ee won't think of yer duty, if the old 'un comes for 'ee. 'Ee'll do what he tells yer. Only it'll be too late. For 'ee.'

Mrs Parsons thought of the whole august system of the General Register Office, of the rule of law, of the phone by her elbow, and of the police.

'None o' that will help 'ee, if he comes,' said the woman. 'I told 'ee. He comes in the dark.'

Mrs Parsons thought of the dark. Of getting out of the car in her own tree-lined drive, when her husband wasn't home yet, and her house in darkness. She thought of the dimness of the multi-storey car park, when she had to be in town late in winter. She thought of lying awake in the small hours, when her husband was away on business. She suddenly realised that half the world, half of life, lay in the dark. She'd never realised it was so much, because she'd spent most of it going to the theatre or watching telly, or sleeping. The dark had seemed such a small part of her life . . . Now she realised how much it was there; out across the Fens; between the thin lines of streetlamps, thin as necklaces that might snap.

She came to her crossroads, quite suddenly.

You either belonged to the dark, or you belonged to the light. As you might belong to a hockey team in your youth, or the WI in middle age. The light wasn't a free gift, it was a side you belonged to, an army in battle. As the Bible put it, there were the Children of Light, and the Deeds of Darkness.

And the Deeds of Darkness would never gain an inch, not through her.

She folded her hands together loosely on the desk, almost humbly, and said:

'I'm afraid the father will have to come and see me.'

'Don't blame me. Don't say I didn't warn 'ee.' The woman shot her a look almost of pity. Then walked out in her down-at-heel shoes, clacking off down the corridor, carrying her dreadful child away; into silence.

Mrs Parsons sat on, utterly exhausted. There was no summons, from the receptionist's buzzer, to fetch her to a new customer. Outside the window, the sky darkened and darkened. So *close*! Thunder must be threatening. The fetid smell the woman had left behind seemed to get worse, not better; but Mrs Parsons did not seem able to summon up the energy to cross the room for the air freshener she kept in the cupboard.

Then Mr Brooks was at her door, hand on the door-handle, dishevelled as usual. He must be home on time tonight, would she see to things?

She almost called him back; but he was gone before she could find her voice. Now there were footsteps and echoing female voices in the hall; the rest of the staff were going home.

The big door banged shut, and she knew she was alone. No sound but the far musical drip of the cold tap in the little kitchen at the end of the corridor.

She knew the creature was coming for her. Was she afraid, a small part of her asked?

Oddly, she wasn't. Or only as afraid as she'd been as a child in the bombings of 1940. Tense, worked up, but not afraid. Not terrified. She thought, quite calmly, that this was the best way, here, in the place she knew so well, with her things around her. In the fortress she had defended so long. Better than running away, and then waiting in fear for the dark to come. In the dark she could only grow weaker . . .

In a way, she was glad to end like this. All her life she had been on the fringes of the battle between the light and the dark, good and evil. It made her feel satisfyingly real to be in the centre of the battle at last. She knew her best years were gone; she had a sudden eagerness to spend what was left in a rush. For what she knew was right.

And beyond that, she was filled with a sort of wonder at the creature that would come. If he was real, then she would know for certain that his Adversary, her God, was real too. And it would be a relief, to know that for certain.

There was a vivid flash from the window; then a distant rattle of thunder. Any moment now. She began putting her desk in order . . . the waiting was what was making her drowsy. Her traitorous body was letting down her soul. If the creature caught her dozing . . . She heard her door squeak as it opened.

'Here's your tea, Mrs Parsons! Mrs Parsons! Mrs Parsons!'

A familiar, unfrightening and indeed female hand was gently shaking her shoulder. She looked up at Mrs Meadowes's freckled face and ginger hair with total disbelief.

'But I heard you go home, Mrs Meadowes!'

'Heavens, no, it's only half past three. I've brought your cup of tea. You must have dozed off. It's ever so close this afternoon. I nearly dozed off myself.'

'Was there . . . a woman in black . . . with a baby . . . a gypsy-looking woman with long hair held back with an elastic band? Come to register the baby?'

The receptionist looked baffled, shook her head. 'We've only had three deaths this afternoon, and two notices of marriage. It's been very quiet. Nobody like that – nobody like that at all. You must have been having a dream . . .'

She gave Mrs Parsons a slightly pitying look that roused all Mrs Parsons's cold wrath. Then said hurriedly, 'Don't let your tea get cold,' and left.

Mrs Parsons stirred her cup of tea, for want of anything better to do. It was then that she saw the draft form, filled out in Biro, in her own handwriting. The name stood out quite clearly.

Beelzebub.

A rage seized Mrs Parsons. She strode to the ordnance survey map on the wall. Witchford was there all right. So was Coveny Lane, with its several buildings marked.

It was Mrs Parsons who left Mr Brooks to lock up and see to things that afternoon. It was Mrs Parsons who drove to Coveny Lane, Witchford, full of rage and yearning, hunting for Old Luke Lucifer, hunting for the last battle, for the truth.

She didn't find any of them, of course. All four buildings in Coveny Lane, Witchford, were large and luxurious modern bungalows. Two of their well-kept gardens contained middle-aged women in smocks and green wellies, up to their elbows in mowing, pruning and weeding. Neither had ever heard of any family called Smith, or seen the woman Mrs Parsons described. Which wasn't really surprising, for Witchford itself wasn't really darkest Fenland at all, but a pleasant prosperous village mainly inhabited by people who commuted to well-paid jobs in Ely. Shaking her head and lambasting herself, back in her car, Mrs Parsons had to admit she'd really always known that.

So where had those creatures come from, the terrible hating babe, the earthy slut in black, and Old Luke Lucifer who came in the night and was as cold as clay?

There was only one place they could have come from.

Inside herself. They lived there. Always.

For a long minute, Mrs Parsons seemed to teeter on a precipice above endless chasms of darkness, where slimy things coiled and twisted through and round each other, hating, fearing, devouring endlessly, without pity. The truth.

Then she murmured, 'Stuff and nonsense.'

And drove away to get her husband's tea ready.